BAB★USHKA

Criminals whisper her name in fear!

BAB★USHKA

The enigmatic heiress to a noble Russian line
— socialite by day, assassin by night!

BAB★USHKA

Blackmailed by the US government to carry out
dirty jobs even the CIA can't sanction!

BAB★USHKA

You might think she's a hero.
That would be a mistake.

image

★ MISSION BRIEFING ★
ANTONY JOHNSTON

★ HIDDEN CAMERAS ★
SHARI CHANKHAMMA

★ TRANSCRIPT ★
SIMON BOWLAND

★ EXTERNAL STAGING ★
SHARI CHANKHAMMA

★ CONTINGENCIES ★
BECKY CLOONAN
MEGAN LEVENS
ROBIN HOELZEMANN
EMMA VIECELI

IMAGE COMICS, INC.

Robert Kirkman—Chief Operating Officer
Erik Larsen—Chief Financial Officer
Todd McFarlane—President
Marc Silvestri—Chief Executive Officer
Jim Valentino—Vice President

Eric Stephenson—Publisher
Corey Hart—Director of Sales
Jeff Boison—Director of Publishing Planning
& Book Trade Sales
Chris Ross—Director of Digital Sales
Jeff Stang—Director of Specialty Sales
Kat Salazar—Director of PR & Marketing
Drew Gill—Art Director
Heather Doornink—Production Director

CODENAME BABOUSHKA, VOL 2: GHOST STATION ZERO.
FIRST PRINTING. FEBRUARY 2018.

Published by Image Comics, Inc. Office of publication: 2701 NW Vaughn St., Suite 780, Portland, OR 9721◦

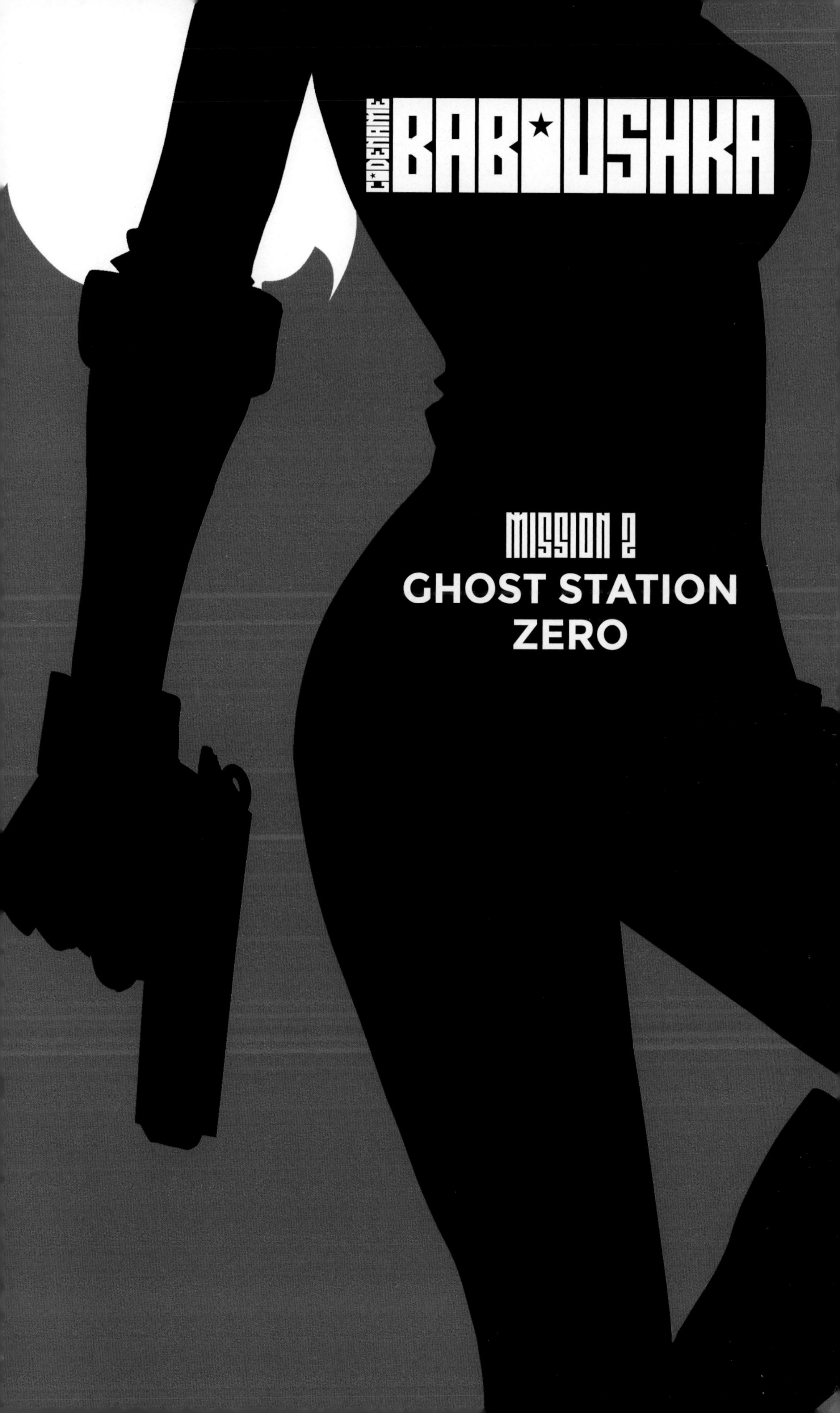
CODENAME
BABOUSHKA
MISSION 2
GHOST STATION
ZERO

PART ★ ONE

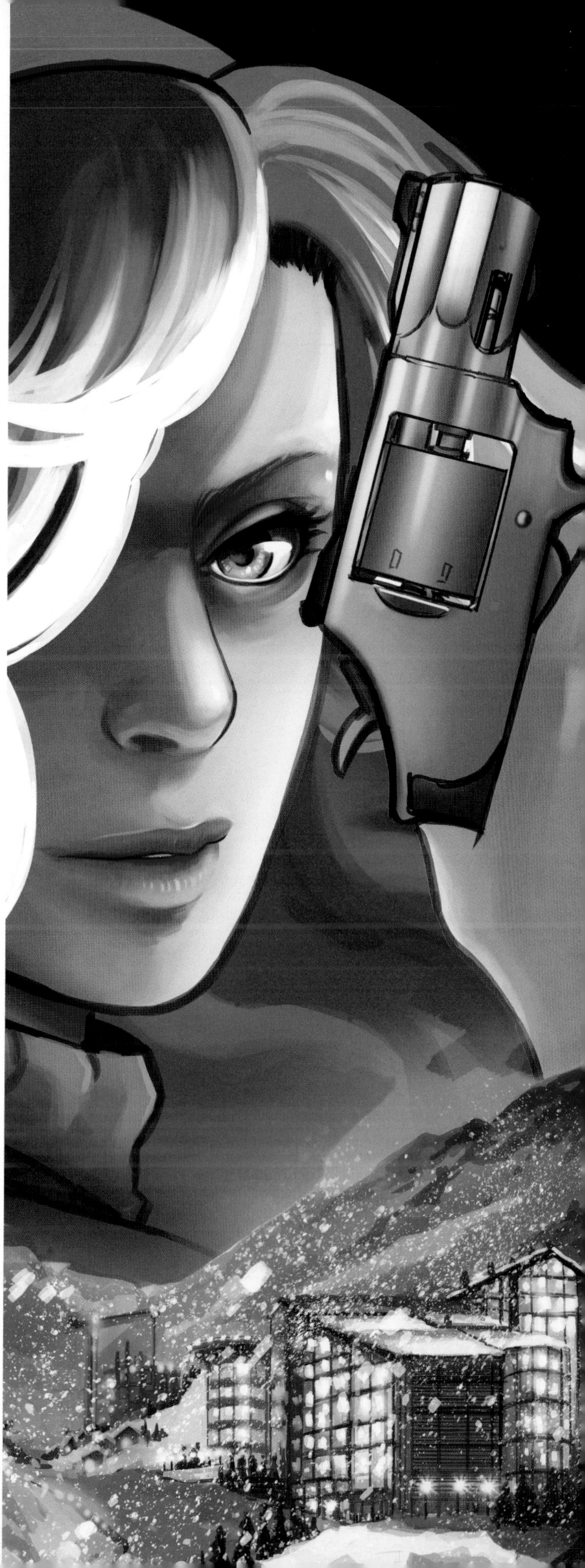

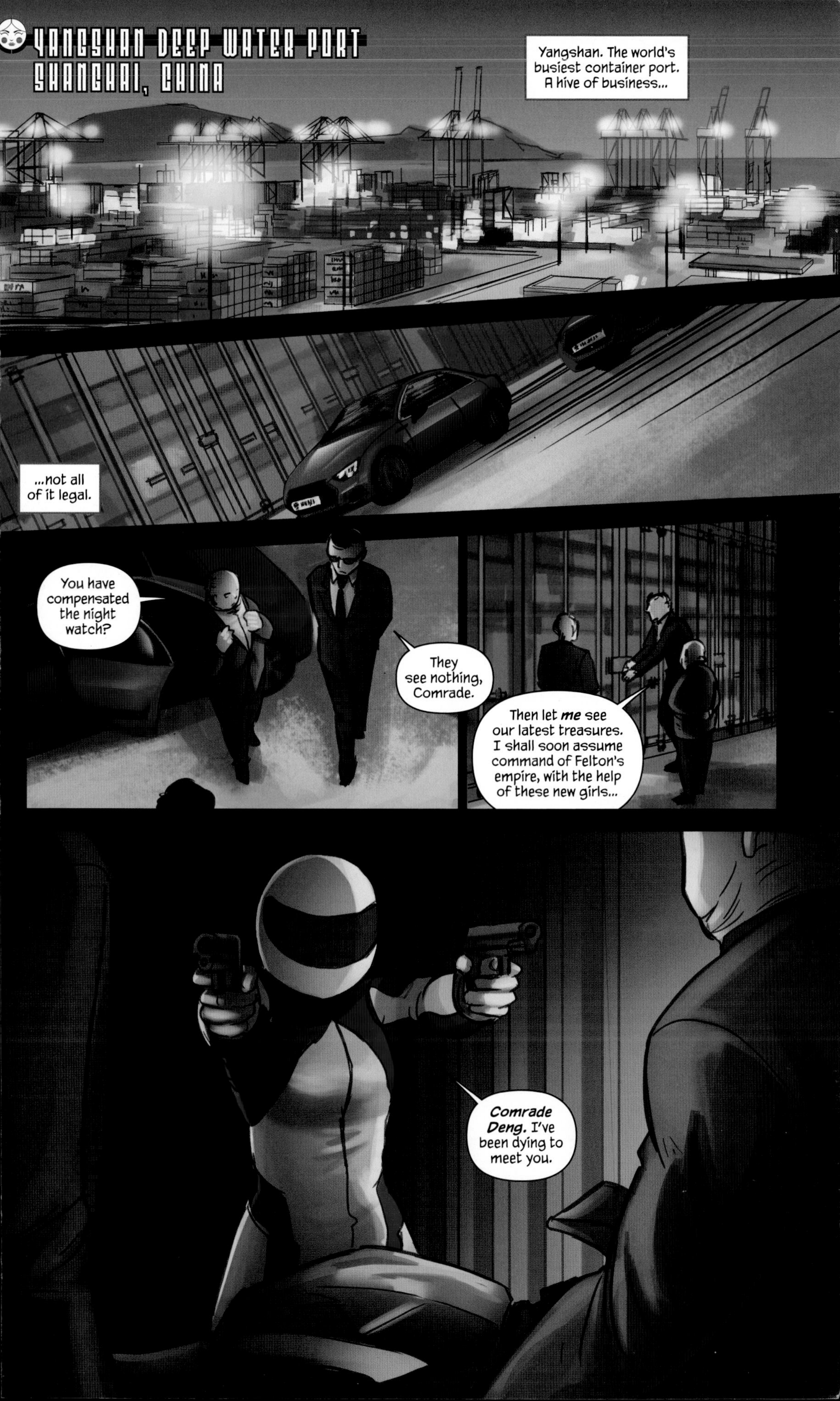
YANGSHAN DEEP WATER PORT
SHANGHAI, CHINA
Yangshan. The world's busiest container port. A hive of business...
...not all of it legal.
You have compensated the night watch?
They see nothing, Comrade.
Then let *me* see our latest treasures. I shall soon assume command of Felton's empire, with the help of these new girls...
Comrade Deng. I've been dying to meet you.

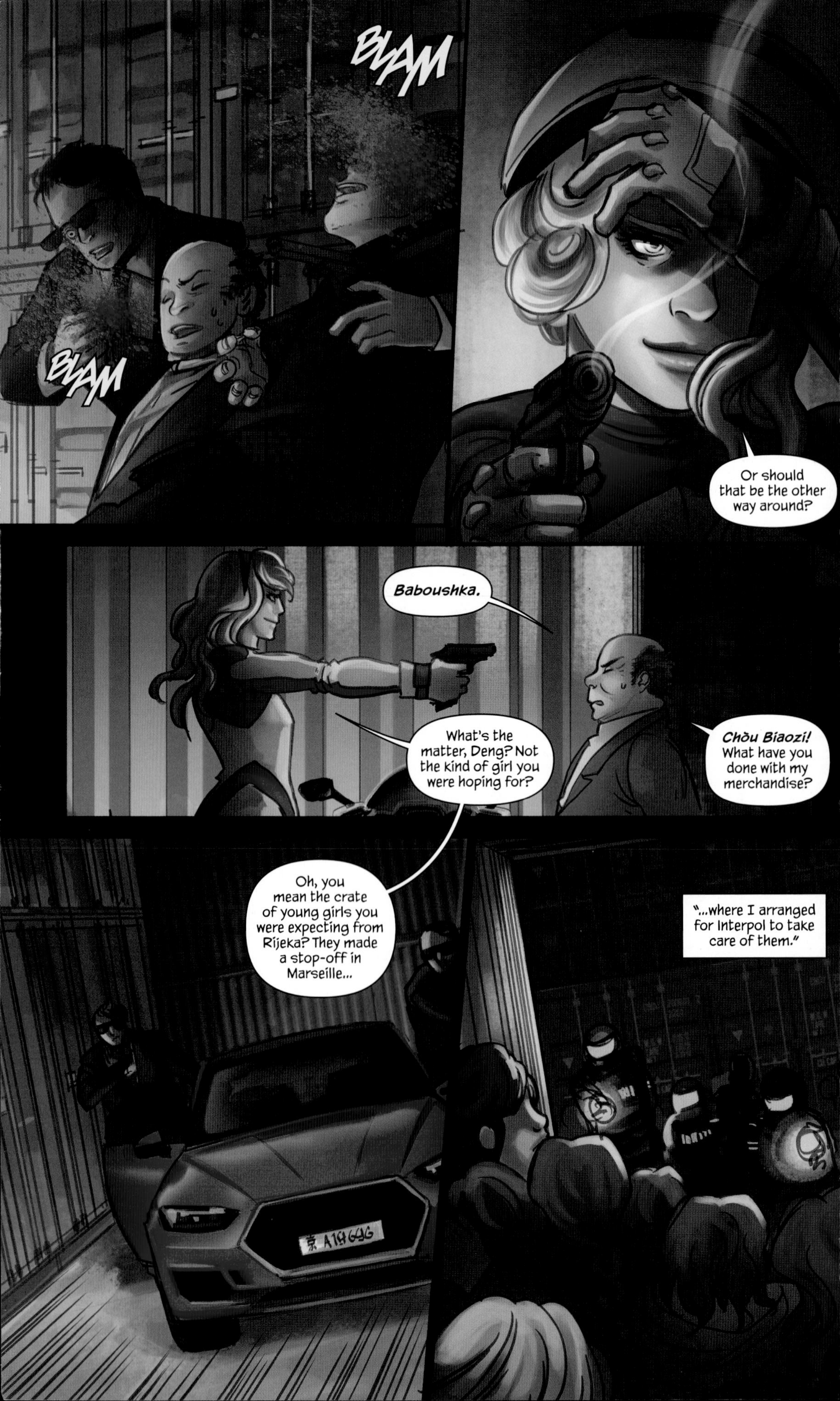
BLAM
BLAM
Or should that be the other way around?
Baboushka.
Chòu Biaozi! What have you done with my merchandise?
What's the matter, Deng? Not the kind of girl you were hoping for?
Oh, you mean the crate of young girls you were expecting from Rijeka? They made a stop-off in Marseille...
"...where I arranged for Interpol to take care of them."

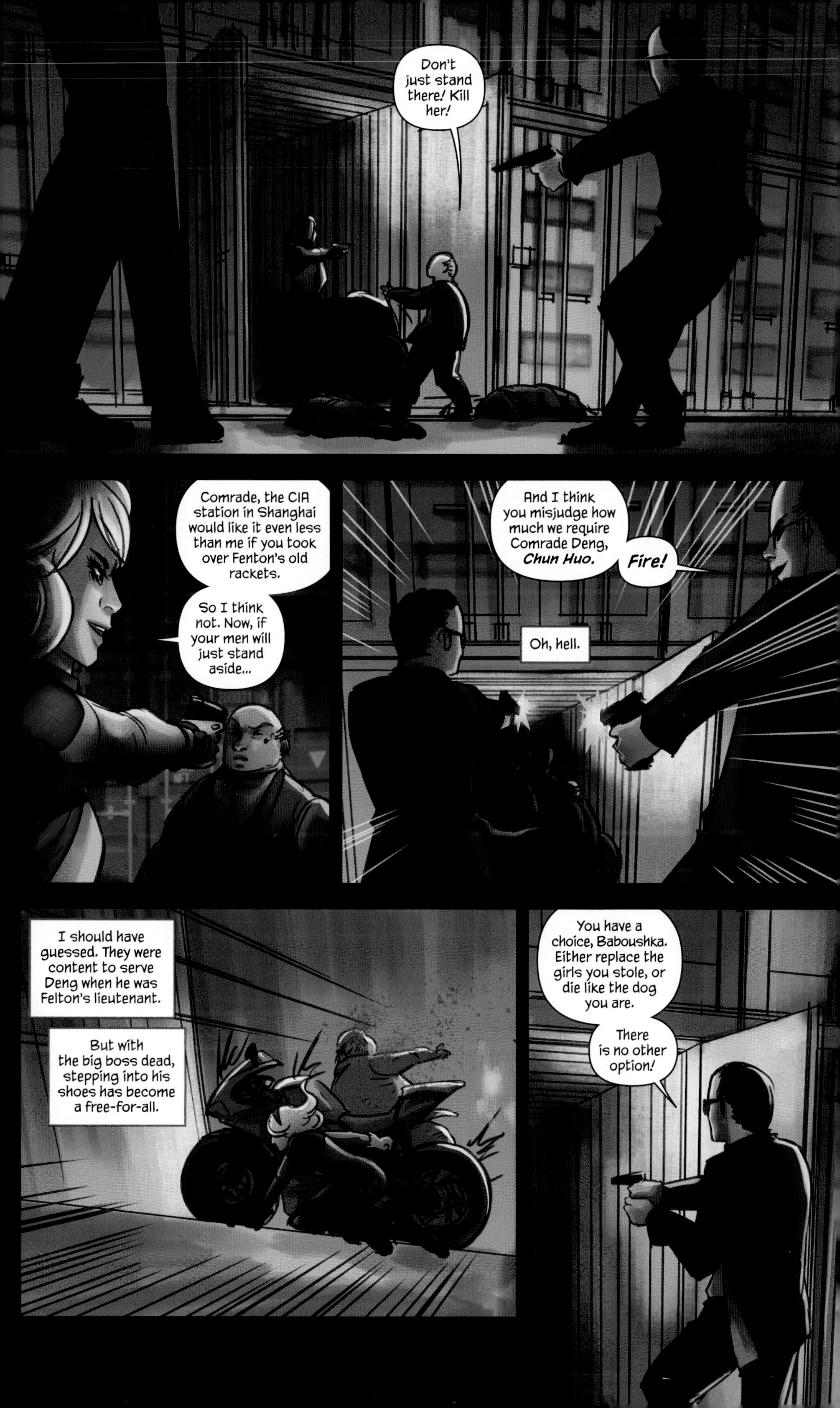
Don't just stand there! Kill her!
Comrade, the CIA station in Shanghai would like it even less than me if you took over Fenton's old rackets.
So I think not. Now, if your men will just stand aside...
And I think you misjudge how much we require Comrade Deng, *Chun Huo.*
Fire!
Oh, hell.
I should have guessed. They were content to serve Deng when he was Felton's lieutenant.
But with the big boss dead, stepping into his shoes has become a free-for-all.
You have a choice, Baboushka. Either replace the girls you stole, or die like the dog you are.
There is no other option!

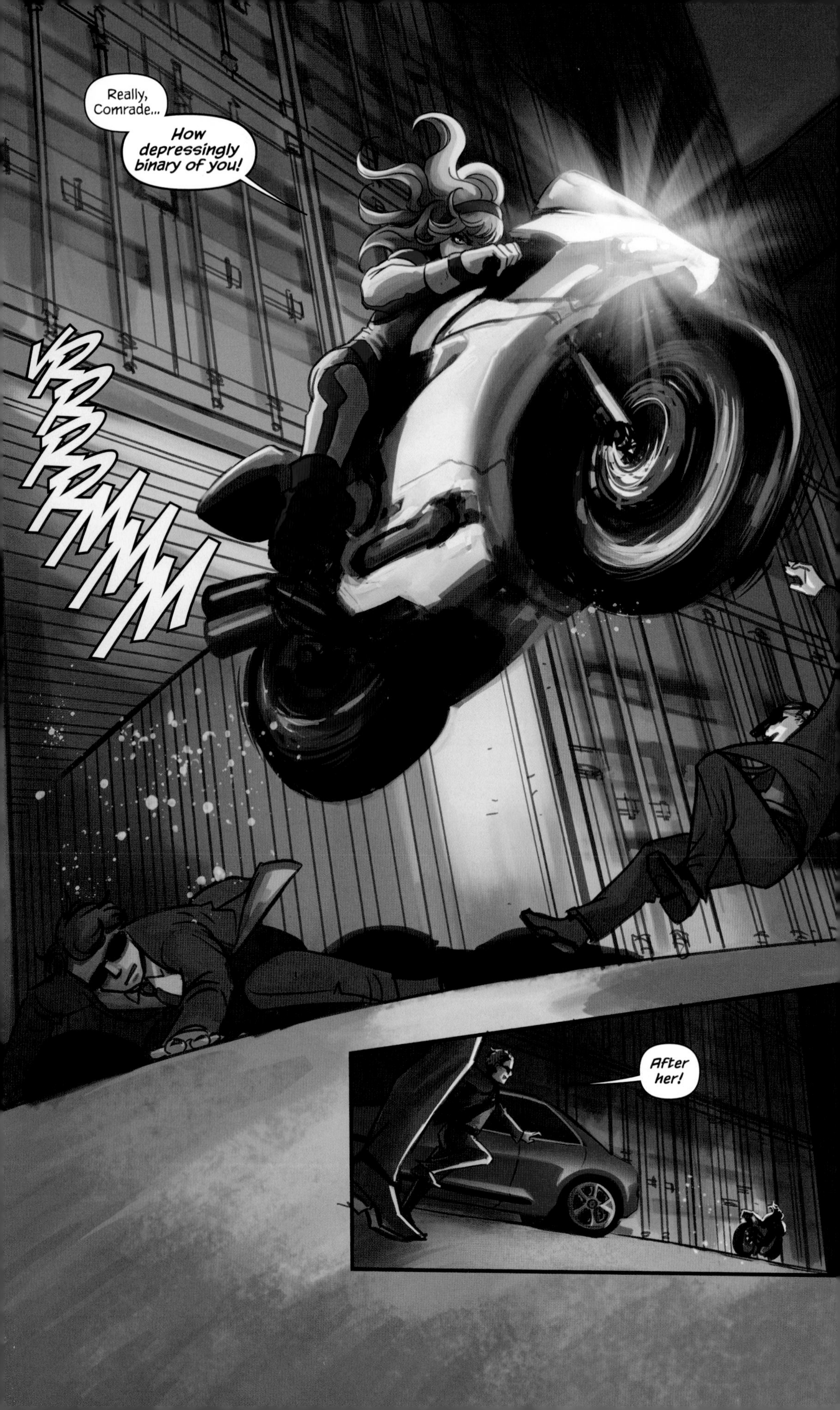
Really, Comrade...
How depressingly binary of you!
VRRRMMM
After her!

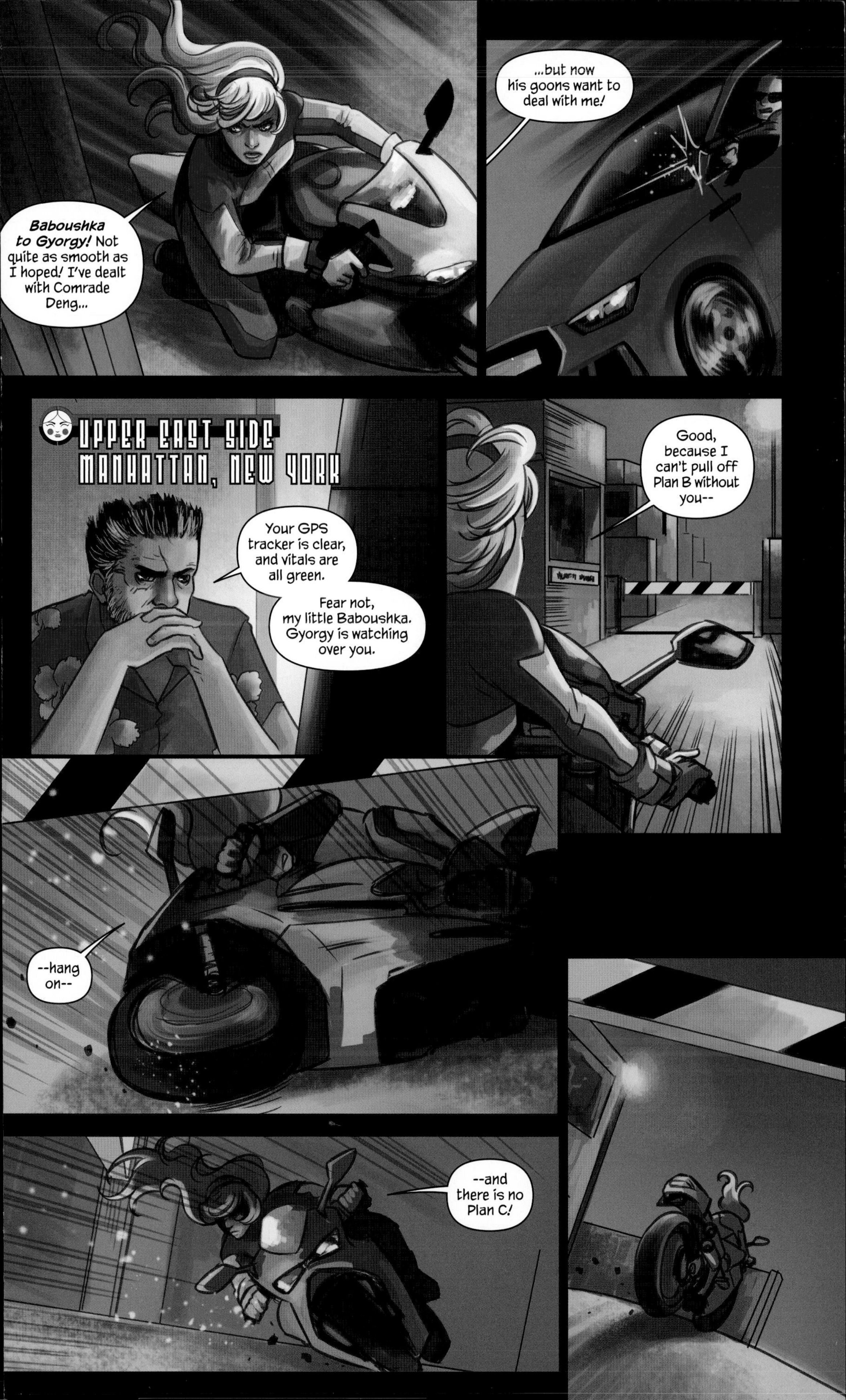

Baboushka to Gyorgy! Not quite as smooth as I hoped! I've dealt with Comrade Deng...
...but now his goons want to deal with me!
UPPER EAST SIDE MANHATTAN, NEW YORK
Your GPS tracker is clear, and vitals are all green.
Fear not, my little Baboushka. Gyorgy is watching over you.
Good, because I can't pull off Plan B without you--
--hang on--
--and there is no Plan C!

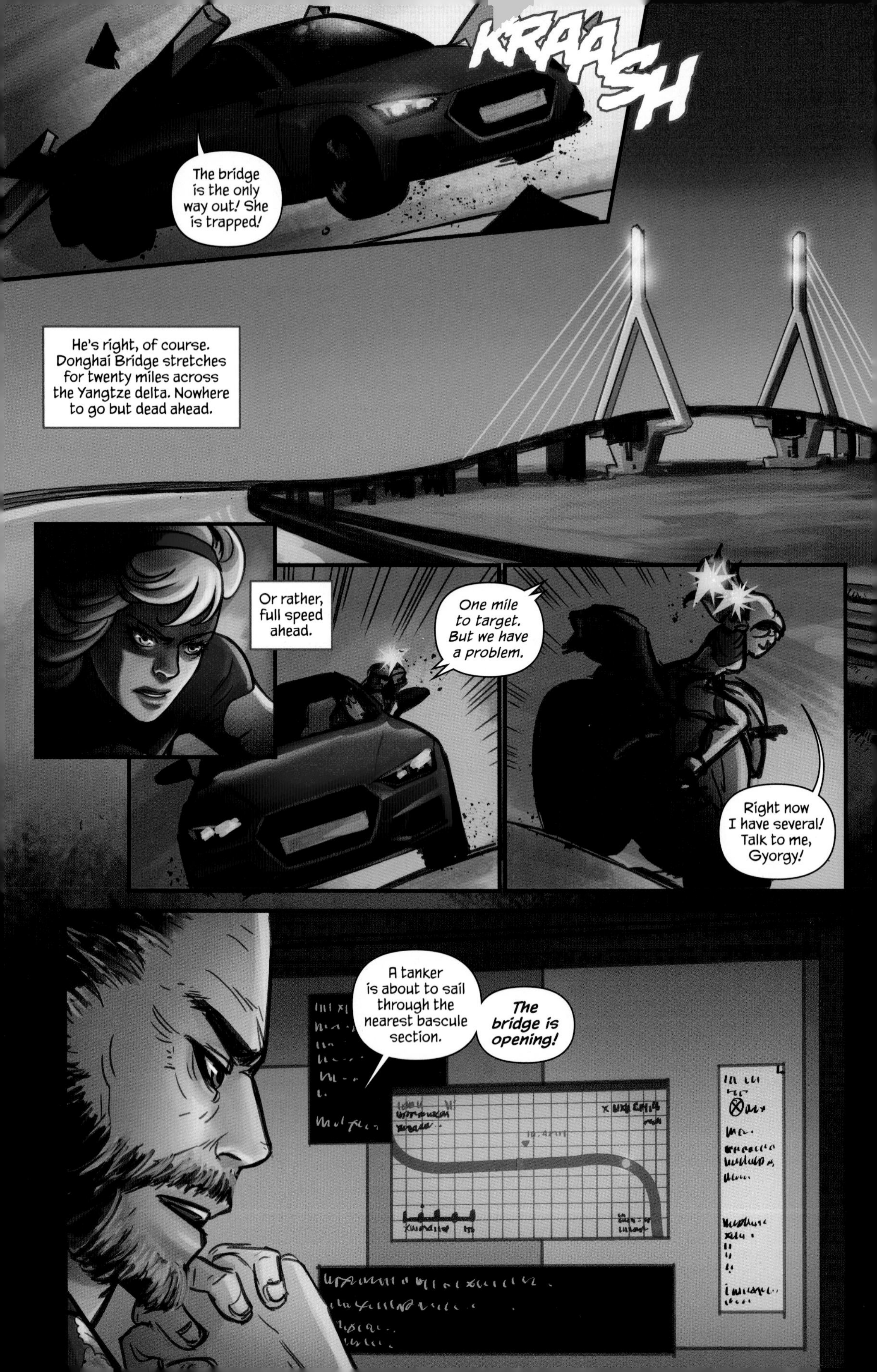
KRAASH
The bridge is the only way out! She is trapped!
He's right, of course. Donghai Bridge stretches for twenty miles across the Yangtze delta. Nowhere to go but dead ahead.
Or rather, full speed ahead.
One mile to target. But we have a problem.
Right now I have several! Talk to me, Gyorgy!
A tanker is about to sail through the nearest bascule section.
The bridge is opening!

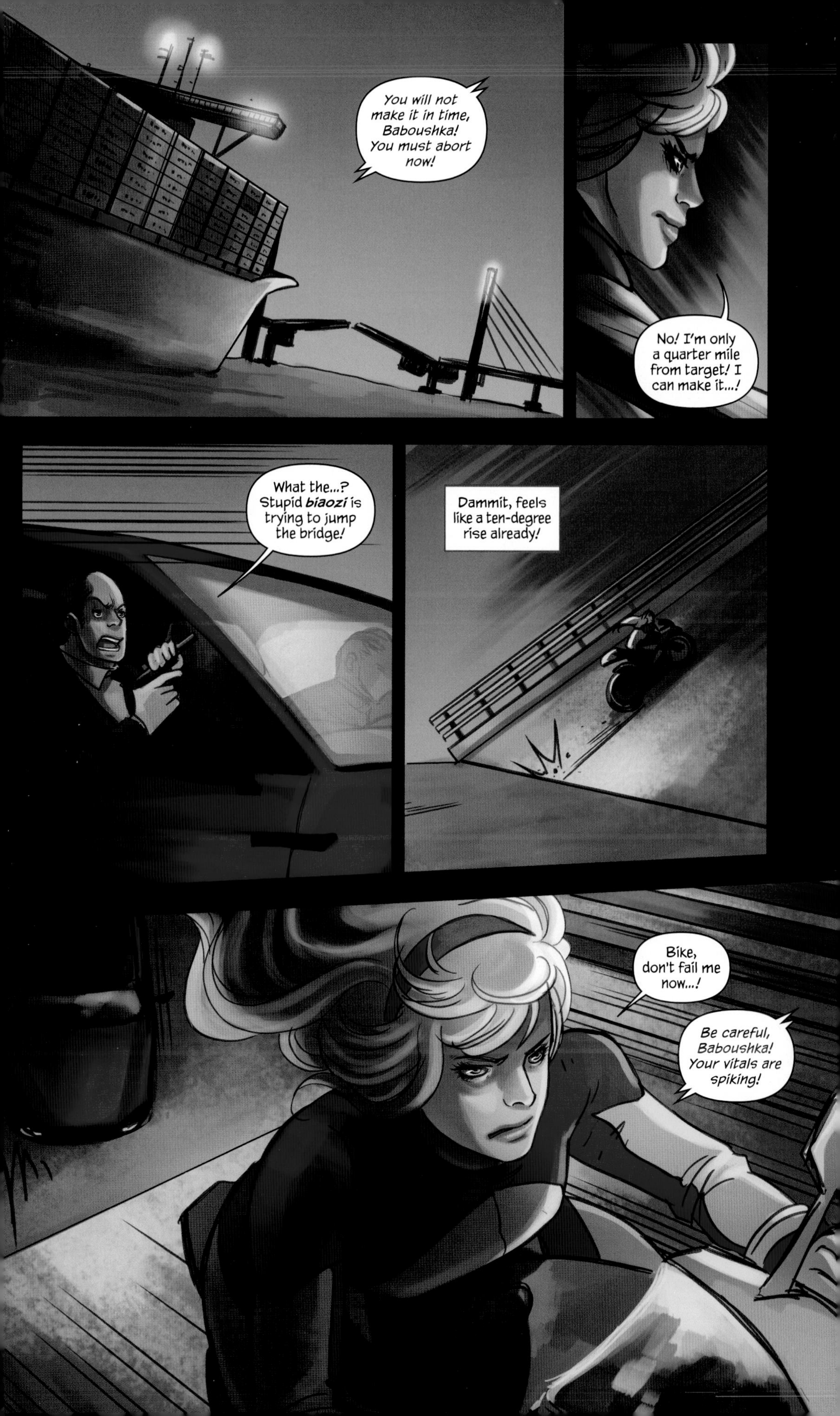
You will not make it in time, Baboushka! You must abort now!
No! I'm only a quarter mile from target! I can make it...!
What the...? Stupid *biaozi* is trying to jump the bridge!
Dammit, feels like a ten-degree rise already!
Bike, don't fail me now...!
Be careful, Baboushka! Your vitals are spiking!

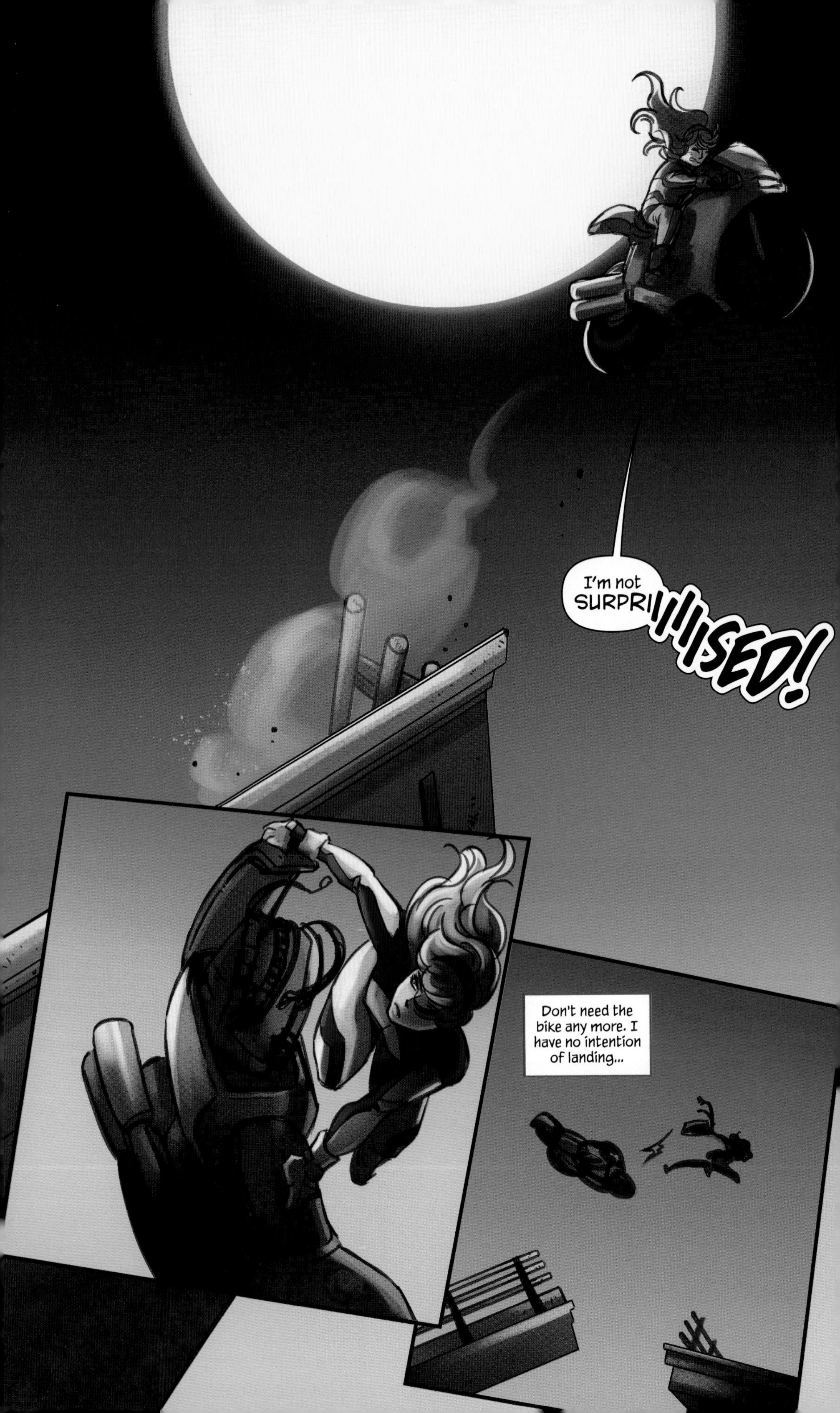
I'm not SURPRIIIIIISED!
Don't need the bike any more. I have no intention of landing...

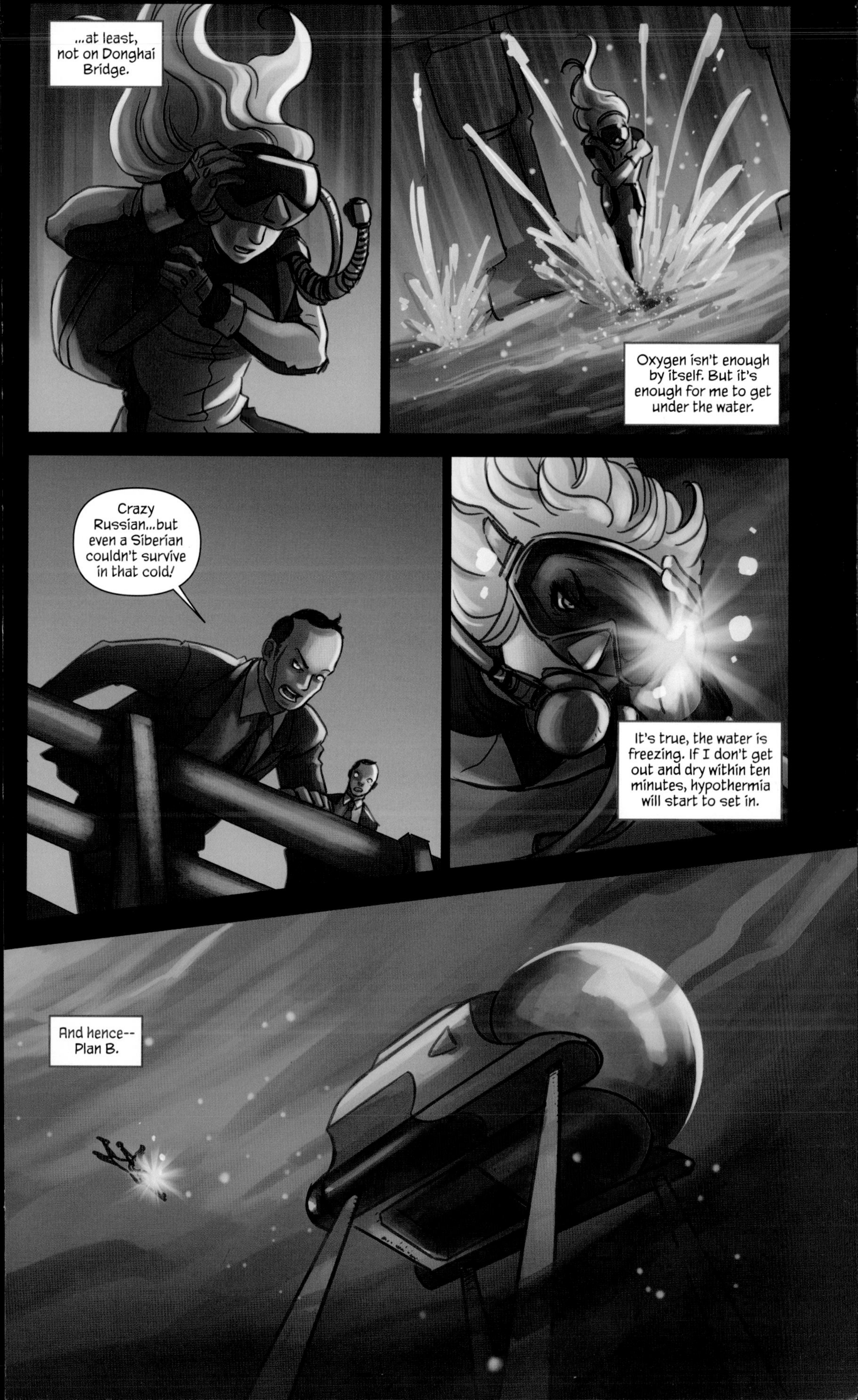
...at least, not on Donghai Bridge.
Oxygen isn't enough by itself. But it's enough for me to get under the water.
Crazy Russian...but even a Siberian couldn't survive in that cold!
It's true, the water is freezing. If I don't get out and dry within ten minutes, hypothermia will start to set in.
And hence-- Plan B.

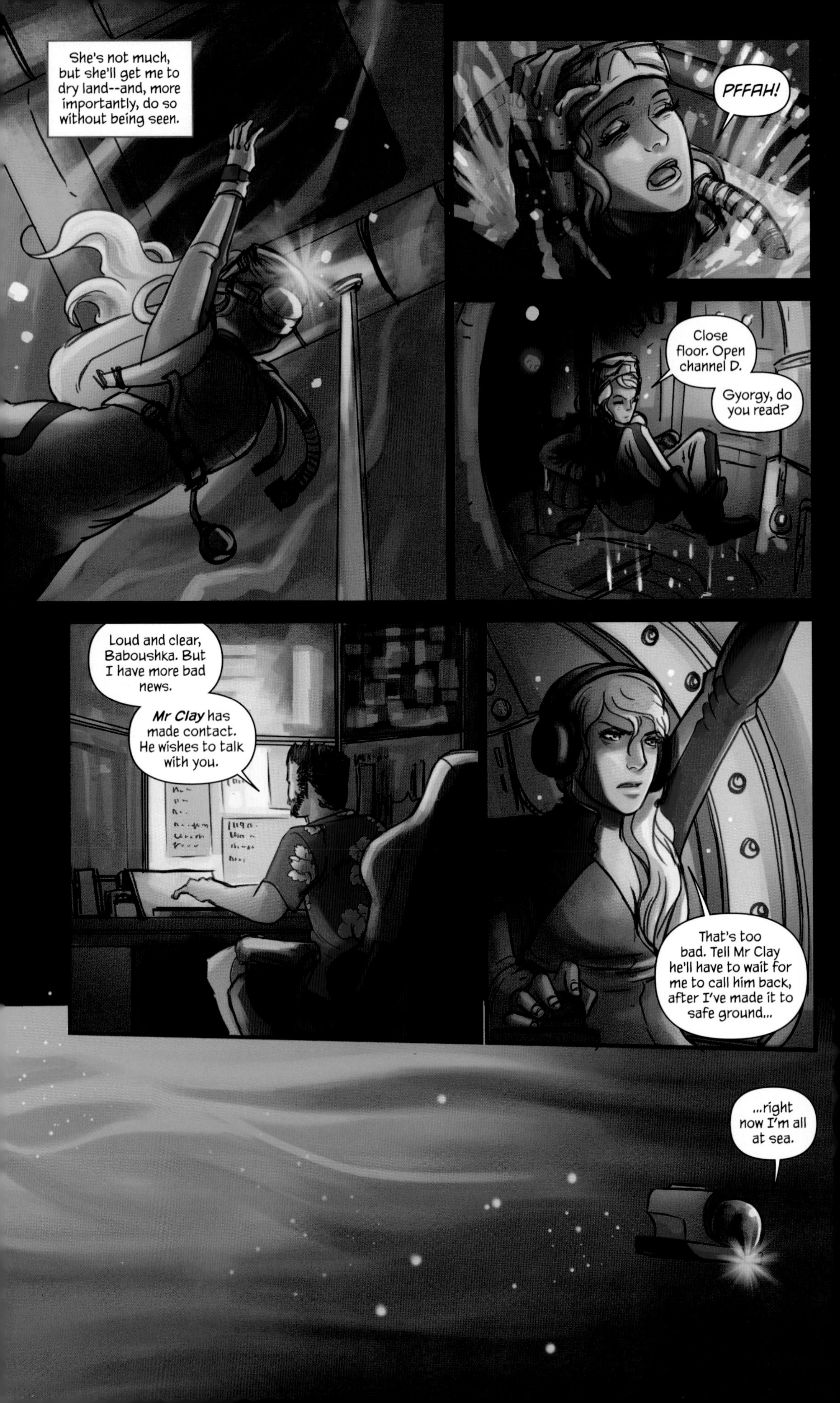
She's not much, but she'll get me to dry land--and, more importantly, do so without being seen.
PFFAH!
Close floor. Open channel D.
Gyorgy, do you read?
Loud and clear, Baboushka. But I have more bad news.
Mr Clay has made contact. He wishes to talk with you.
That's too bad. Tell Mr Clay he'll have to wait for me to call him back, after I've made it to safe ground...
...right now I'm all at sea.

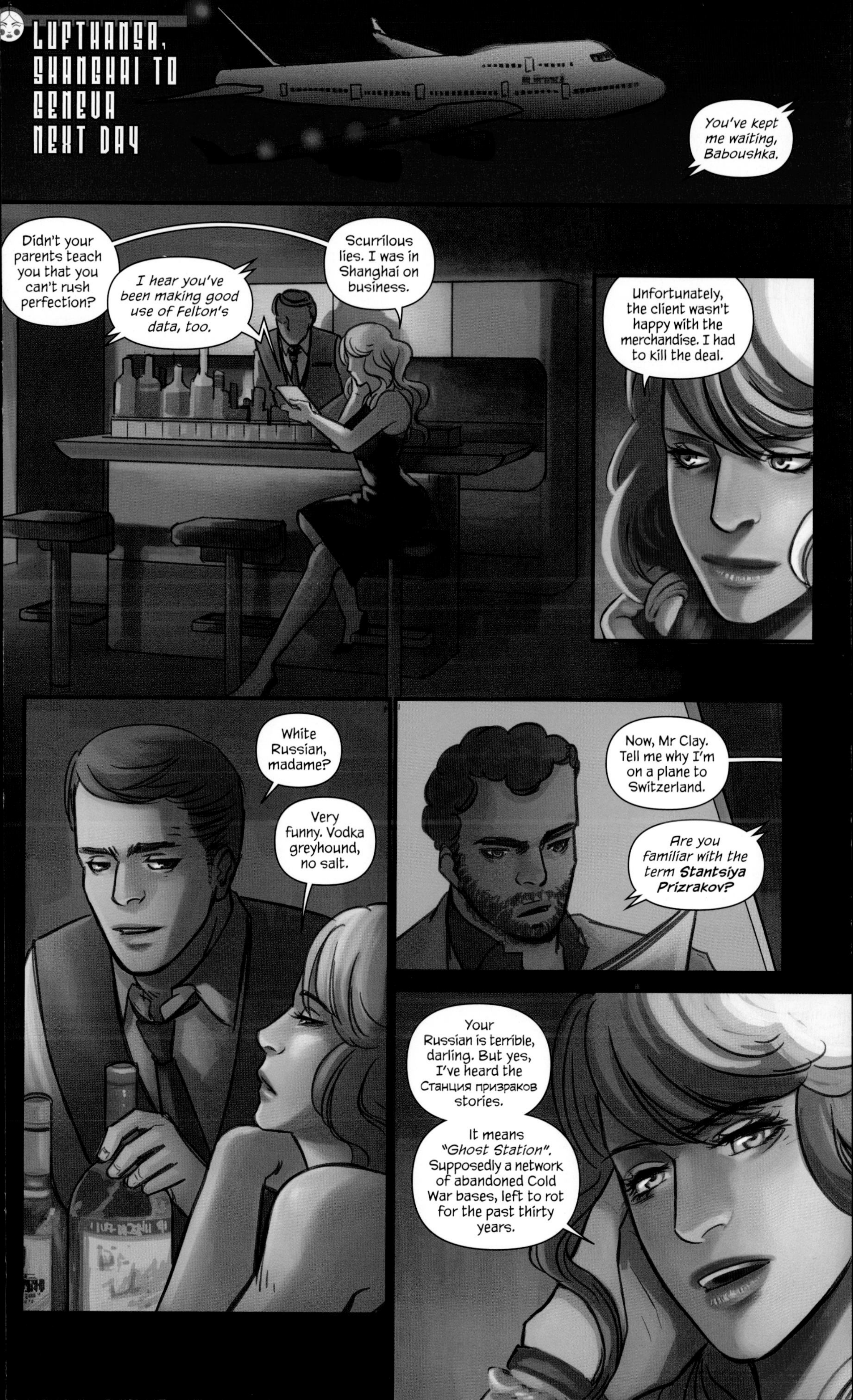
LUFTHANSA, SHANGHAI TO GENEVA NEXT DAY
You've kept me waiting, Baboushka.
Didn't your parents teach you that you can't rush perfection?
I hear you've been making good use of Felton's data, too.
Scurrilous lies. I was in Shanghai on business.
Unfortunately, the client wasn't happy with the merchandise. I had to kill the deal.
White Russian, madame?
Very funny. Vodka greyhound, no salt.
Now, Mr Clay. Tell me why I'm on a plane to Switzerland.
Are you familiar with the term Stantsiya Prizrakov?
Your Russian is terrible, darling. But yes, I've heard the Станция призраков stories.
It means "Ghost Station". Supposedly a network of abandoned Cold War bases, left to rot for the past thirty years.

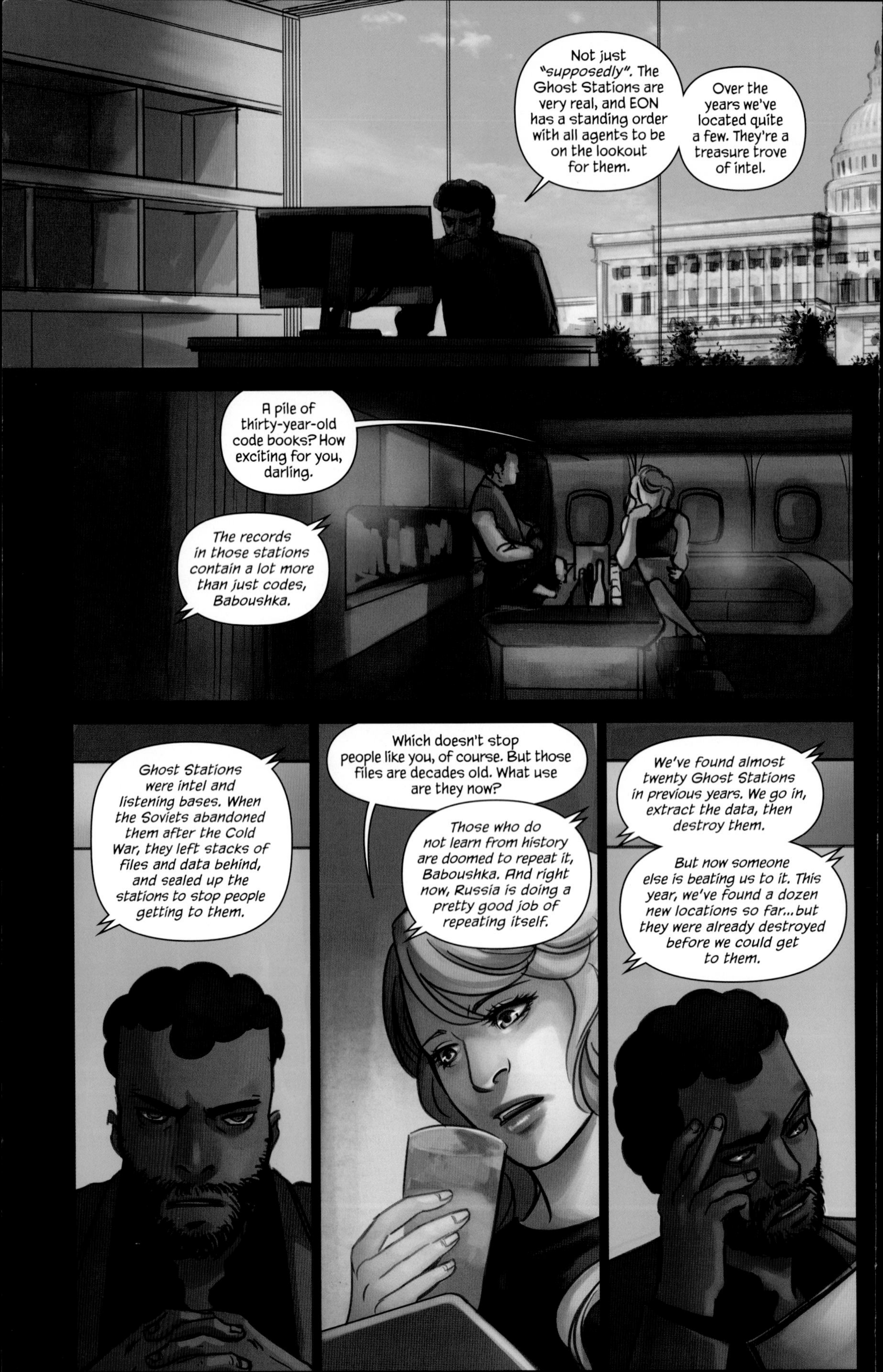

Not just *"supposedly"*. The Ghost Stations are very real, and EON has a standing order with all agents to be on the lookout for them.
Over the years we've located quite a few. They're a treasure trove of intel.
A pile of thirty-year-old code books? How exciting for you, darling.
The records in those stations contain a lot more than just codes, Baboushka.
Ghost Stations were intel and listening bases. When the Soviets abandoned them after the Cold War, they left stacks of files and data behind, and sealed up the stations to stop people getting to them.
Which doesn't stop people like you, of course. But those files are decades old. What use are they now?
Those who do not learn from history are doomed to repeat it, Baboushka. And right now, Russia is doing a pretty good job of repeating itself.
We've found almost twenty Ghost Stations in previous years. We go in, extract the data, then destroy them.
But now someone else is beating us to it. This year, we've found a dozen new locations so far...but they were already destroyed before we could get to them.

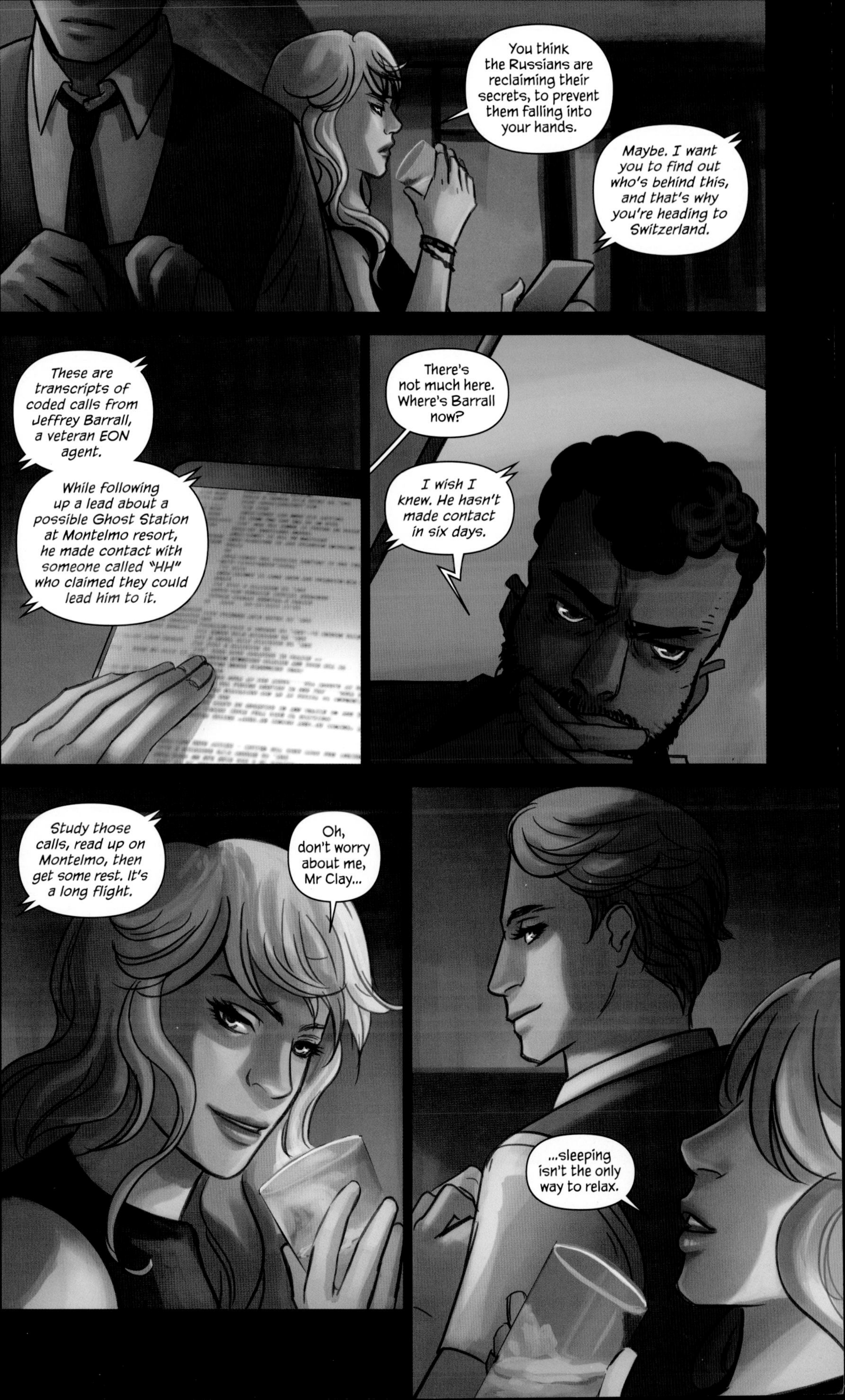
You think the Russians are reclaiming their secrets, to prevent them falling into your hands.
Maybe. I want you to find out who's behind this, and that's why you're heading to Switzerland.
These are transcripts of coded calls from Jeffrey Barrall, a veteran EON agent.
While following up a lead about a possible Ghost Station at Montelmo resort, he made contact with someone called "HH" who claimed they could lead him to it.
There's not much here. Where's Barrall now?
I wish I knew. He hasn't made contact in six days.
Study those calls, read up on Montelmo, then get some rest. It's a long flight.
Oh, don't worry about me, Mr Clay...
...sleeping isn't the only way to relax.

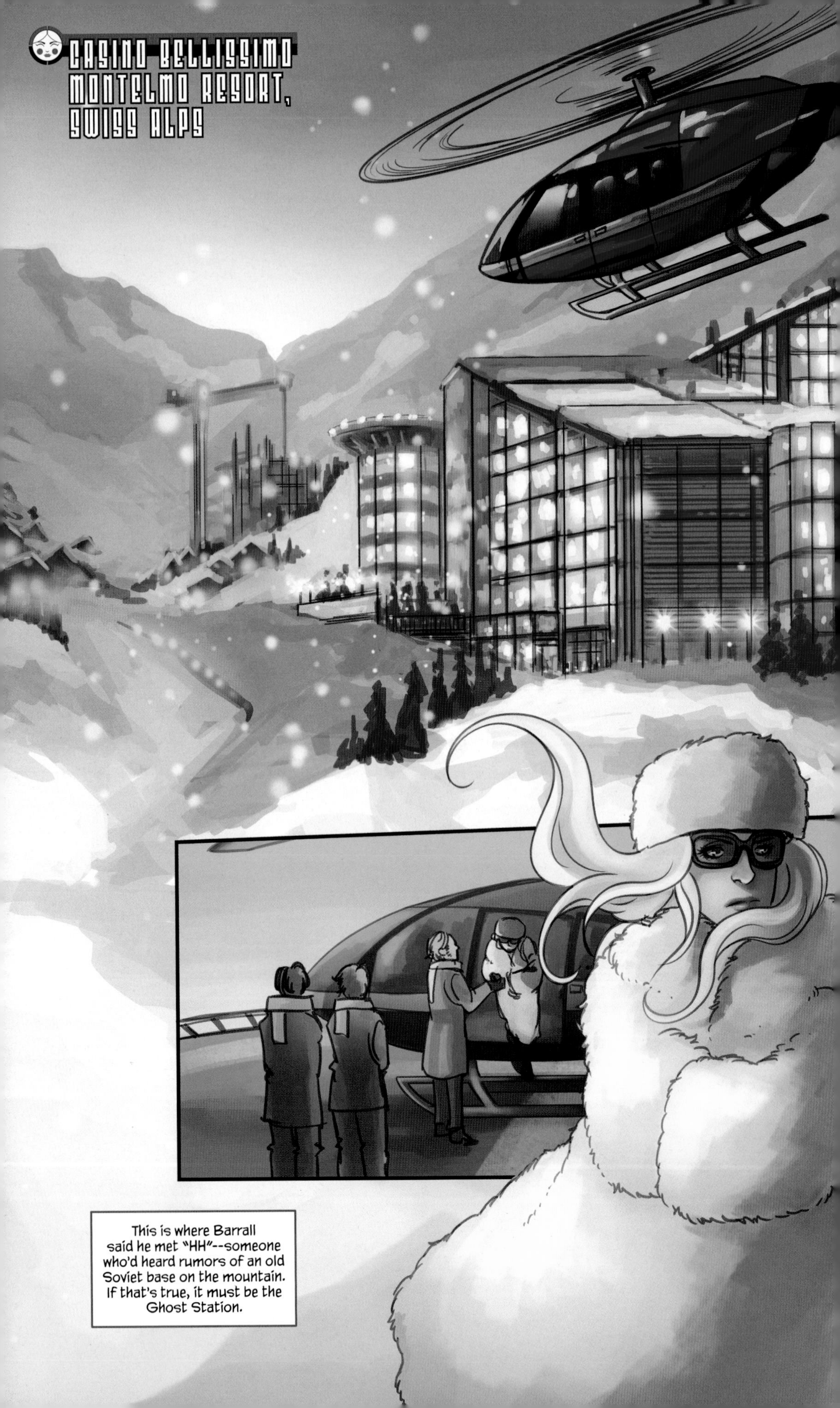
CASINO BELLISSIMO
MONTELMO RESORT,
SWISS ALPS
This is where Barrall said he met "HH"--someone who'd heard rumors of an old Soviet base on the mountain. If that's true, it must be the Ghost Station.

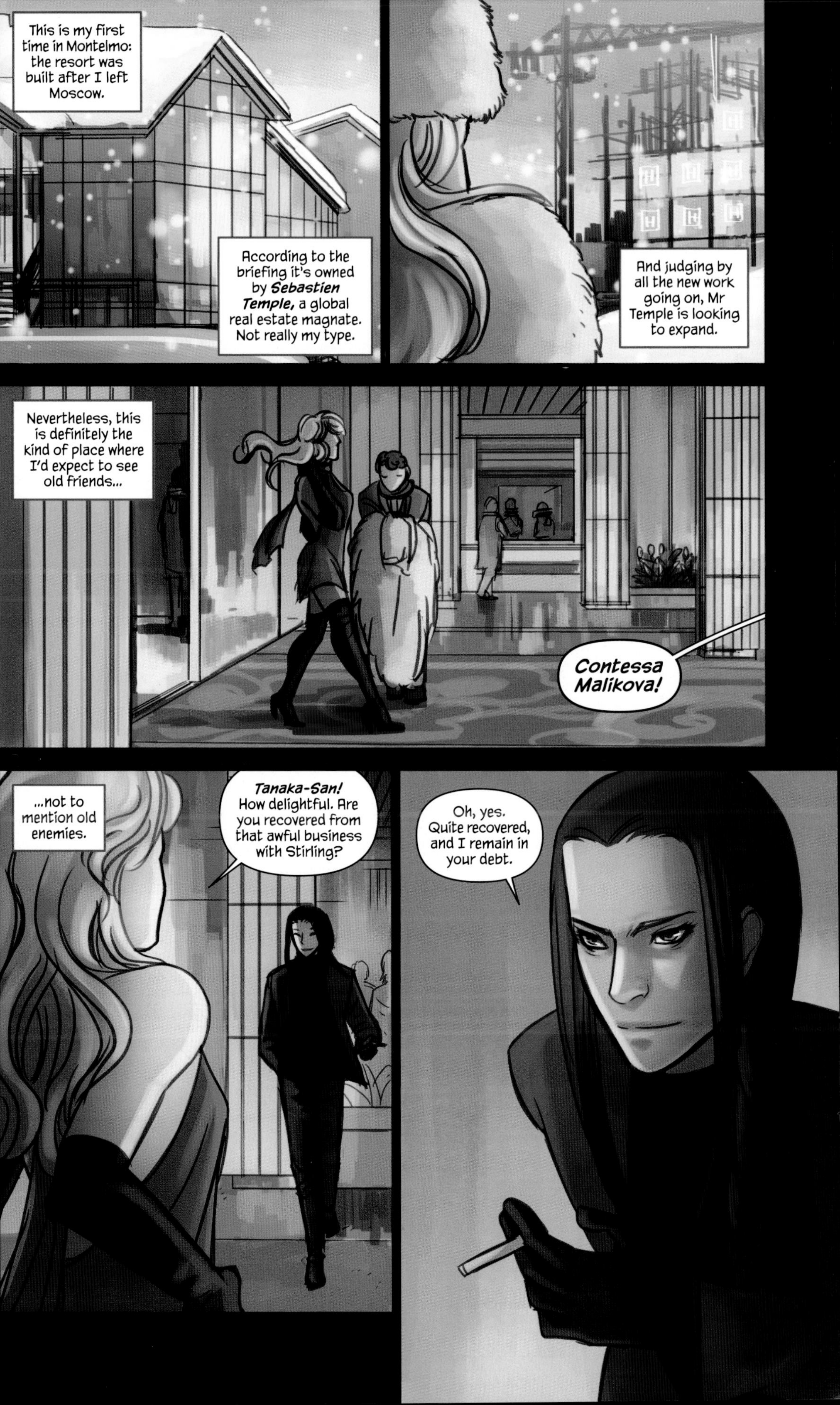
This is my first time in Montelmo: the resort was built after I left Moscow.
According to the briefing it's owned by Sebastien Temple, a global real estate magnate. Not really my type.
And judging by all the new work going on, Mr Temple is looking to expand.
Nevertheless, this is definitely the kind of place where I'd expect to see old friends...
Contessa Malikova!
...not to mention old enemies.
Tanaka-San! How delightful. Are you recovered from that awful business with Stirling?
Oh, yes. Quite recovered, and I remain in your debt.

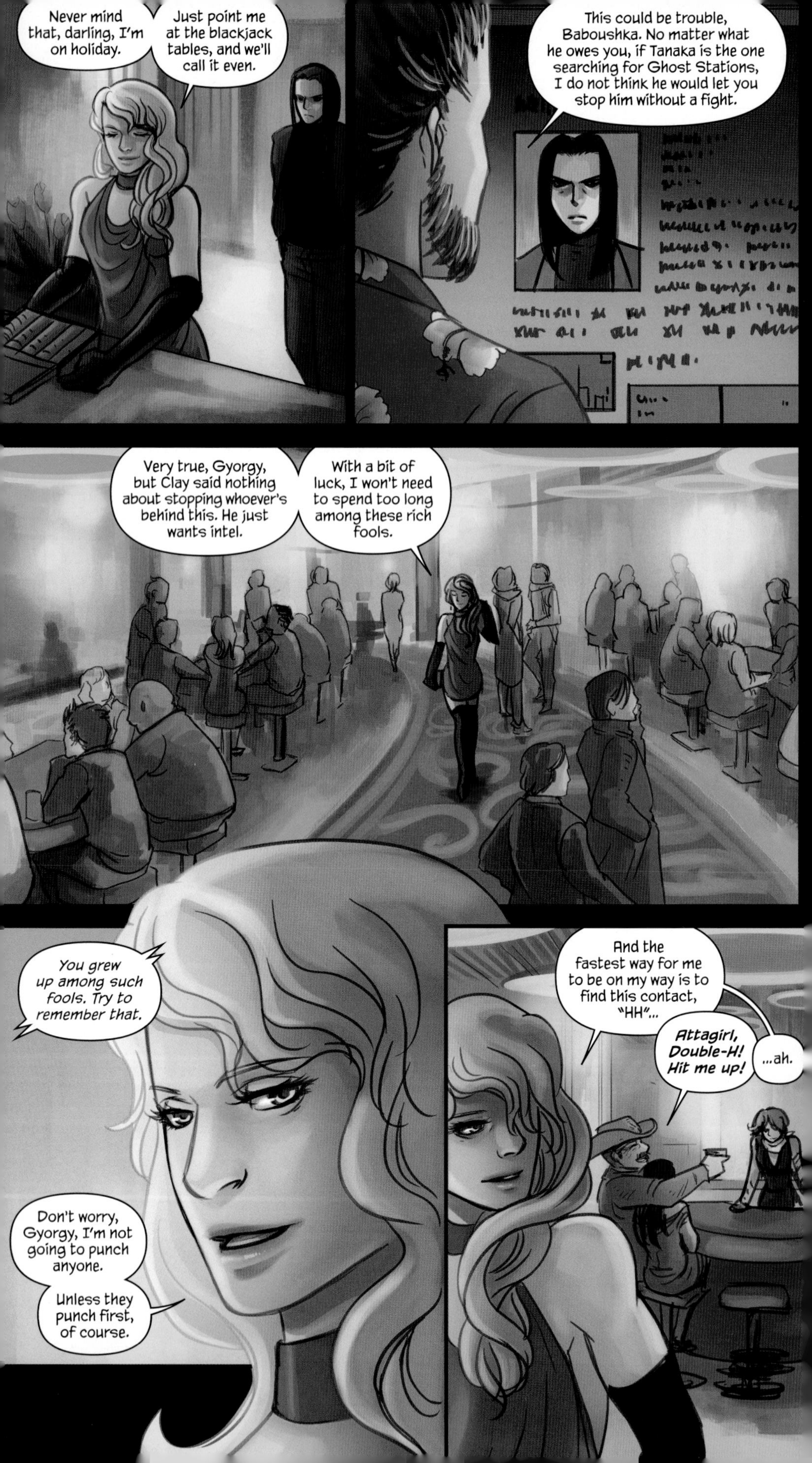
Never mind that, darling, I'm on holiday.
Just point me at the blackjack tables, and we'll call it even.
This could be trouble, Baboushka. No matter what he owes you, if Tanaka is the one searching for Ghost Stations, I do not think he would let you stop him without a fight.
Very true, Gyorgy, but Clay said nothing about stopping whoever's behind this. He just wants intel.
With a bit of luck, I won't need to spend too long among these rich fools.
You grew up among such fools. Try to remember that.
Don't worry, Gyorgy, I'm not going to punch anyone.
Unless they punch first, of course.
And the fastest way for me to be on my way is to find this contact, "HH"...
Attagirl, Double-H! Hit me up!
...ah.

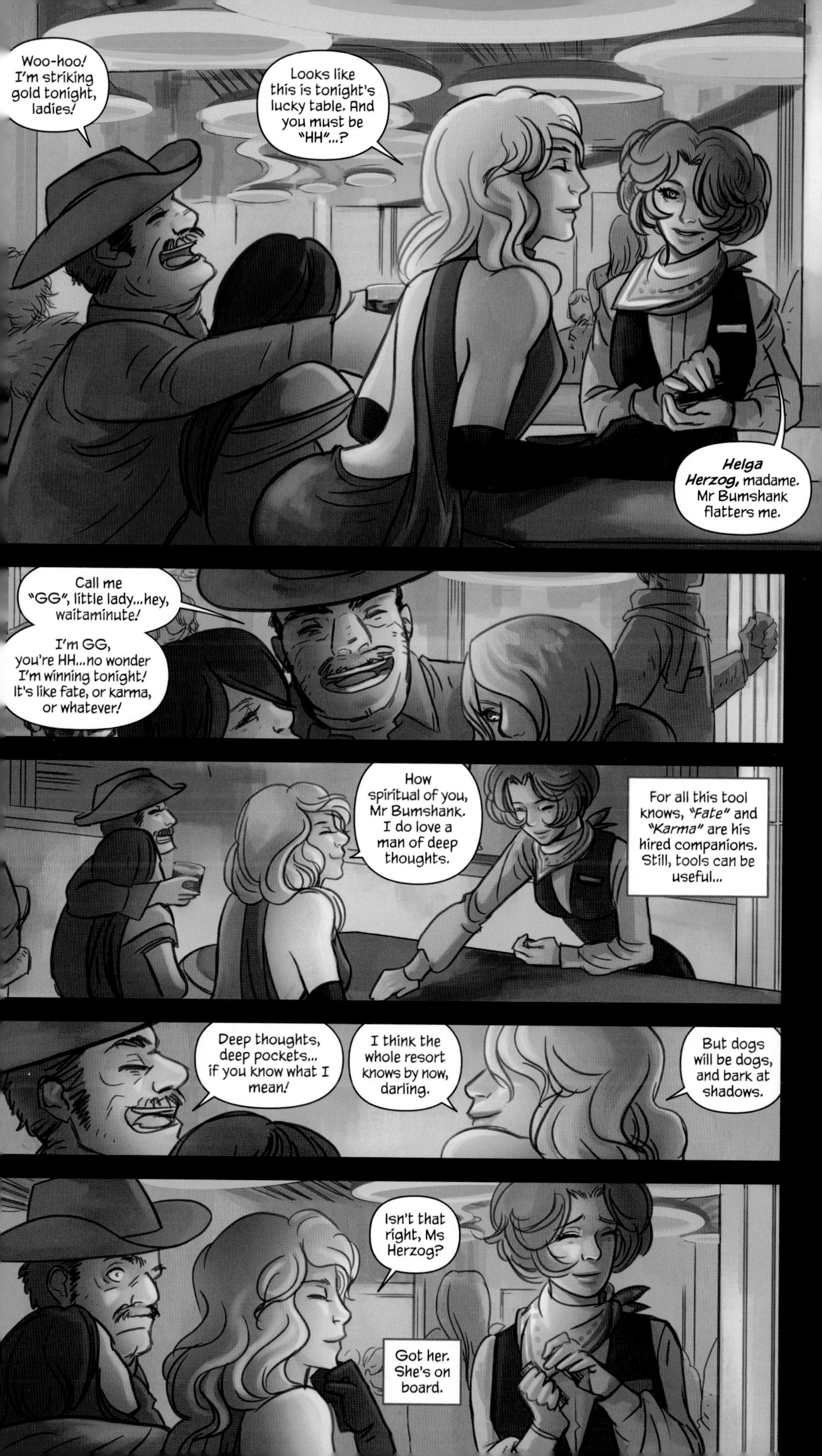
Woo-hoo! I'm striking gold tonight, ladies!
Looks like this is tonight's lucky table. And you must be "HH"...?
Helga Herzog, madame. Mr Bumshank flatters me.
Call me "GG", little lady...hey, waitaminute!
I'm GG, you're HH...no wonder I'm winning tonight! It's like fate, or karma, or whatever!
How spiritual of you, Mr Bumshank. I do love a man of deep thoughts.
For all this tool knows, *"Fate"* and *"Karma"* are his hired companions. Still, tools can be useful...
Deep thoughts, deep pockets... if you know what I mean!
I think the whole resort knows by now, darling.
But dogs will be dogs, and bark at shadows.
Isn't that right, Ms Herzog?
Got her. She's on board.

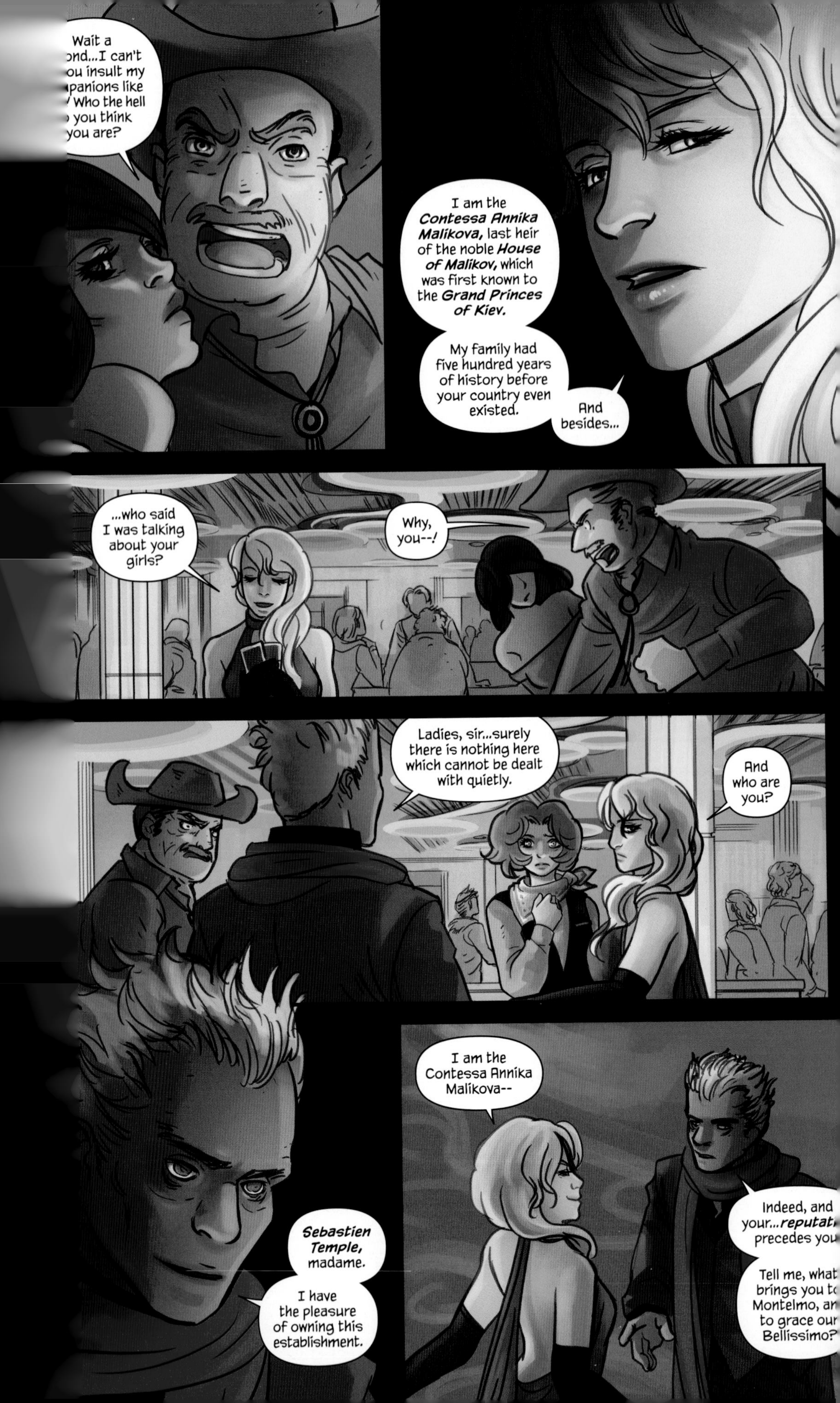

Wait a
ond...I can't
ou insult my
panions like
Who the hell
you think
you are?
I am the Contessa Annika Malikova, last heir of the noble House of Malikov, which was first known to the Grand Princes of Kiev.
My family had five hundred years of history before your country even existed.
And besides...
...who said I was talking about your girls?
Why, you--!
Ladies, sir...surely there is nothing here which cannot be dealt with quietly.
And who are you?
I am the Contessa Annika Malikova--
Sebastien Temple, madame.
I have the pleasure of owning this establishment.
Indeed, and your...reputat
precedes you
Tell me, what
brings you t
Montelmo, an
to grace our
Bellissimo?

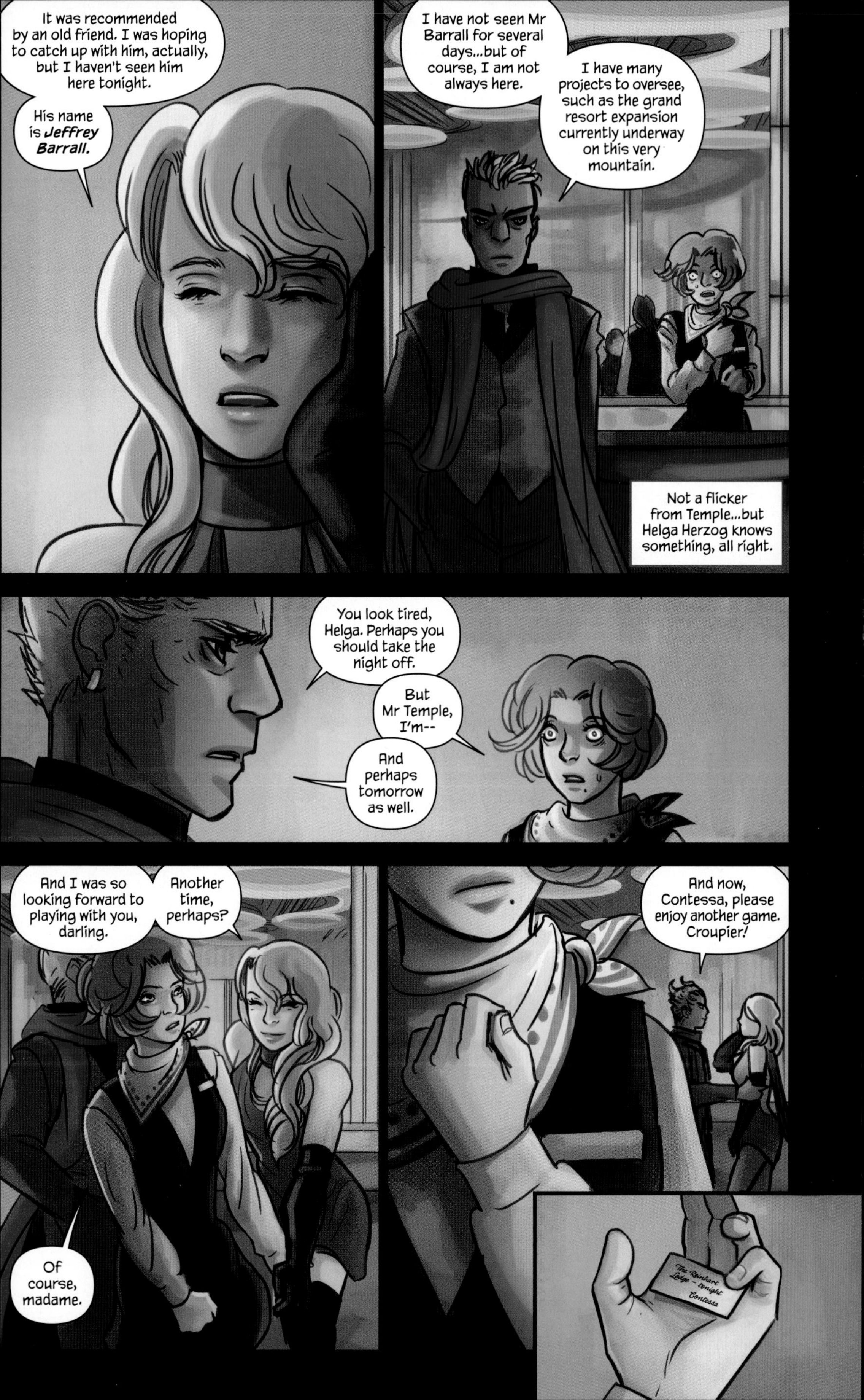
It was recommended by an old friend. I was hoping to catch up with him, actually, but I haven't seen him here tonight.
His name is ***Jeffrey Barrall.***
I have not seen Mr Barrall for several days...but of course, I am not always here.
I have many projects to oversee, such as the grand resort expansion currently underway on this very mountain.
Not a flicker from Temple...but Helga Herzog knows something, all right.
You look tired, Helga. Perhaps you should take the night off.
But Mr Temple, I'm--
And perhaps tomorrow as well.
And I was so looking forward to playing with you, darling.
Another time, perhaps?
Of course, madame.
And now, Contessa, please enjoy another game. Croupier!
The Reinhart Lodge – tonight
Contessa

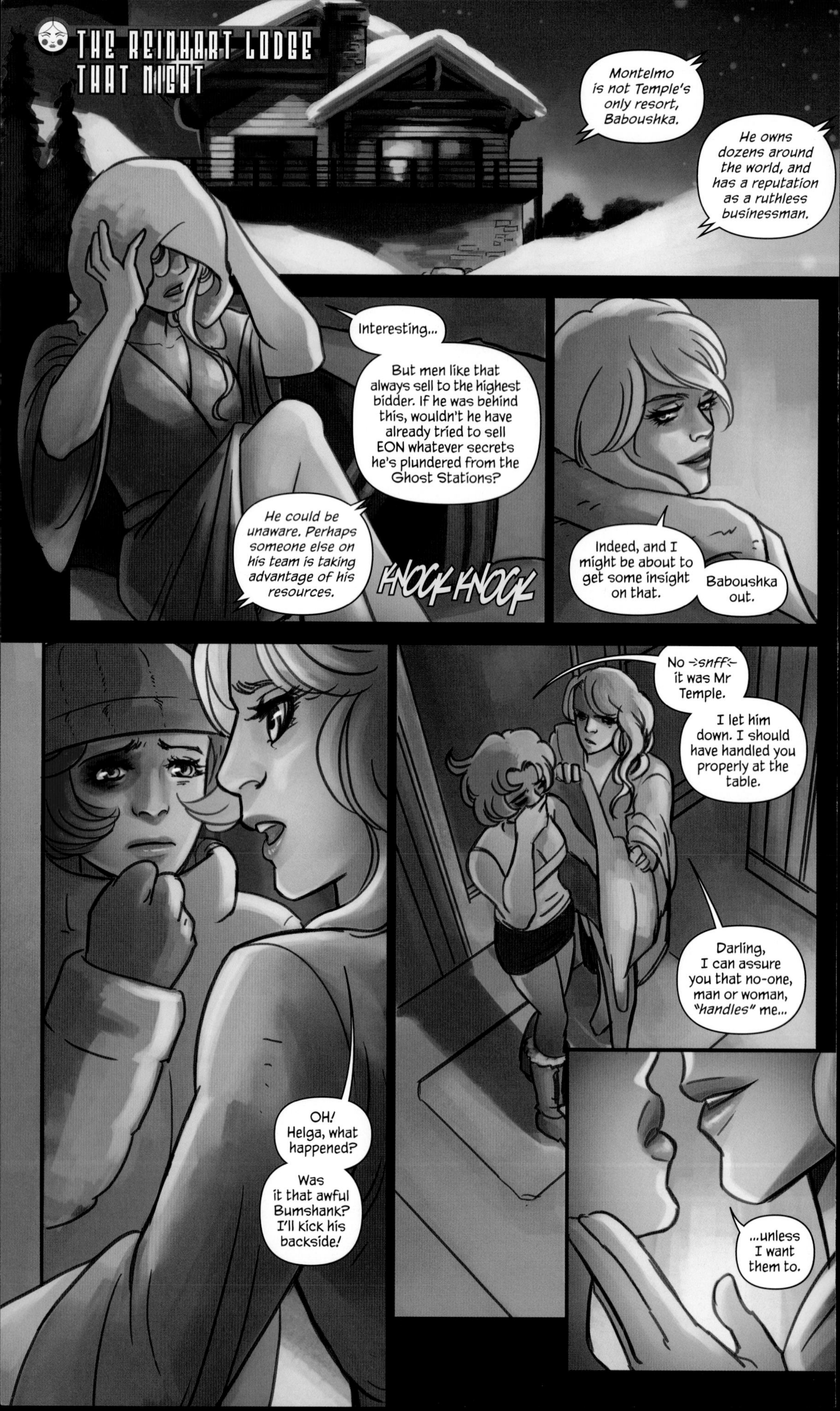
THE REINHART LODGE
THAT NIGHT
Montelmo is not Temple's only resort, Baboushka.
He owns dozens around the world, and has a reputation as a ruthless businessman.
Interesting...
But men like that always sell to the highest bidder. If he was behind this, wouldn't he have already tried to sell EON whatever secrets he's plundered from the Ghost Stations?
He could be unaware. Perhaps someone else on his team is taking advantage of his resources.
KNOCK KNOCK
Indeed, and I might be about to get some insight on that.
Baboushka out.
OH! Helga, what happened?
Was it that awful Bumshank? I'll kick his backside!
No -snff- it was Mr Temple.
I let him down. I should have handled you properly at the table.
Darling, I can assure you that no-one, man or woman, "handles" me...
...unless I want them to.

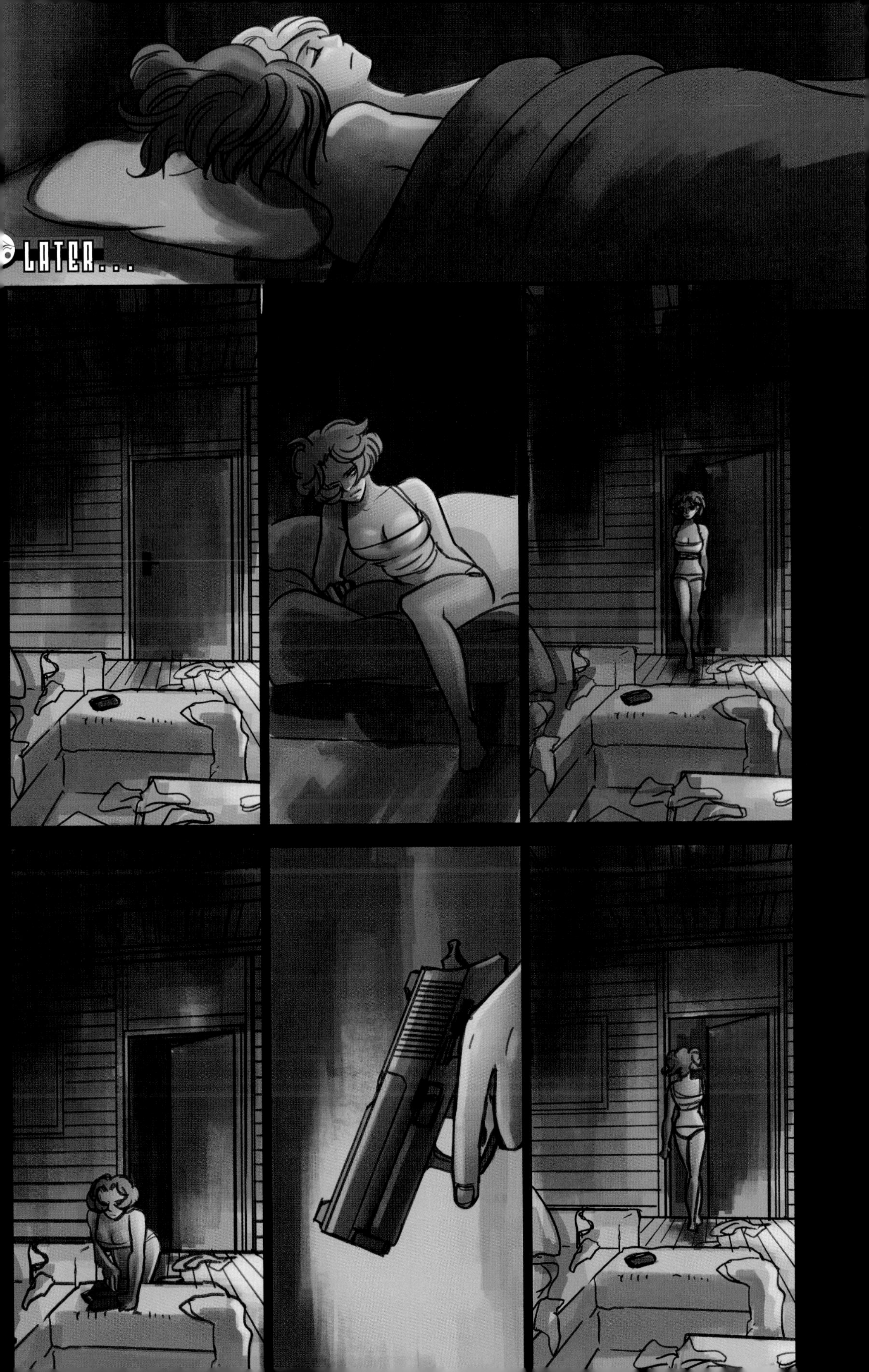
LATER...

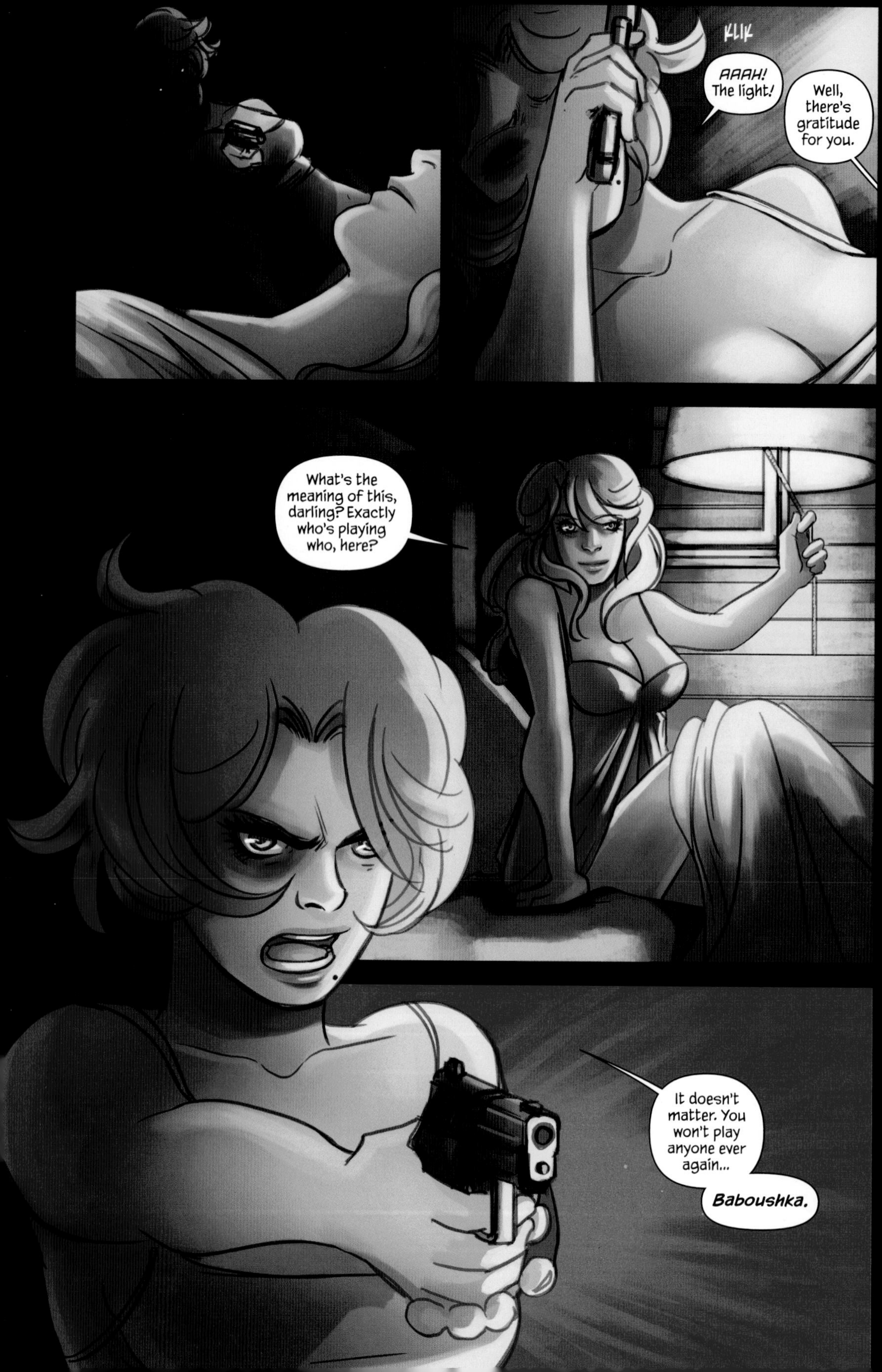
KLIK
AAAH! The light!
Well, there's gratitude for you.
What's the meaning of this, darling? Exactly who's playing who, here?
It doesn't matter. You won't play anyone ever again...
Baboushka.

PART ★ TWO

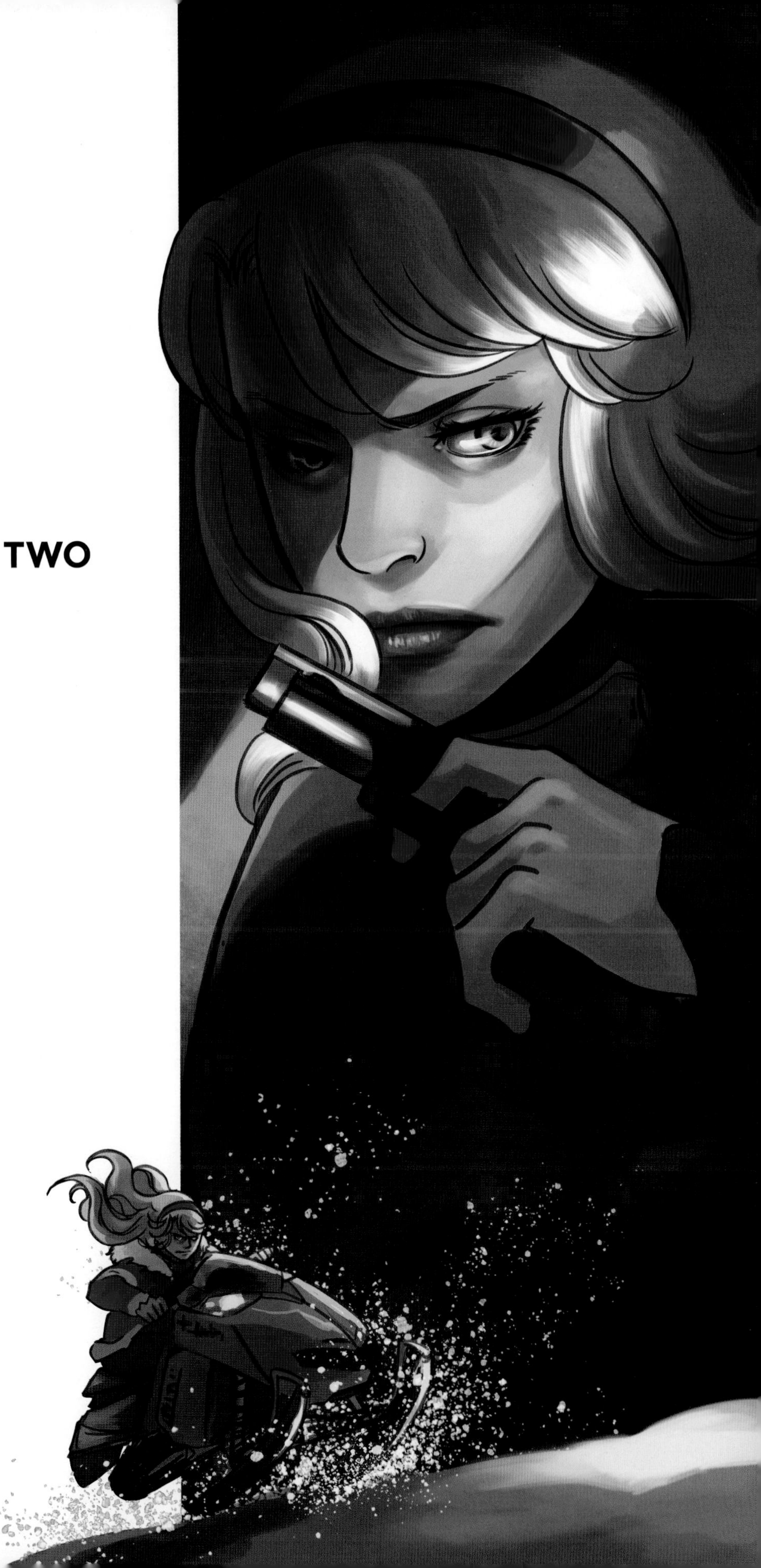

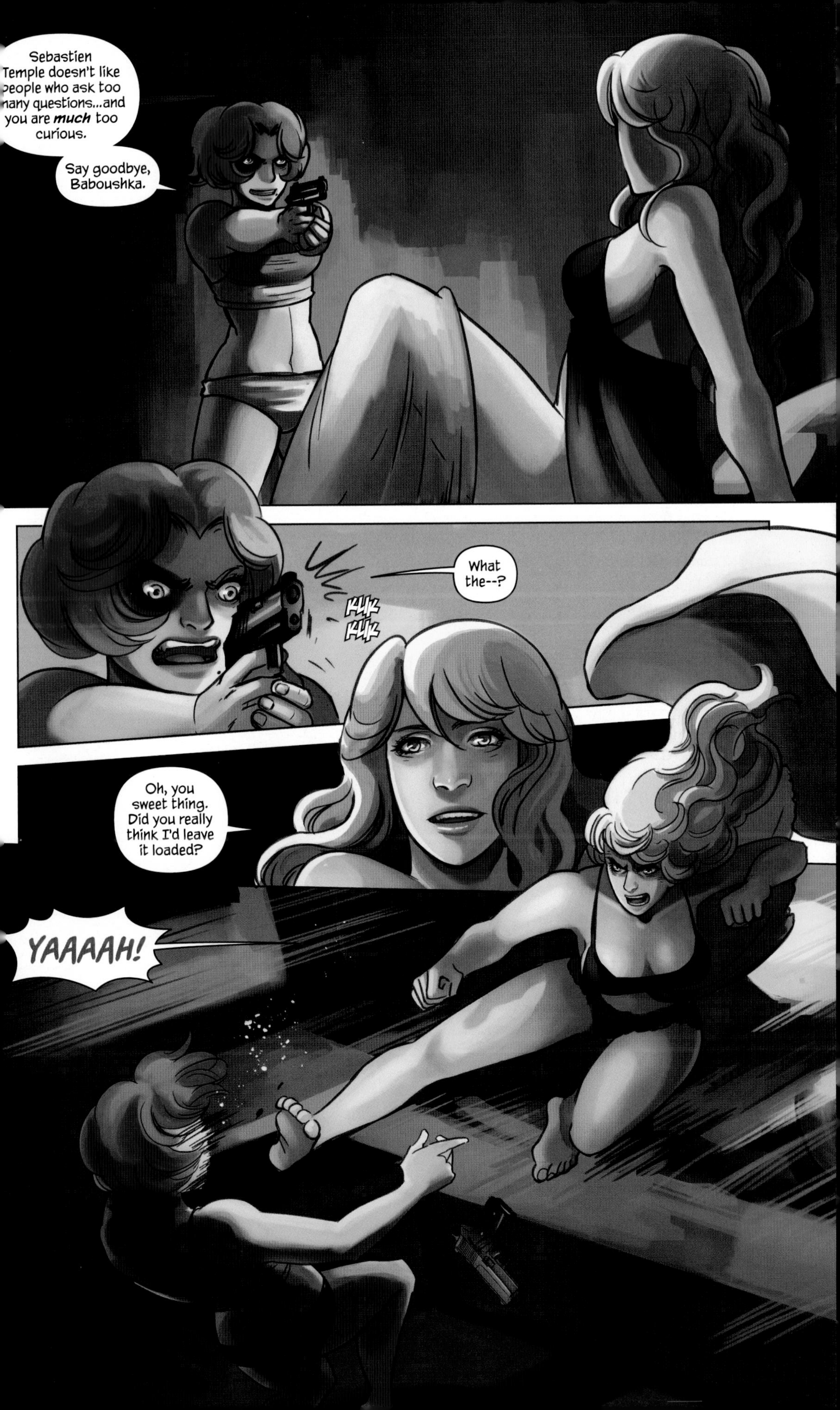
Sebastien Temple doesn't like people who ask too many questions...and you are *much* too curious.
Say goodbye, Baboushka.
What the--?
KLIK KLIK
Oh, you sweet thing. Did you really think I'd leave it loaded?
YAAAAH!

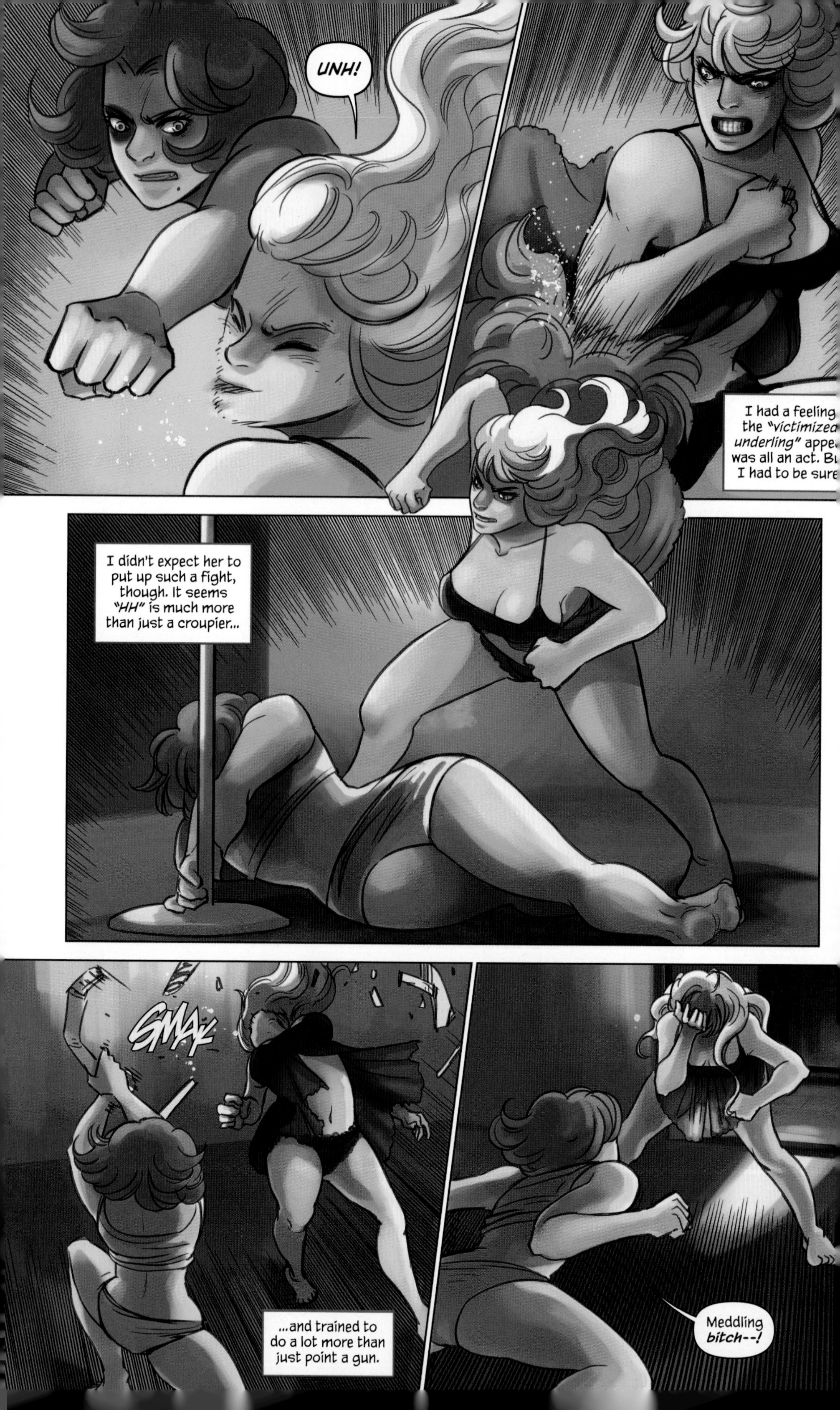
UNH!
I had a feeling the "victimized underling" appe... was all an act. Bu... I had to be sure
I didn't expect her to put up such a fight, though. It seems "HH" is much more than just a croupier...
SMAK
...and trained to do a lot more than just point a gun.
Meddling bitch--!

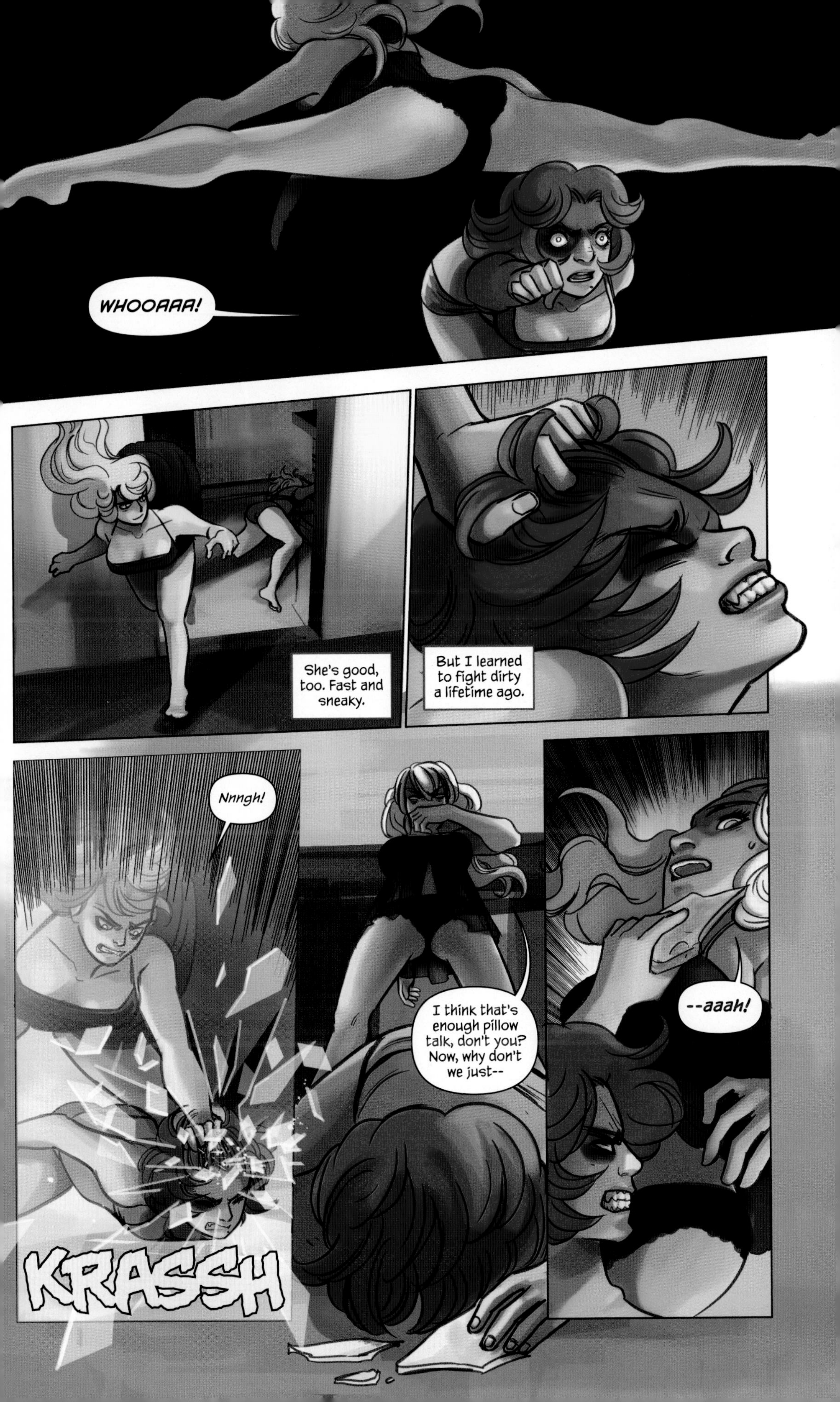
WHOOAAA!
She's good, too. Fast and sneaky.
But I learned to fight dirty a lifetime ago.
Nnngh!
KRASSH
I think that's enough pillow talk, don't you? Now, why don't we just--
--aaah!

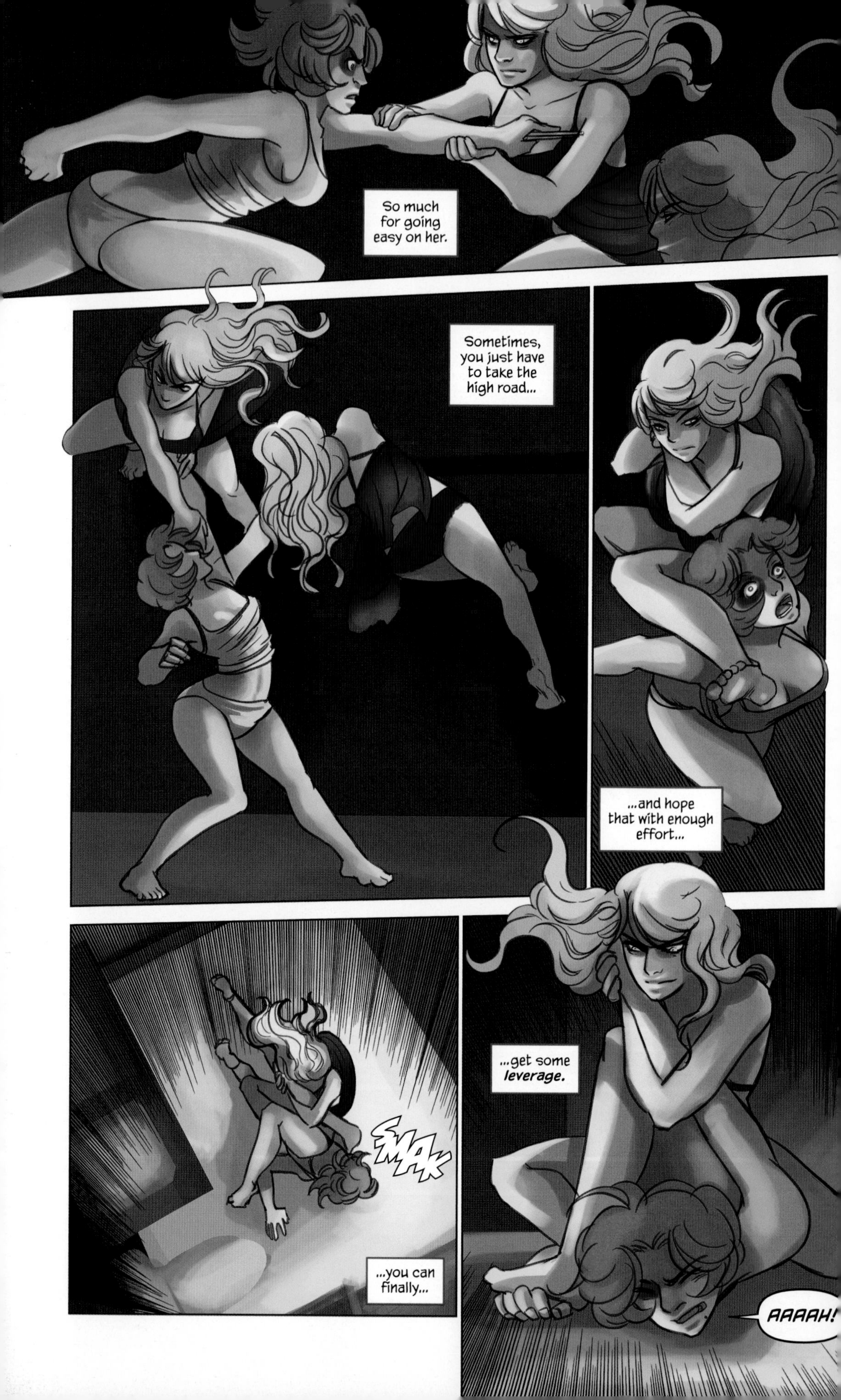
So much for going easy on her.
Sometimes, you just have to take the high road...
...and hope that with enough effort...
...you can finally...
SMAK
...get some *leverage.*
AAAAH!

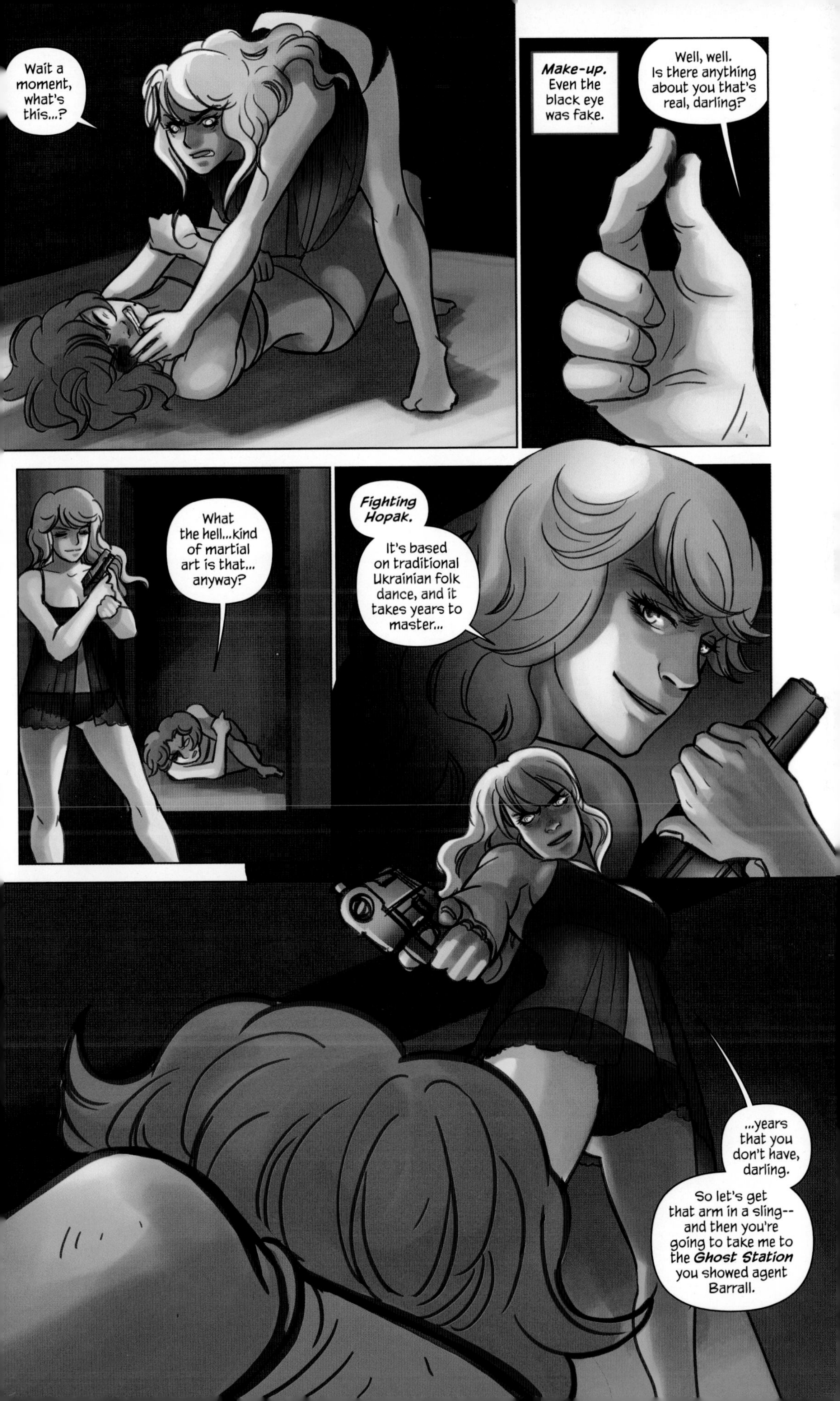
Wait a moment, what's this...?
Make-up. Even the black eye was fake.
Well, well. Is there anything about you that's real, darling?
What the hell...kind of martial art is that... anyway?
Fighting Hopak.
It's based on traditional Ukrainian folk dance, and it takes years to master...
...years that you don't have, darling.
So let's get that arm in a sling-- and then you're going to take me to the Ghost Station you showed agent Barrall.

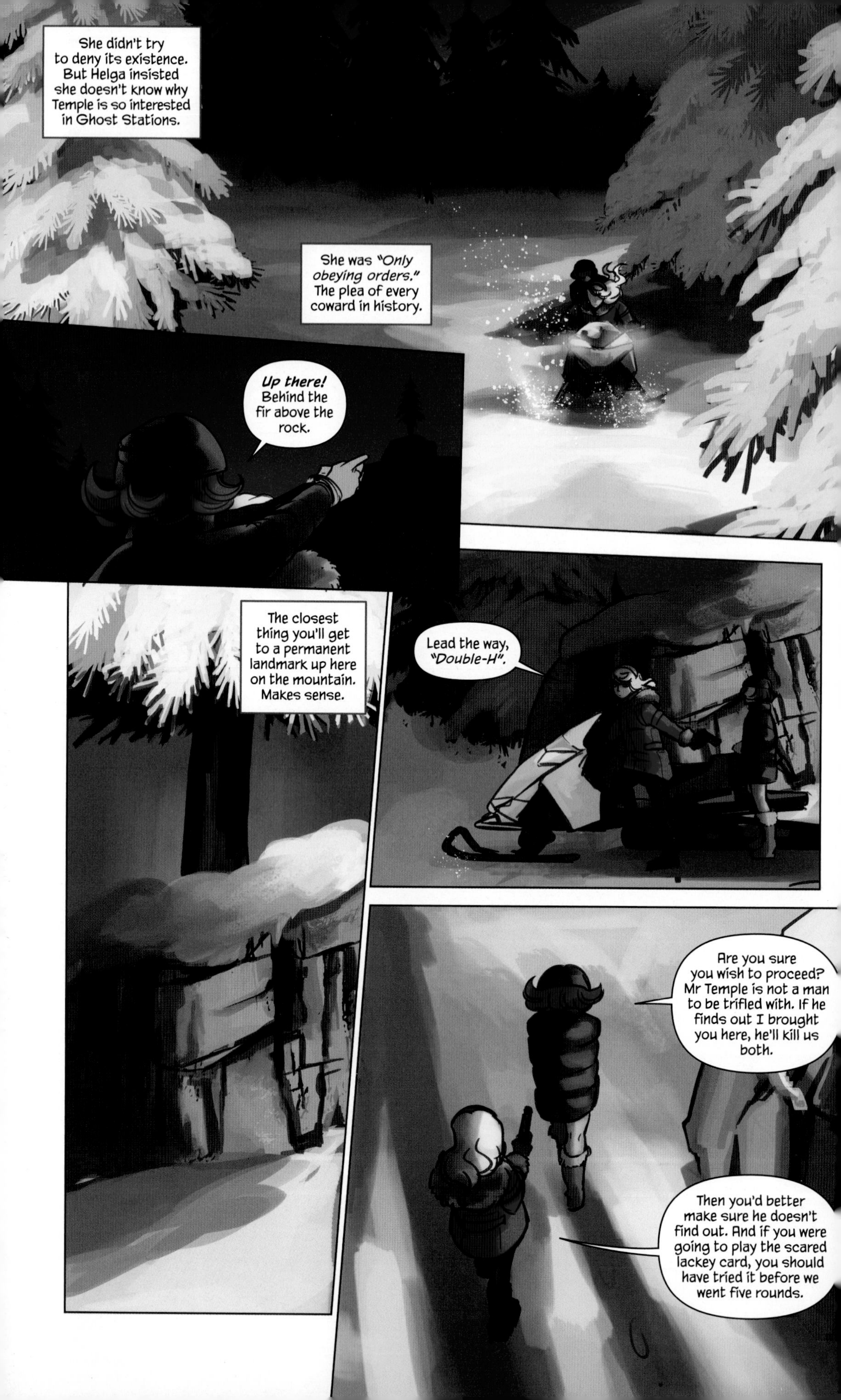
She didn't try to deny its existence. But Helga insisted she doesn't know why Temple is so interested in Ghost Stations.
She was *"Only obeying orders."* The plea of every coward in history.
Up there! Behind the fir above the rock.
The closest thing you'll get to a permanent landmark up here on the mountain. Makes sense.
Lead the way, *"Double-H"*.
Are you sure you wish to proceed? Mr Temple is not a man to be trifled with. If he finds out I brought you here, he'll kill us both.
Then you'd better make sure he doesn't find out. And if you were going to play the scared lackey card, you should have tried it before we went five rounds.

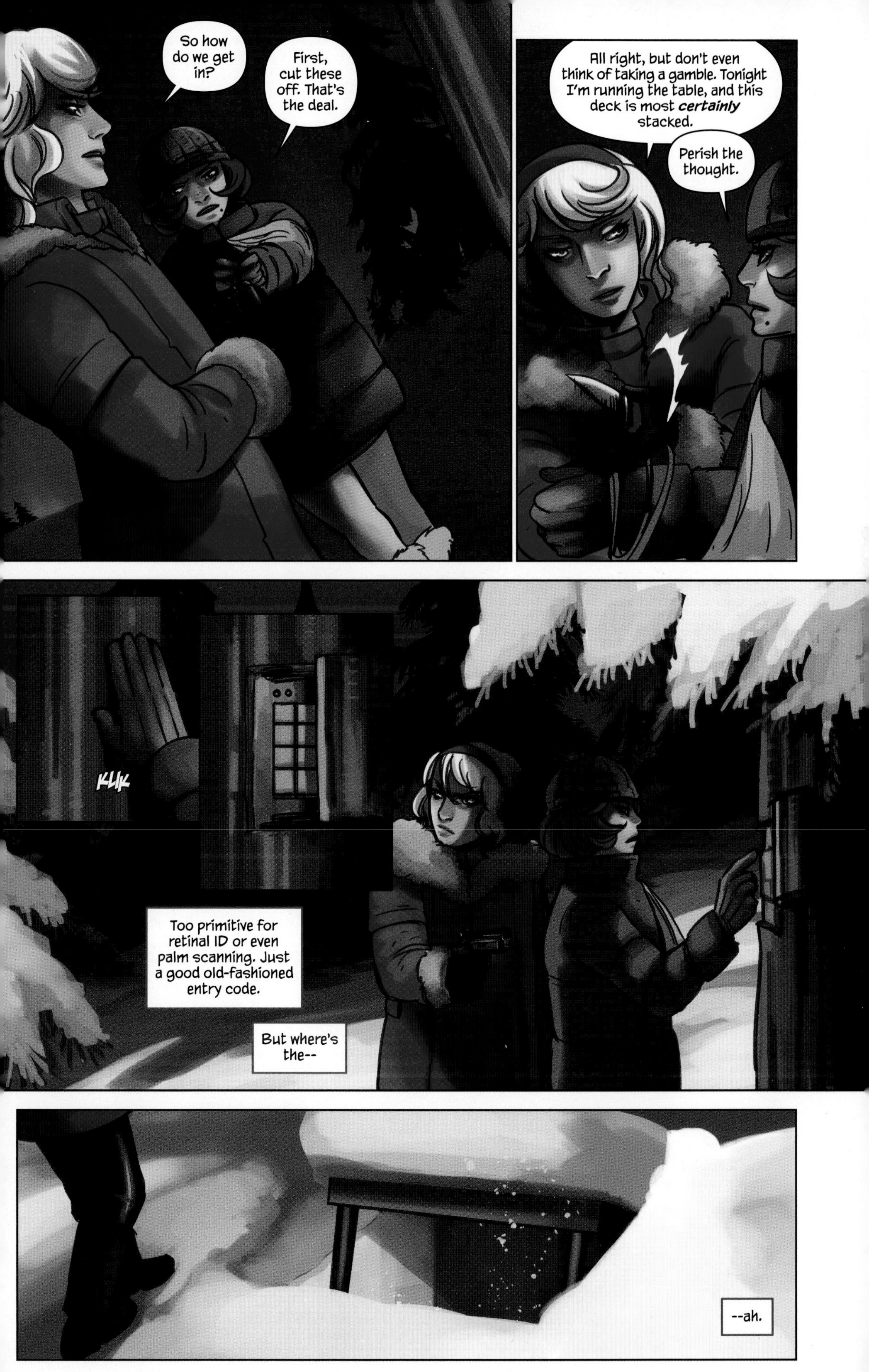
So how do we get in?
First, cut these off. That's the deal.
All right, but don't even think of taking a gamble. Tonight I'm running the table, and this deck is most *certainly* stacked.
Perish the thought.
KLIK
Too primitive for retinal ID or even palm scanning. Just a good old-fashioned entry code.
But where's the--
--ah.

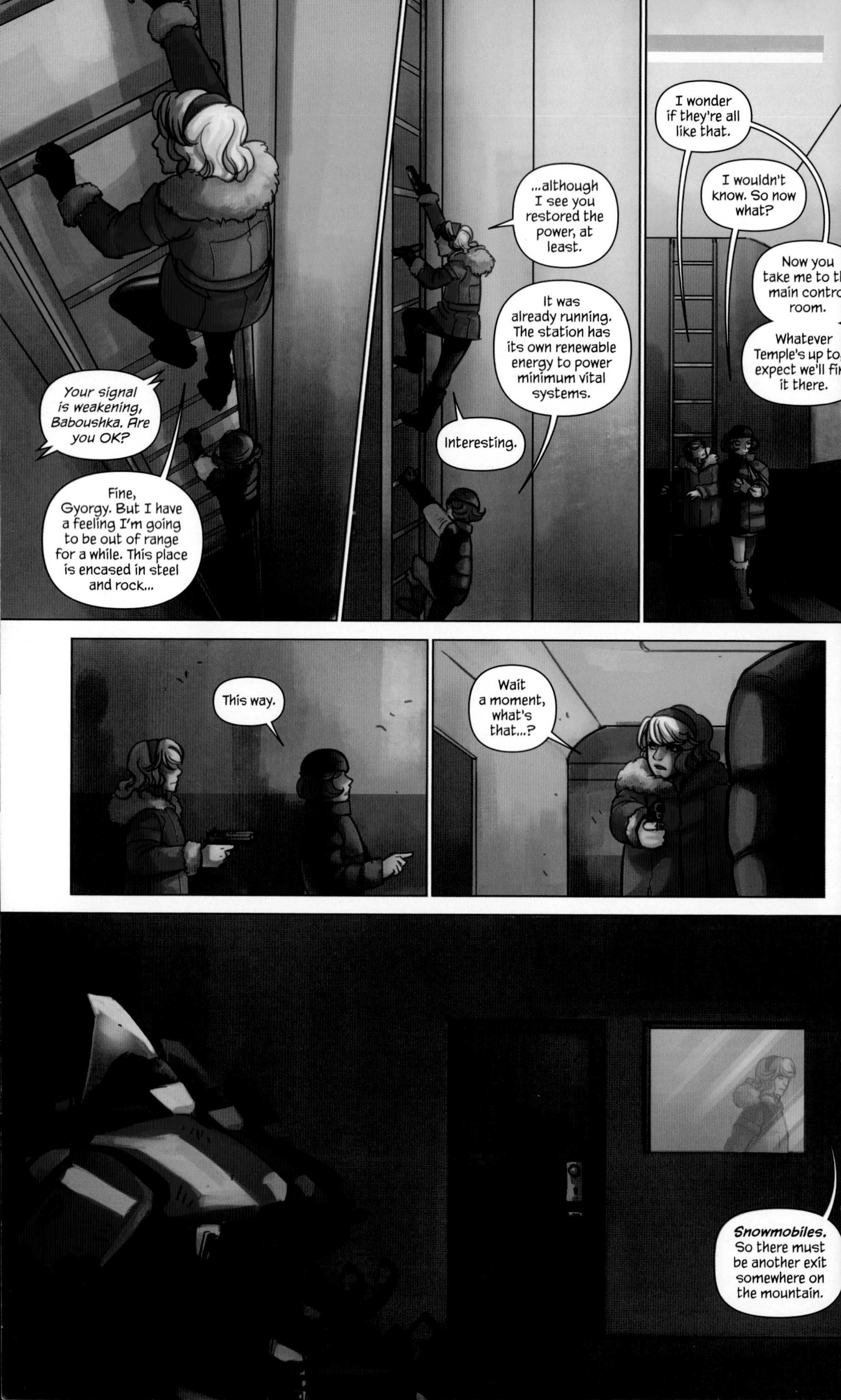

Your signal is weakening, Baboushka. Are you OK?
Fine, Gyorgy. But I have a feeling I'm going to be out of range for a while. This place is encased in steel and rock...
...although I see you restored the power, at least.
Interesting.
It was already running. The station has its own renewable energy to power minimum vital systems.
I wonder if they're all like that.
I wouldn't know. So now what?
Now you take me to th main contro room.
Whatever Temple's up to expect we'll fi it there.
This way.
Wait a moment, what's that...?
Snowmobiles. So there must be another exit somewhere on the mountain.

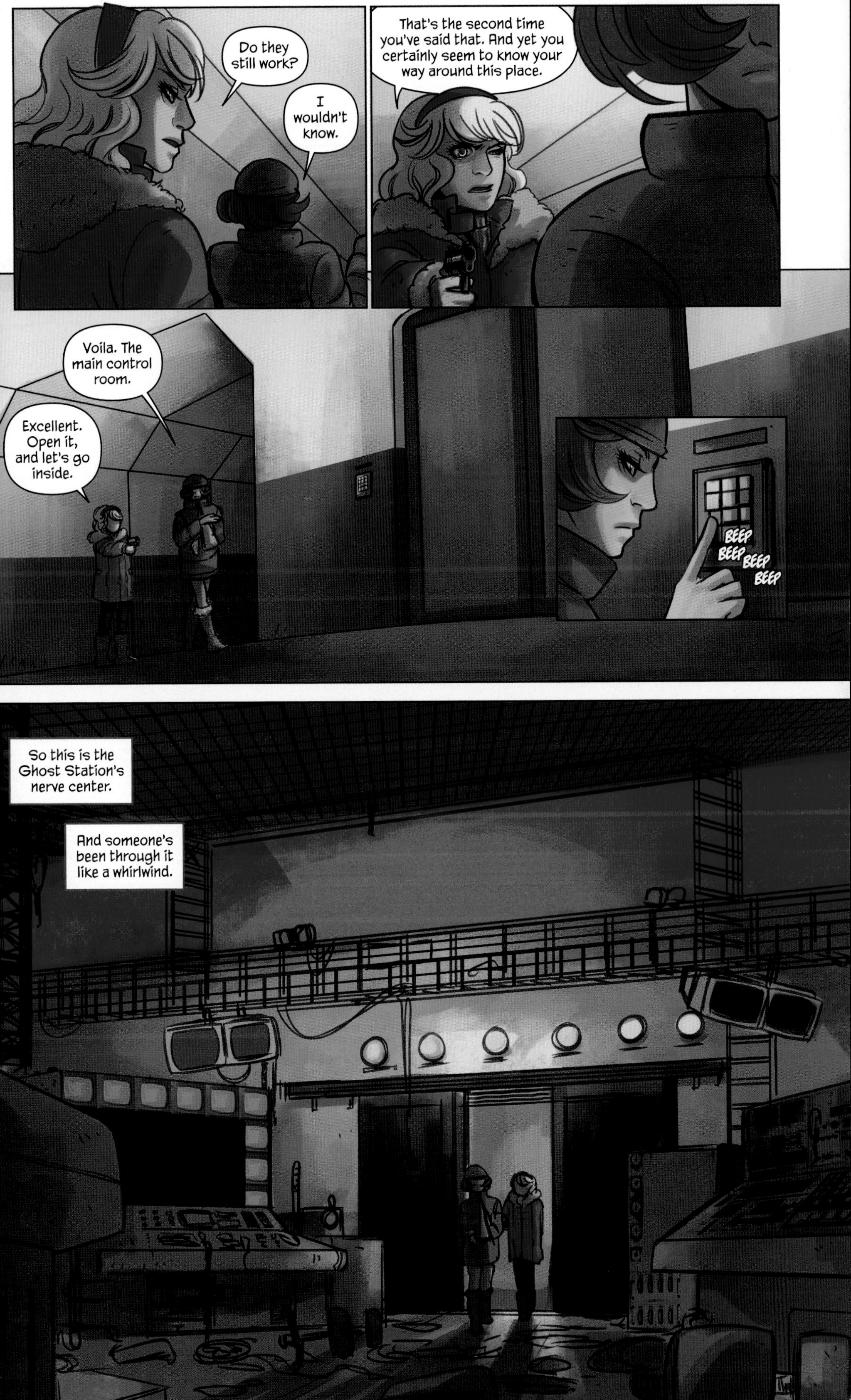
Do they still work?
I wouldn't know.
That's the second time you've said that. And yet you certainly seem to know your way around this place.
Voila. The main control room.
Excellent. Open it, and let's go inside.
BEEP BEEP BEEP BEEP
So this is the Ghost Station's nerve center.
And someone's been through it like a whirlwind.

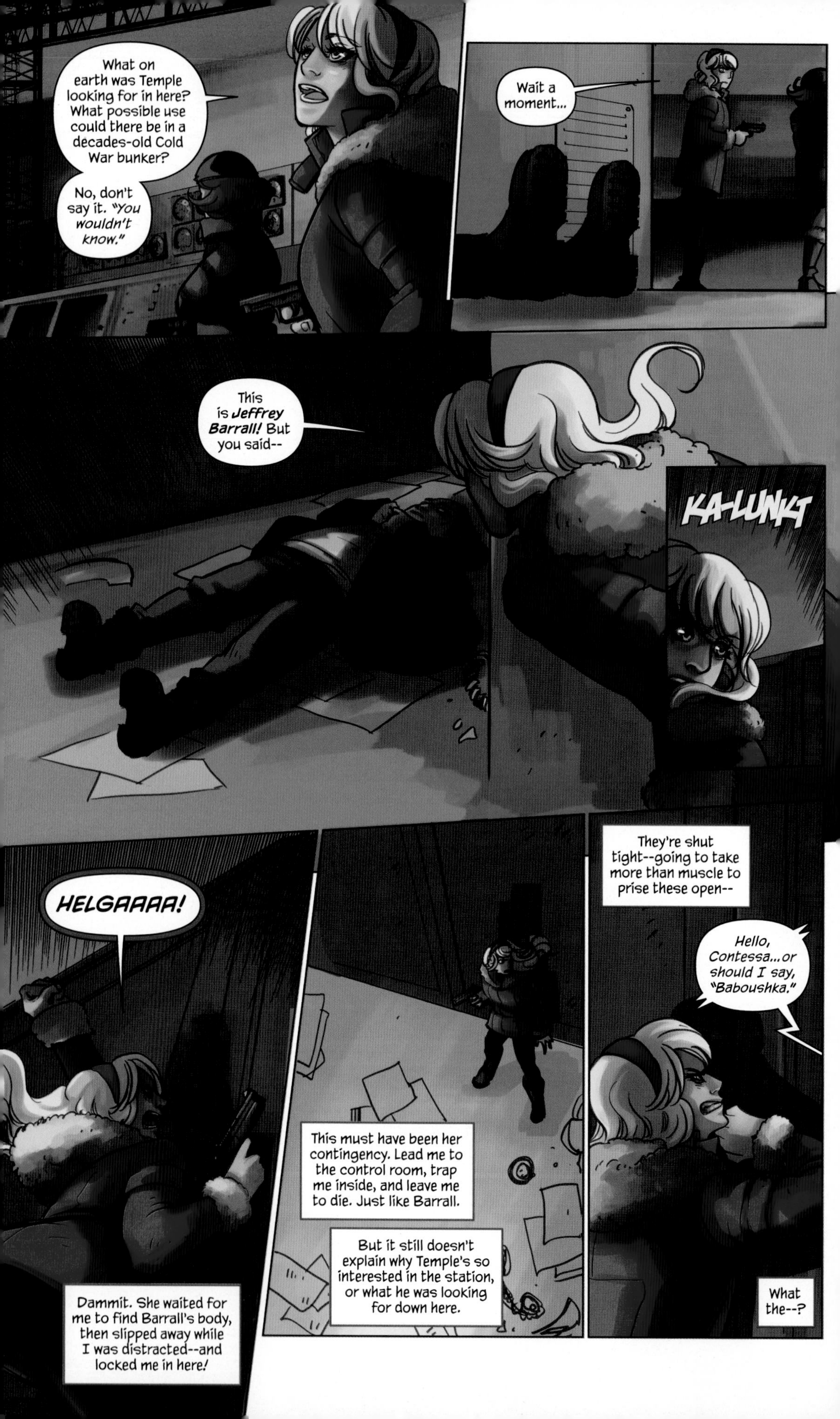
What on earth was Temple looking for in here? What possible use could there be in a decades-old Cold War bunker?
No, don't say it. "You wouldn't know."
Wait a moment...
This is Jeffrey Barrall! But you said--
KA-LUNKT
HELGAAAA!
Dammit. She waited for me to find Barrall's body, then slipped away while I was distracted--and locked me in here!
This must have been her contingency. Lead me to the control room, trap me inside, and leave me to die. Just like Barrall.
But it still doesn't explain why Temple's so interested in the station, or what he was looking for down here.
They're shut tight--going to take more than muscle to prise these open--
Hello, Contessa...or should I say, "Baboushka."
What the--?

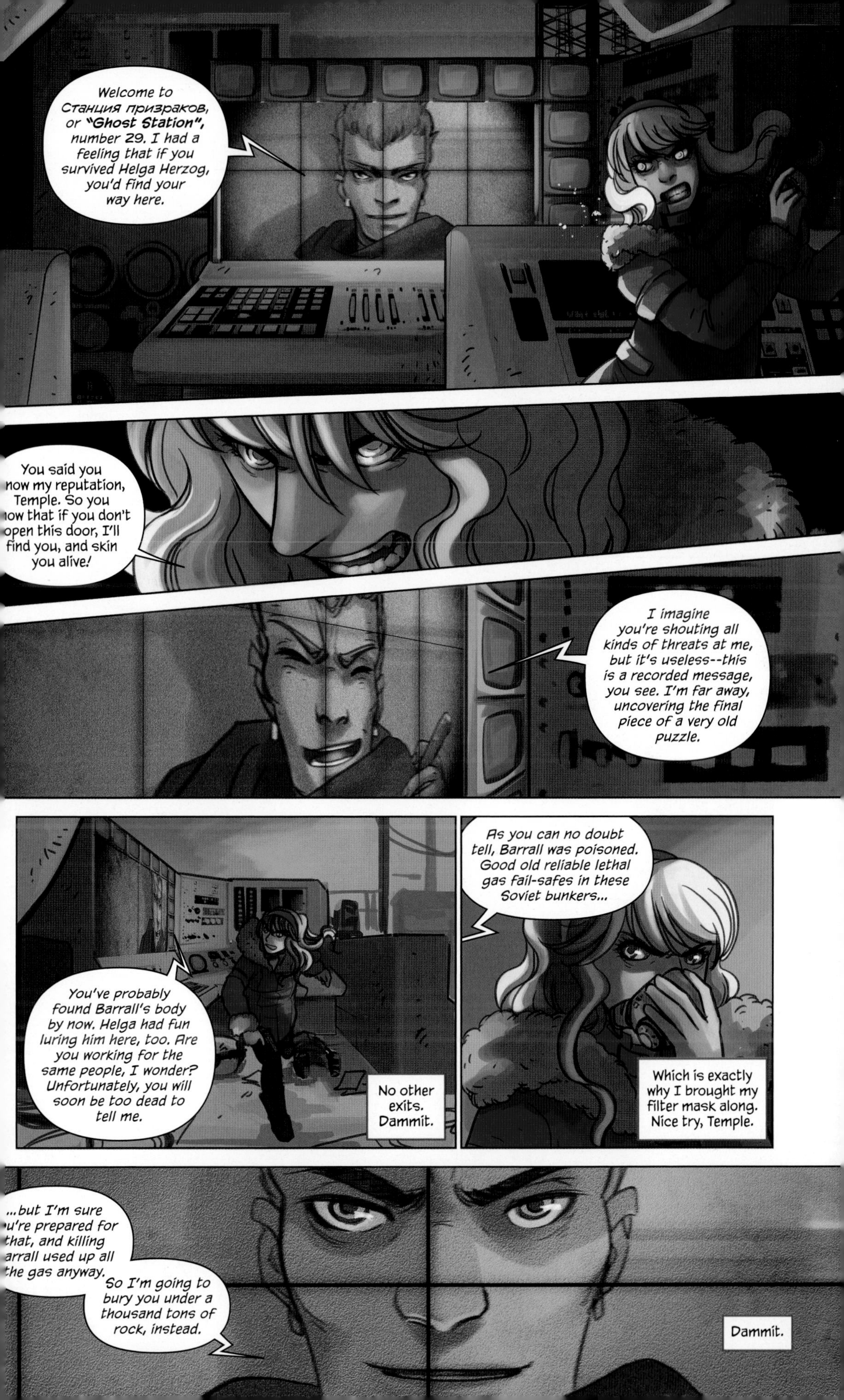
Welcome to Станция призраков, or "Ghost Station", number 29. I had a feeling that if you survived Helga Herzog, you'd find your way here.
You said you now my reputation, Temple. So you now that if you don't open this door, I'll find you, and skin you alive!
I imagine you're shouting all kinds of threats at me, but it's useless--this is a recorded message, you see. I'm far away, uncovering the final piece of a very old puzzle.
You've probably found Barrall's body by now. Helga had fun luring him here, too. Are you working for the same people, I wonder? Unfortunately, you will soon be too dead to tell me.
No other exits. Dammit.
As you can no doubt tell, Barrall was poisoned. Good old reliable lethal gas fail-safes in these Soviet bunkers...
Which is exactly why I brought my filter mask along. Nice try, Temple.
...but I'm sure u're prepared for that, and killing arrall used up all the gas anyway.
So I'm going to bury you under a thousand tons of rock, instead.
Dammit.

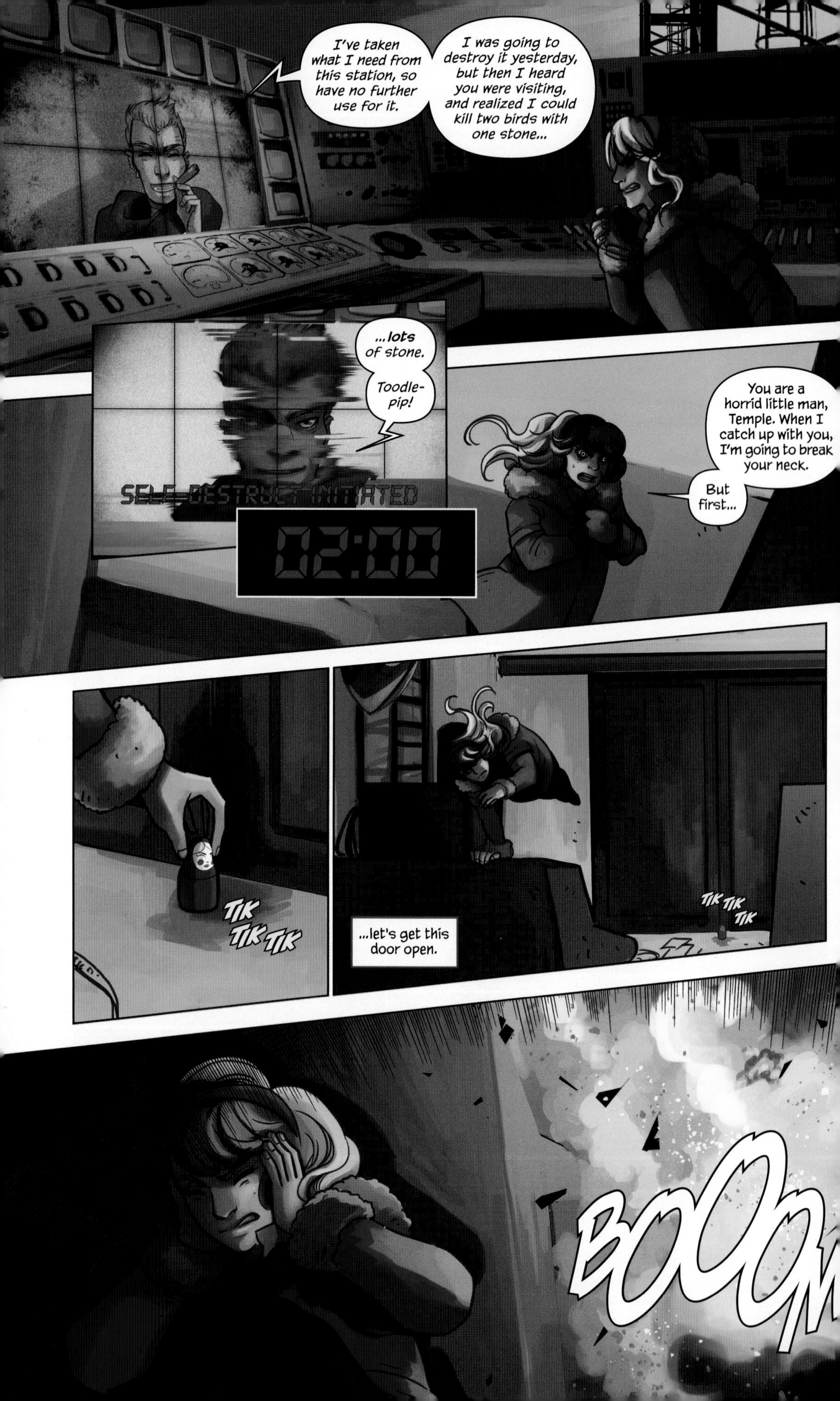
I've taken what I need from this station, so have no further use for it.
I was going to destroy it yesterday, but then I heard you were visiting, and realized I could kill two birds with one stone...
...lots of stone.
Toodle-pip!
SELF-DESTRUCT INITIATED
02:00
You are a horrid little man, Temple. When I catch up with you, I'm going to break your neck.
But first...
TIK TIK TIK
...let's get this door open.
TIK TIK TIK
BOOM

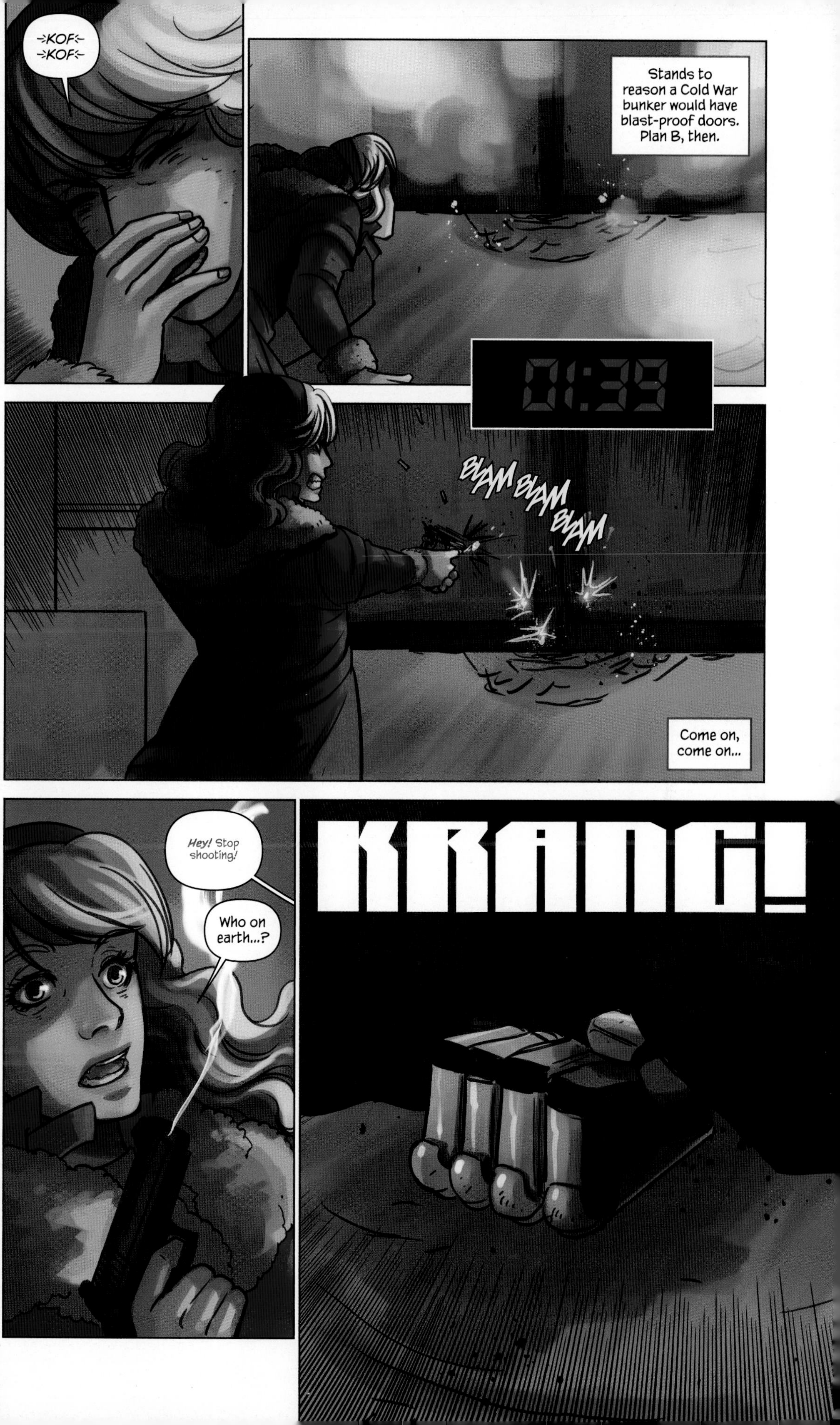

-KOF-
-KOF-
Stands to reason a Cold War bunker would have blast-proof doors. Plan B, then.
01:39
BLAM BLAM BLAM
Come on, come on...
Hey! Stop shooting!
Who on earth...?
KRANG!

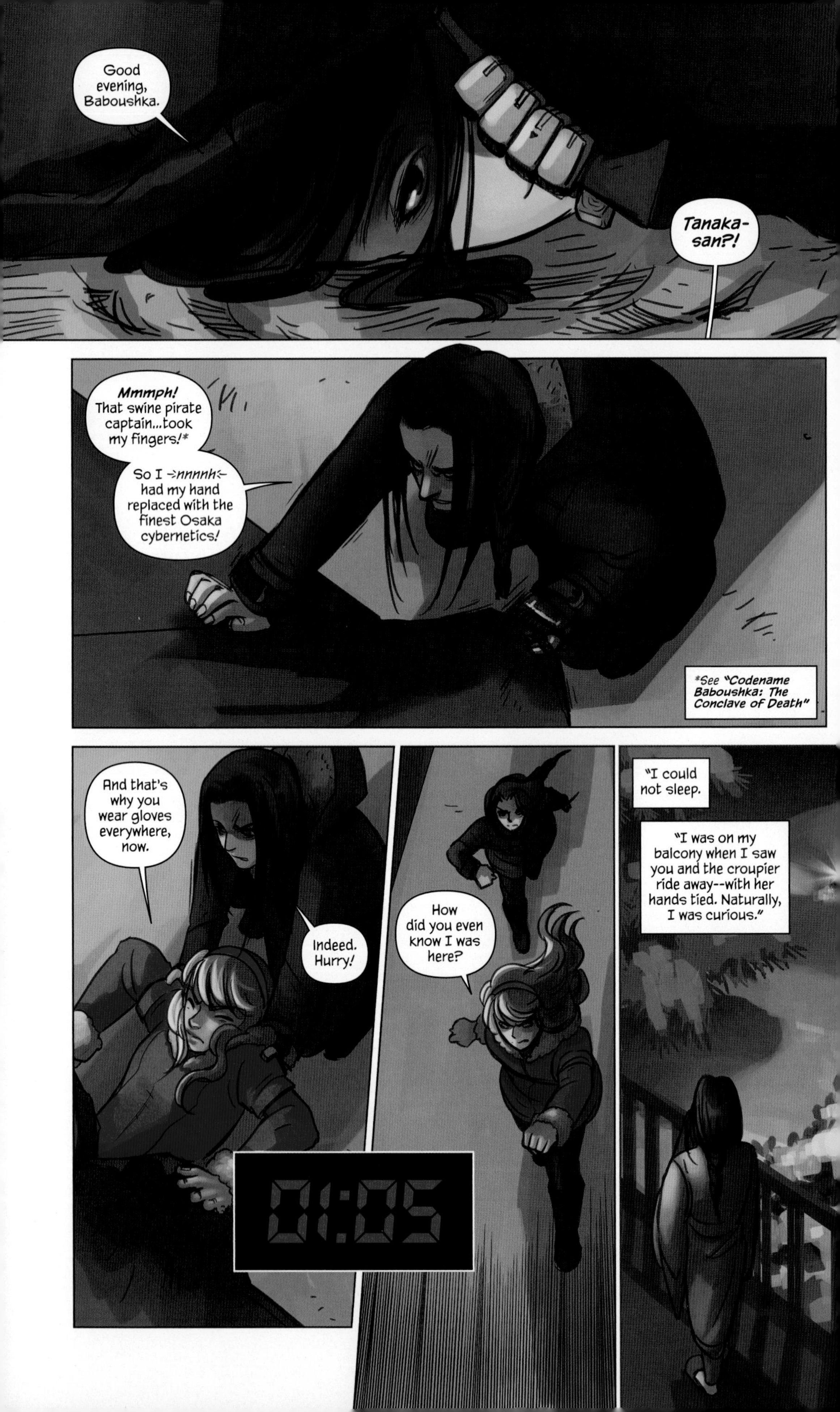
Good evening, Baboushka.
Tanaka-san?!
Mmmph! That swine pirate captain...took my fingers!*
So I ⇢nnnnh⇠ had my hand replaced with the finest Osaka cybernetics!
*See "Codename Baboushka: The Conclave of Death"
And that's why you wear gloves everywhere, now.
Indeed. Hurry!
01:05
How did you even know I was here?
"I could not sleep.
"I was on my balcony when I saw you and the croupier ride away--with her hands tied. Naturally, I was curious."

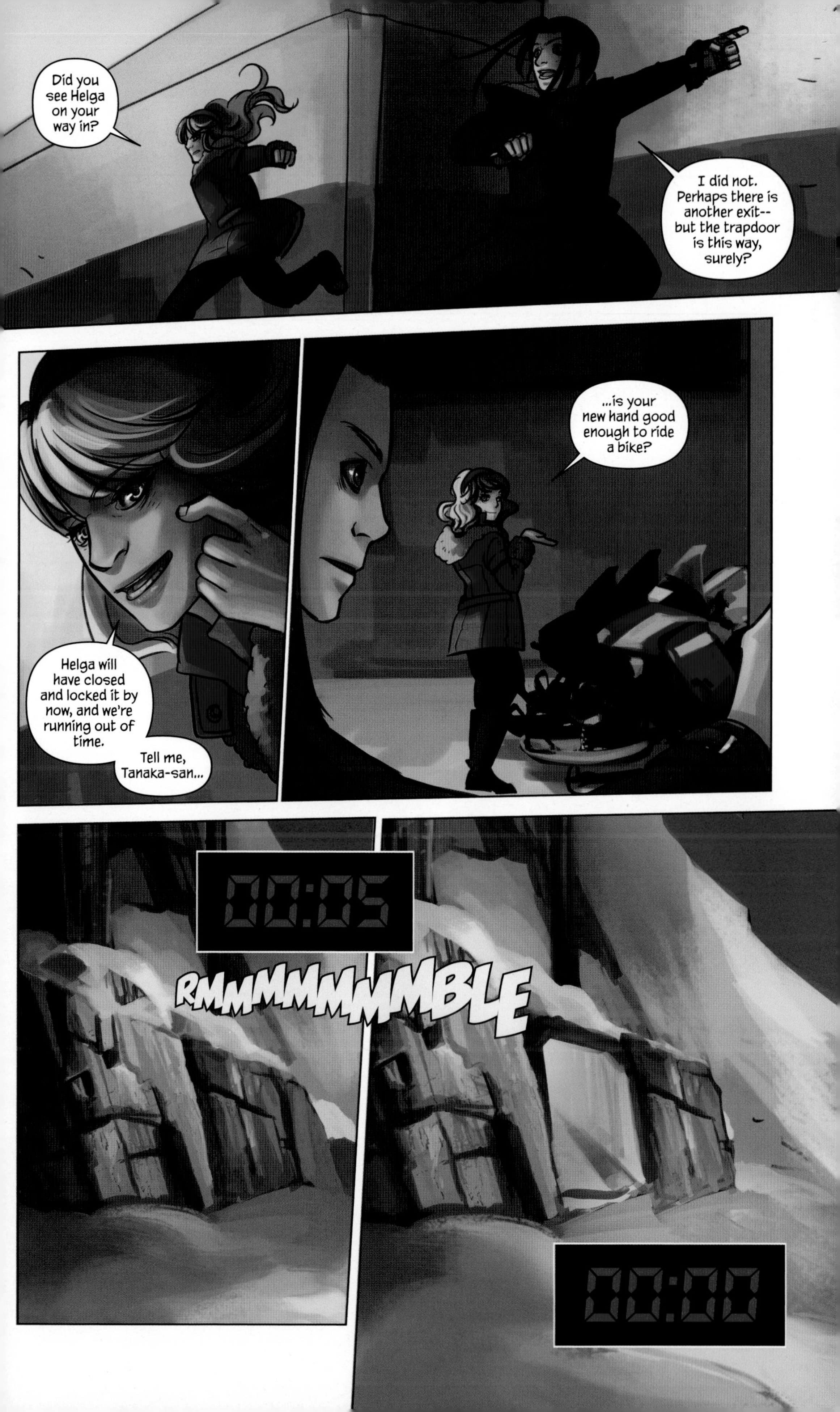

Did you see Helga on your way in?
I did not. Perhaps there is another exit-- but the trapdoor is this way, surely?
Helga will have closed and locked it by now, and we're running out of time.
Tell me, Tanaka-san...
...is your new hand good enough to ride a bike?
00:05
RMMMMMMMMBLE
00:00

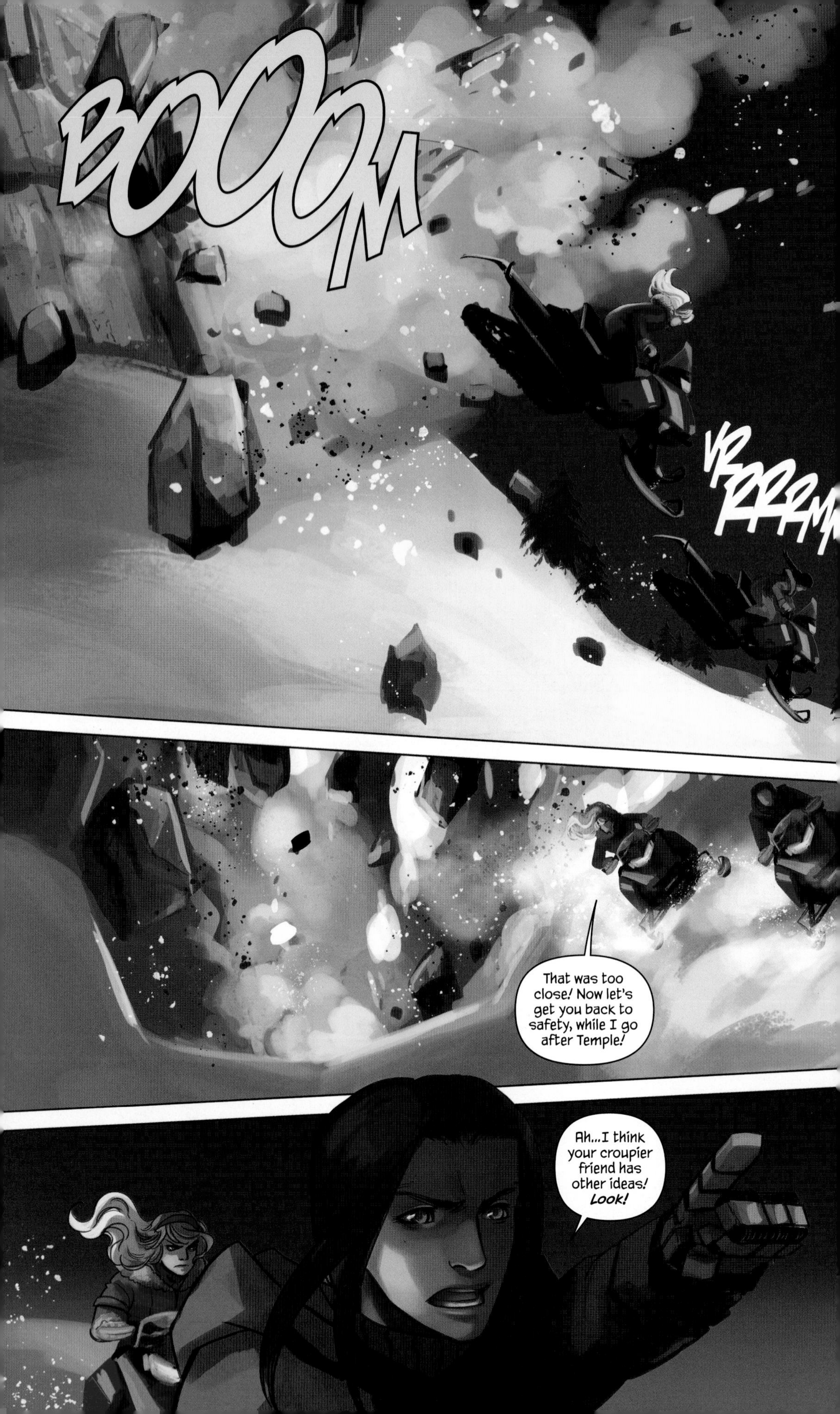
BOOOM
VRRRRMM
That was too close! Now let's get you back to safety, while I go after Temple!
Ah...I think your croupier friend has other ideas! LOOK!

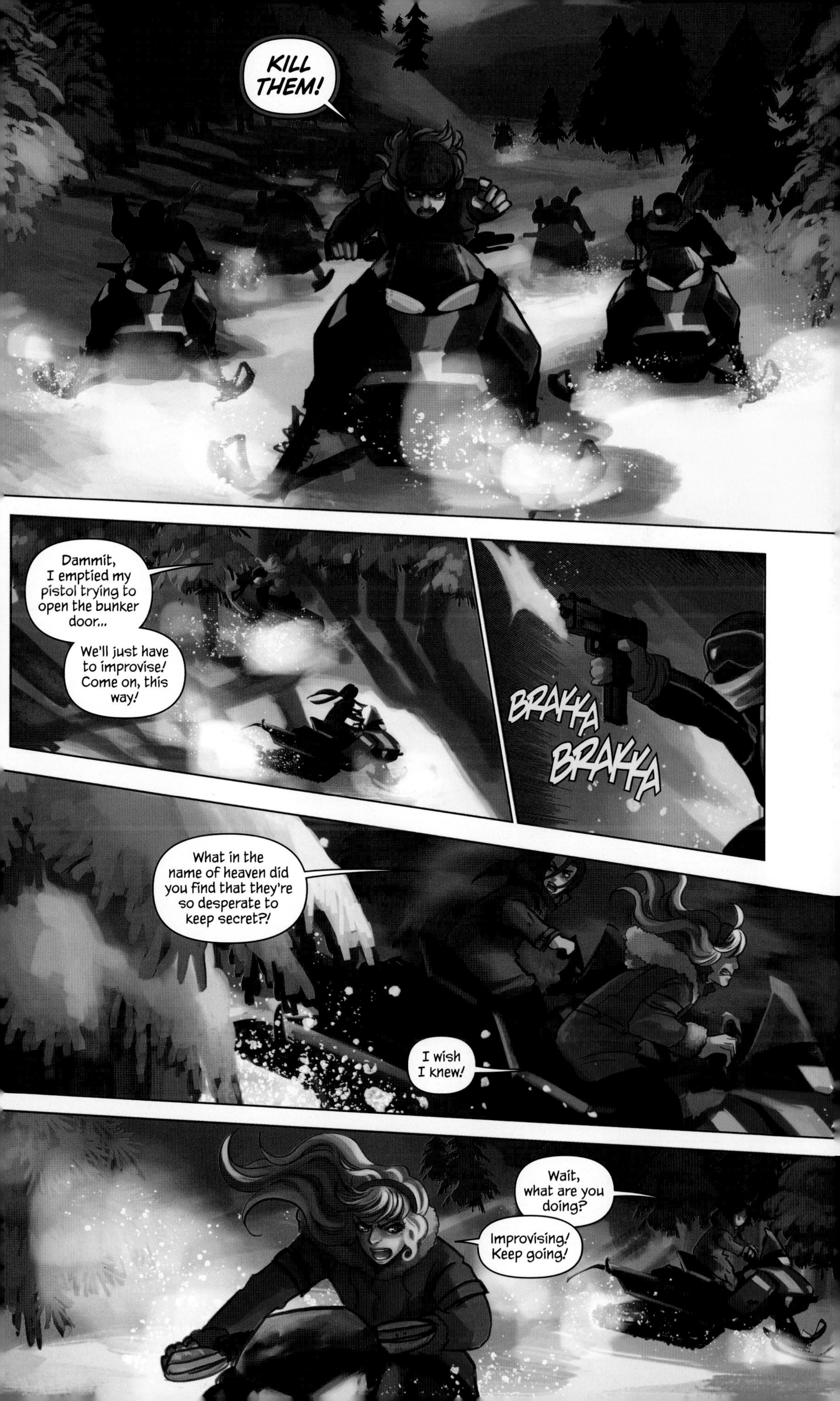
KILL THEM!
Dammit, I emptied my pistol trying to open the bunker door...
We'll just have to improvise! Come on, this way!
BRAKKA BRAKKA
What in the name of heaven did you find that they're so desperate to keep secret?!
I wish I knew!
Wait, what are you doing?
Improvising! Keep going!

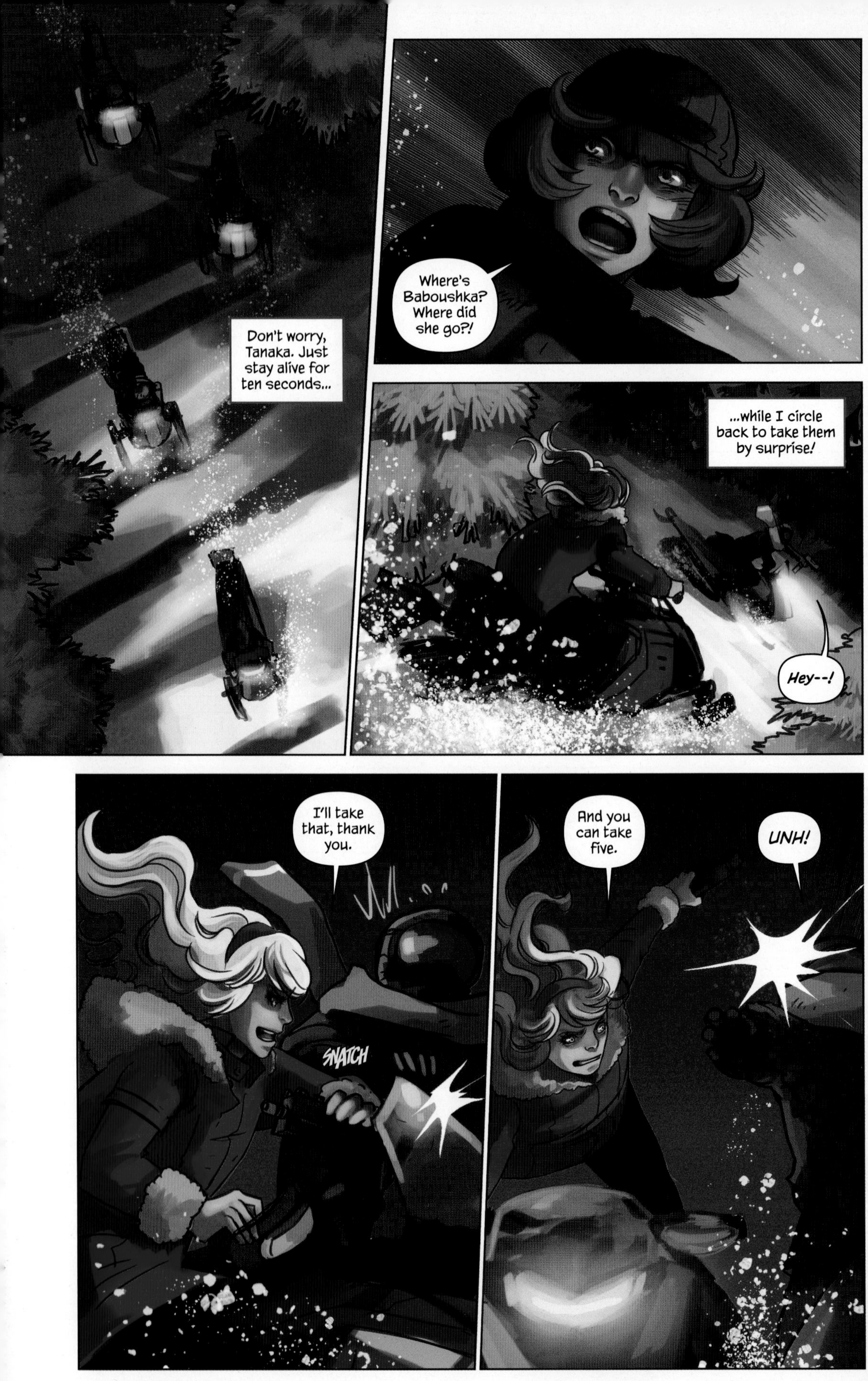

Don't worry, Tanaka. Just stay alive for ten seconds...
Where's Baboushka? Where did she go?!
...while I circle back to take them by surprise!
Hey--!
I'll take that, thank you.
SNATCH
And you can take five.
UNH!

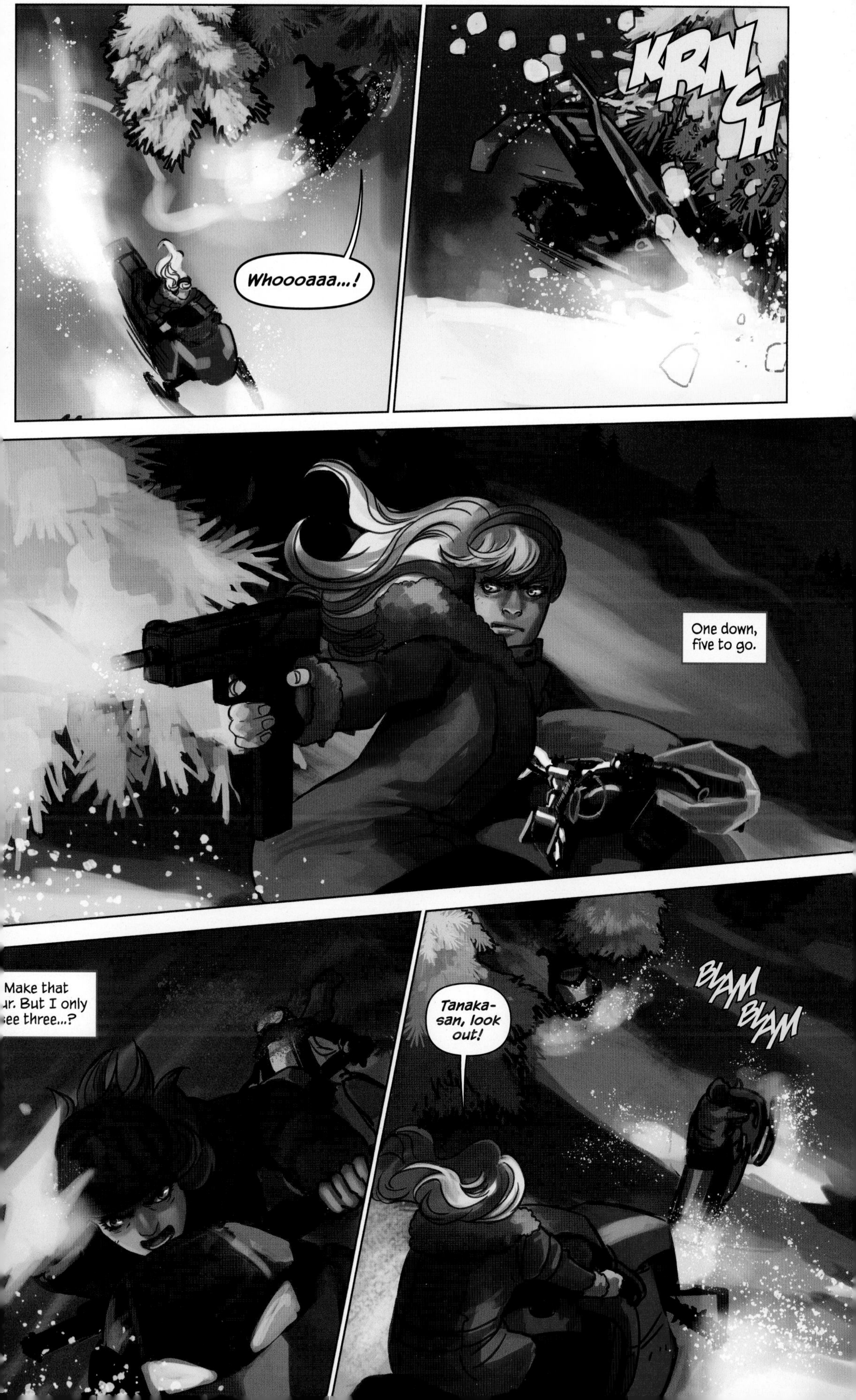

Whoooaaa...!
KRNCH
One down, five to go.
Make that
ur. But I only
see three...?
Tanaka-san, look out!
BLAM BLAM

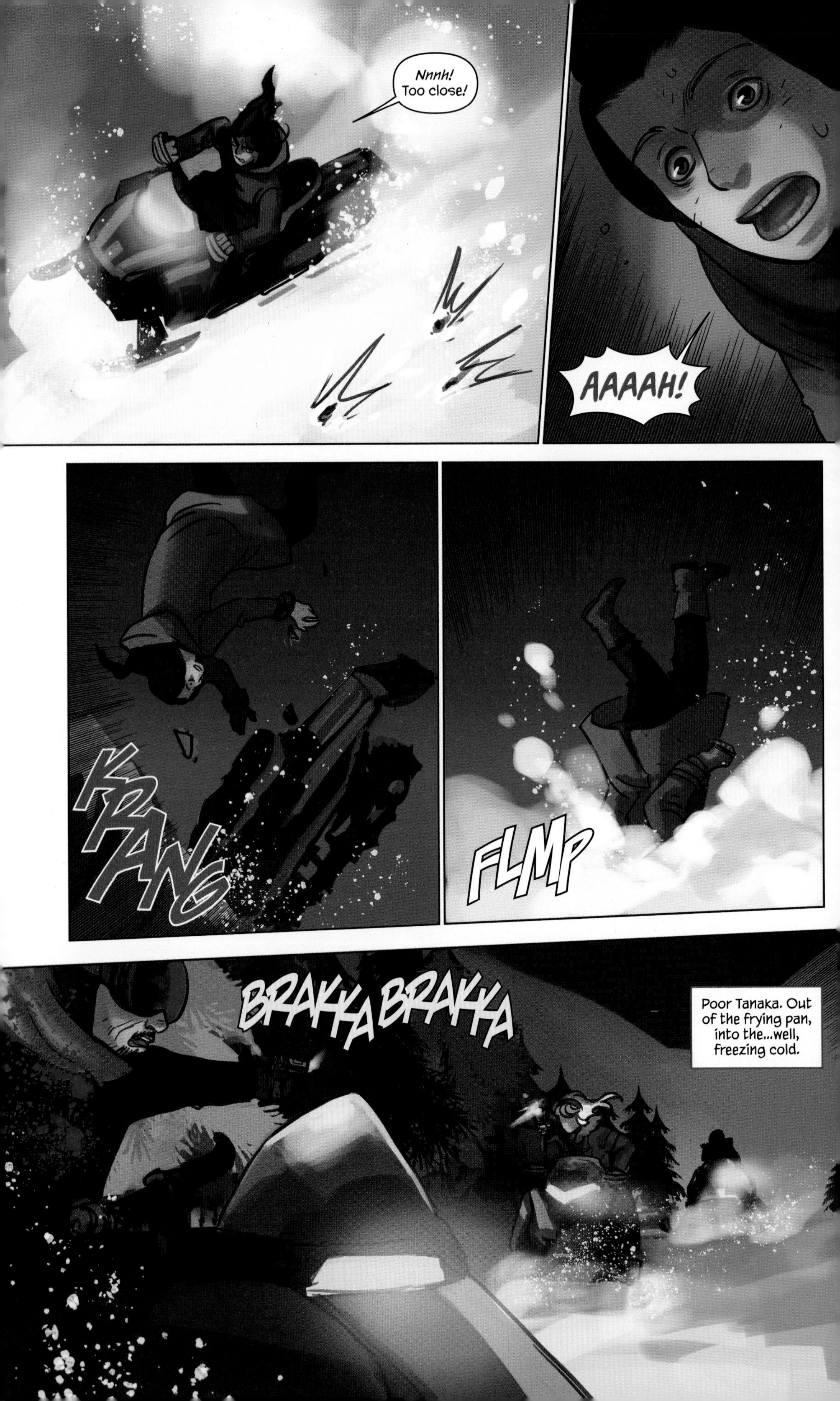
Nnnh! Too close!
AAAAH!
KRANG
FLMP
BRAKKA BRAKKA
Poor Tanaka. Out of the frying pan, into the...well, freezing cold.

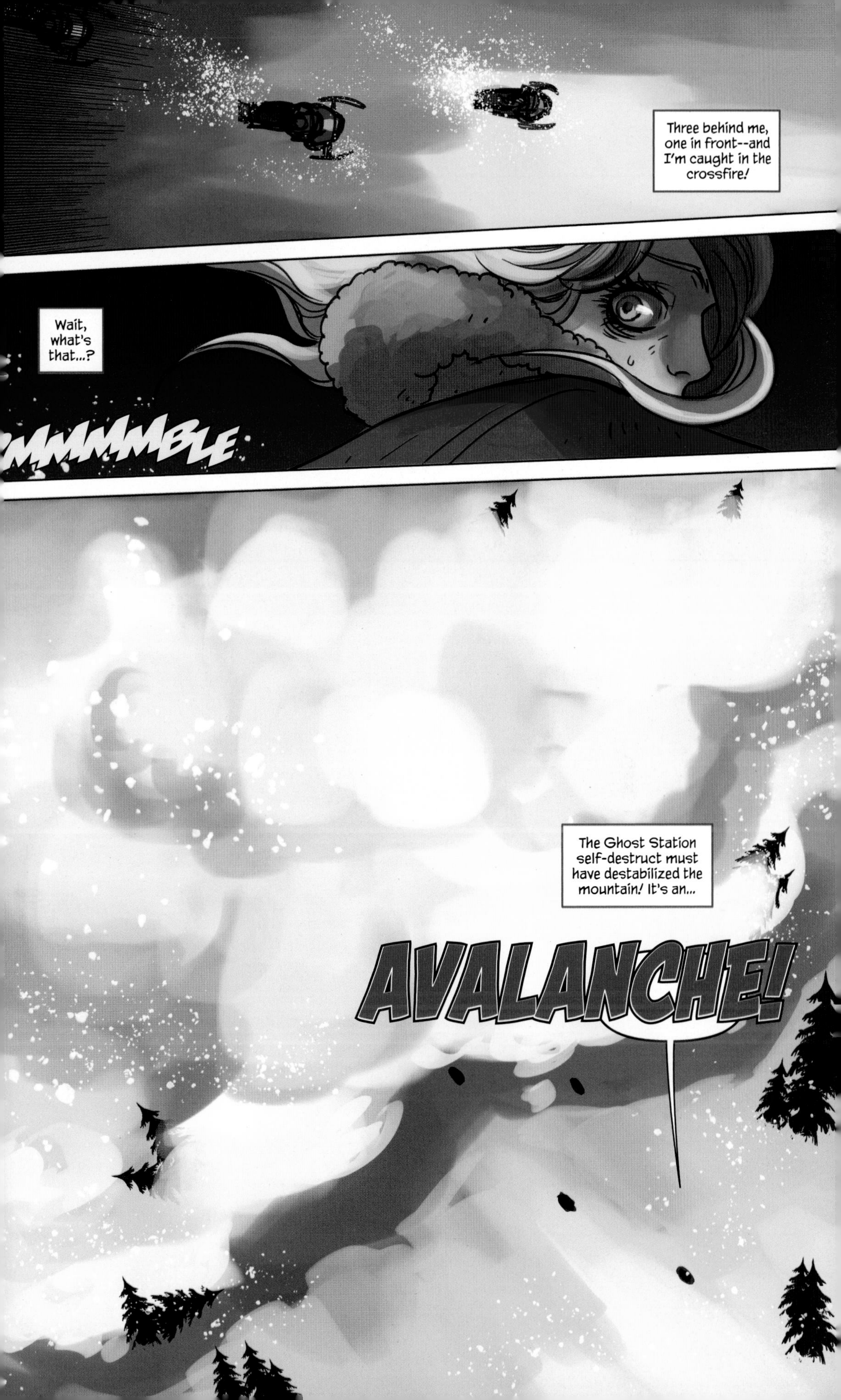
Three behind me, one in front--and I'm caught in the crossfire!
Wait, what's that...?
MMMMMBLE
The Ghost Station self-destruct must have destabilized the mountain! It's an...
AVALANCHE!

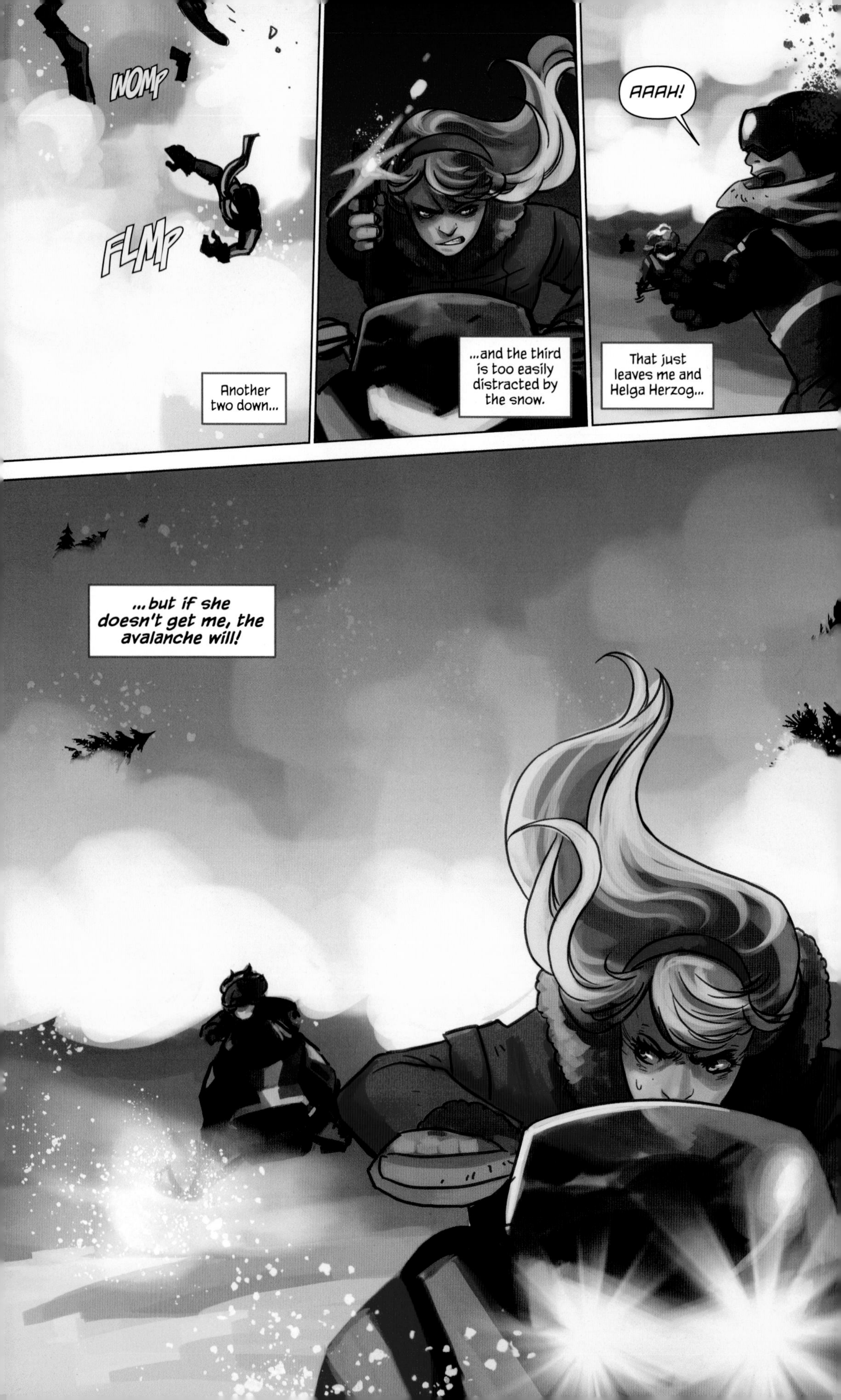
WOMP
FLMP
Another two down...
...and the third is too easily distracted by the snow.
AAAH!
That just leaves me and Helga Herzog...
...but if she doesn't get me, the avalanche will!

PART ★ THREE

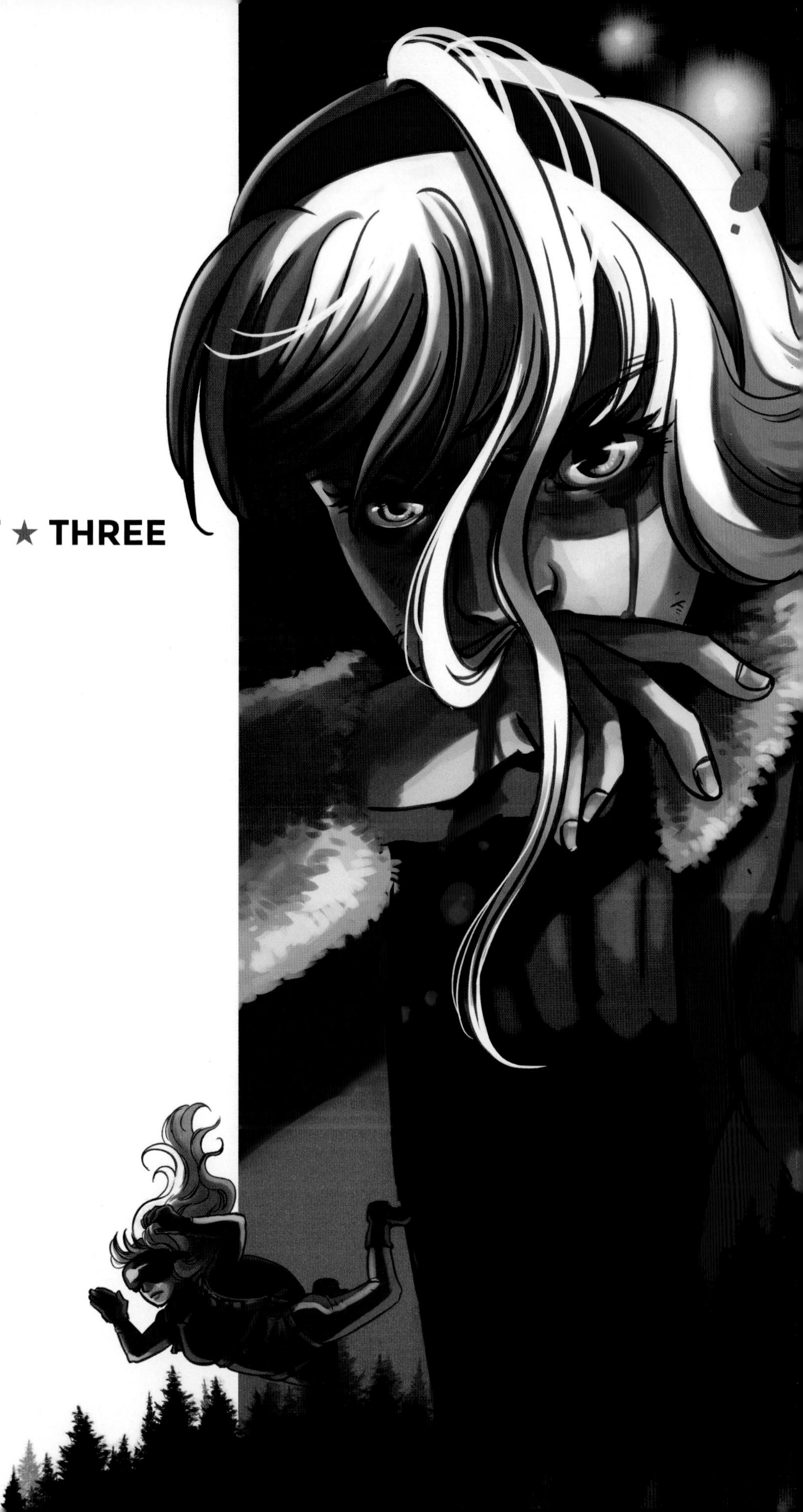

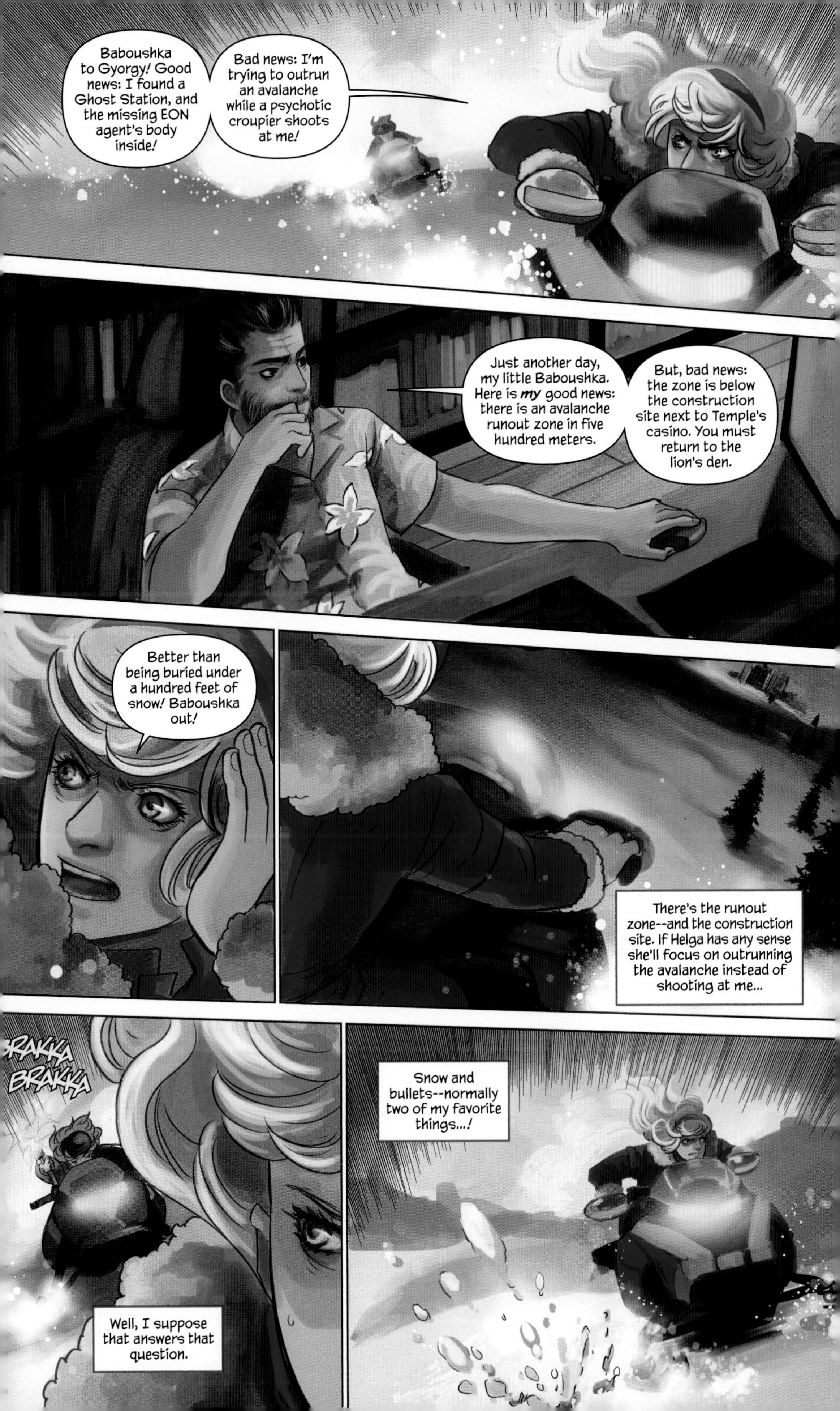
Baboushka to Gyorgy! Good news: I found a Ghost Station, and the missing EON agent's body inside!
Bad news: I'm trying to outrun an avalanche while a psychotic croupier shoots at me!
Just another day, my little Baboushka. Here is *my* good news: there is an avalanche runout zone in five hundred meters.
But, bad news: the zone is below the construction site next to Temple's casino. You must return to the lion's den.
Better than being buried under a hundred feet of snow! Baboushka out!
There's the runout zone--and the construction site. If Helga has any sense she'll focus on outrunning the avalanche instead of shooting at me...
BRAKKA BRAKKA
Well, I suppose that answers that question.
Snow and bullets--normally two of my favorite things...!

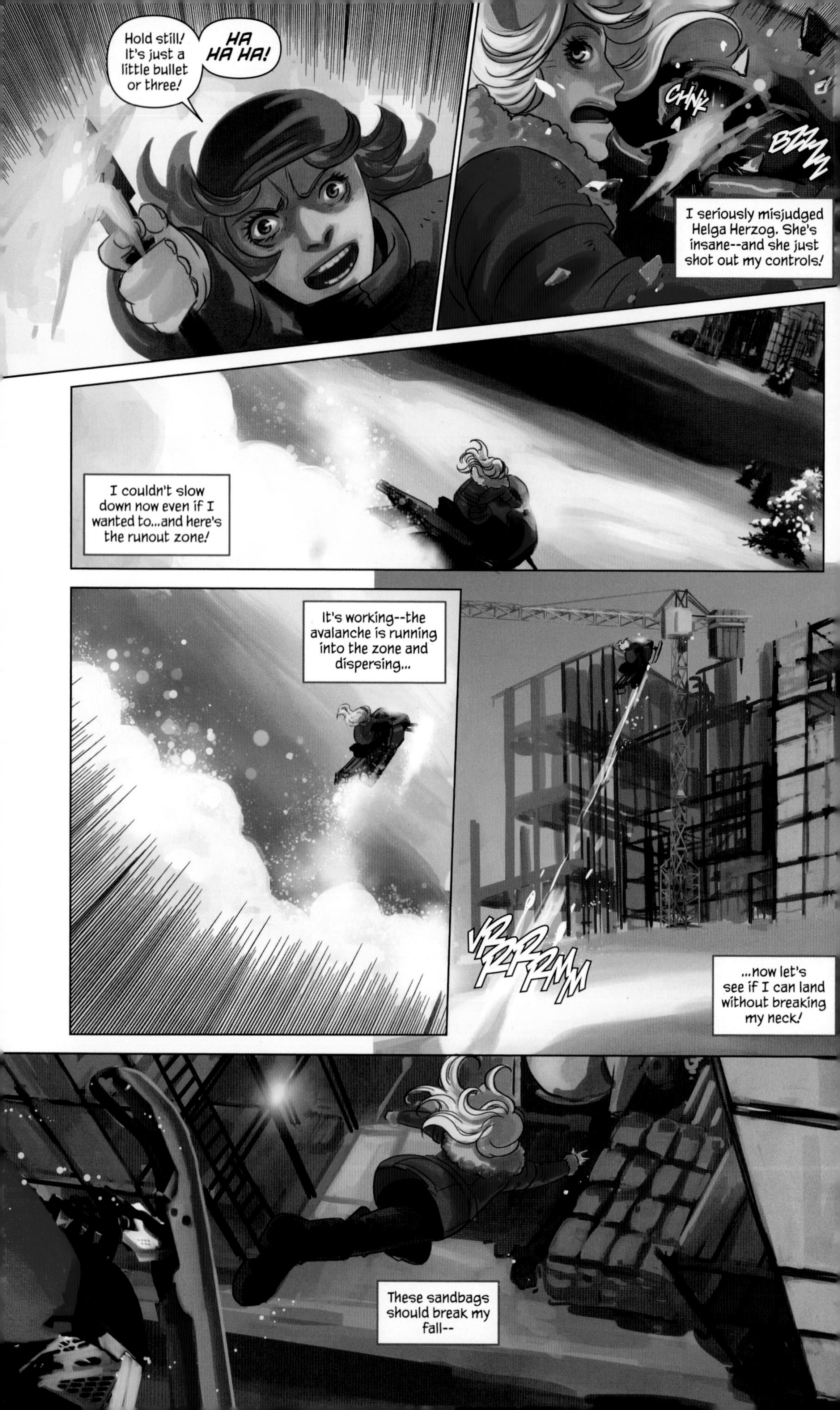

Hold still! It's just a little bullet or three!
HA HA HA!
CHNK
BZZZ
I seriously misjudged Helga Herzog. She's insane--and she just shot out my controls!
I couldn't slow down now even if I wanted to...and here's the runout zone!
It's working--the avalanche is running into the zone and dispersing...
VRRRRMMM
...now let's see if I can land without breaking my neck!
These sandbags should break my fall--

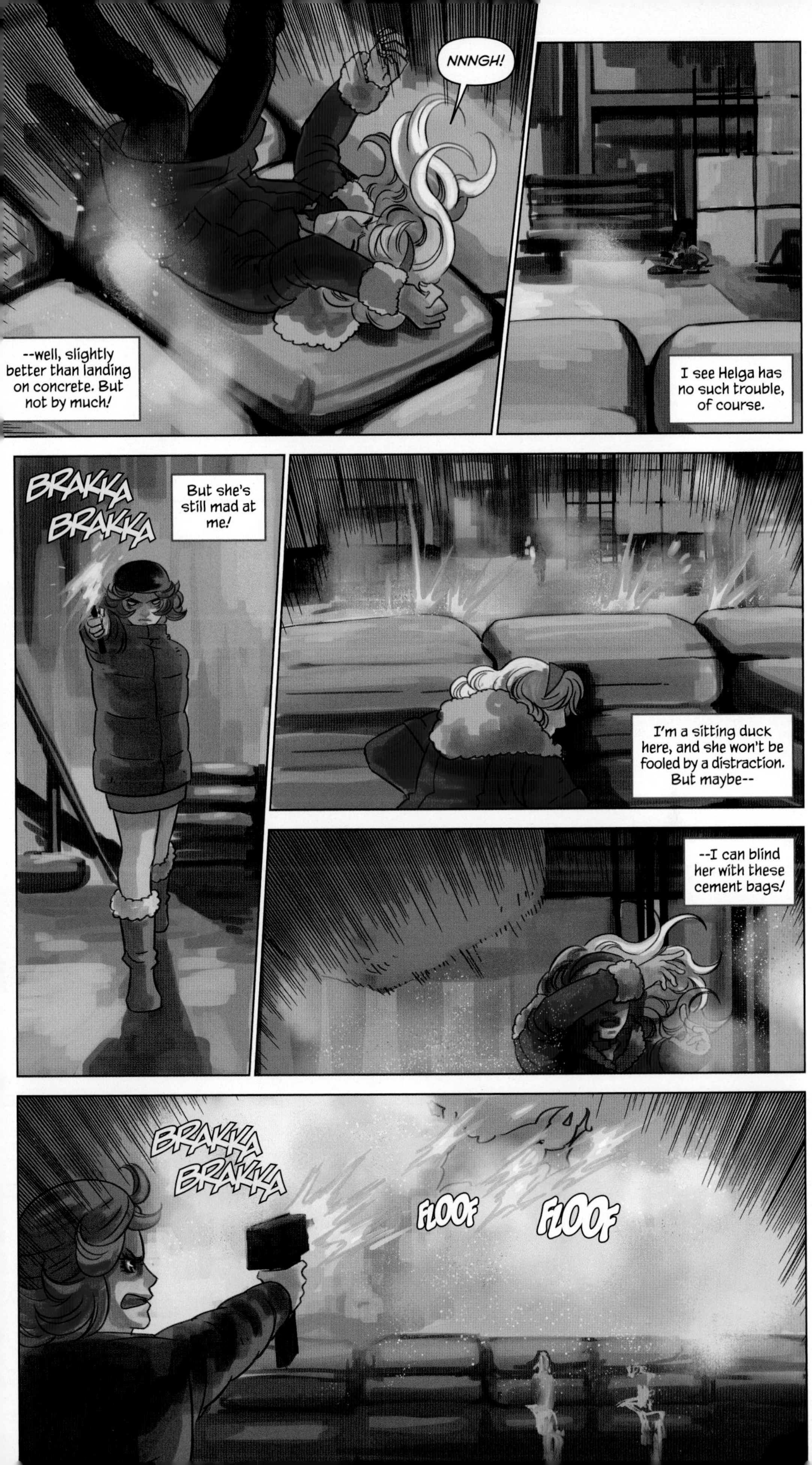
NNNGH!
--well, slightly better than landing on concrete. But not by much!
I see Helga has no such trouble, of course.
BRAKKA BRAKKA
But she's still mad at me!
I'm a sitting duck here, and she won't be fooled by a distraction. But maybe--
--I can blind her with these cement bags!
BRAKKA BRAKKA
FLOOF
FLOOF

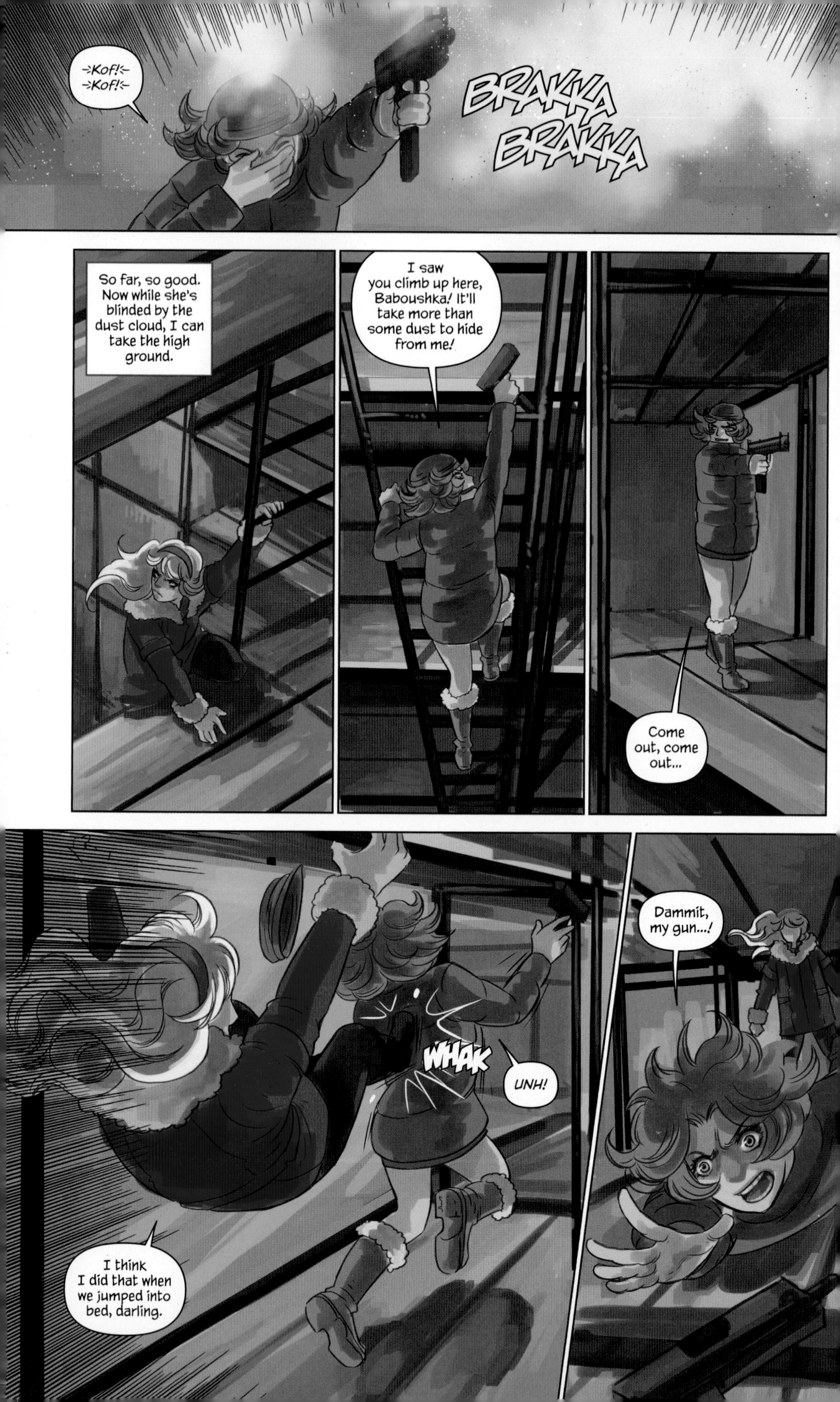

-Kof!-
-Kof!-
BRAKKA BRAKKA
So far, so good. Now while she's blinded by the dust cloud, I can take the high ground.
I saw you climb up here, Baboushka! It'll take more than some dust to hide from me!
Come out, come out...
WHAK
UNH!
I think I did that when we jumped into bed, darling.
Dammit, my gun...!

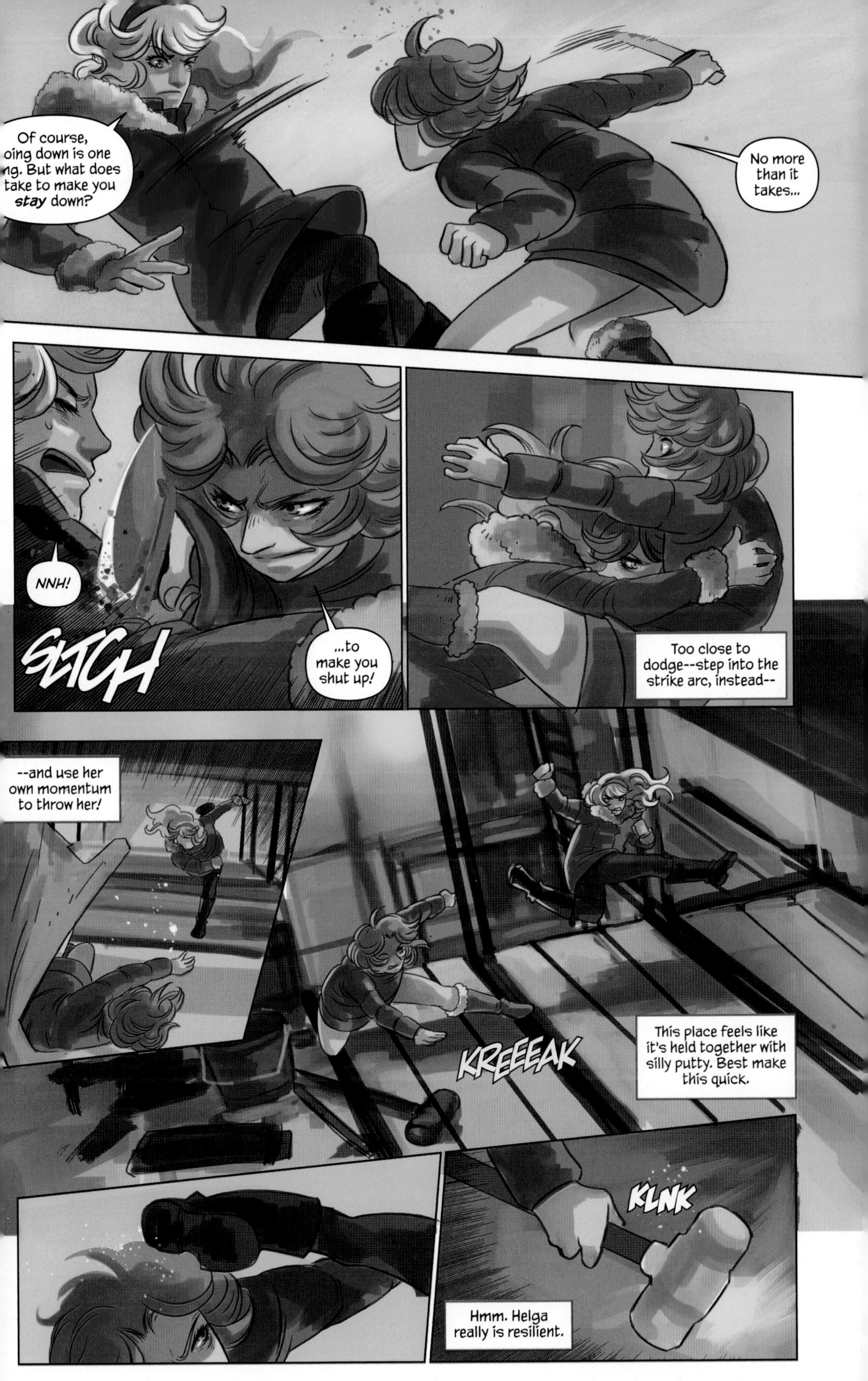

Of course, oing down is one ng. But what does take to make you stay down?
No more than it takes...
NNH!
SLTCH
...to make you shut up!
Too close to dodge--step into the strike arc, instead--
--and use her own momentum to throw her!
KREEEAK
This place feels like it's held together with silly putty. Best make this quick.
KLNK
Hmm. Helga really is resilient.

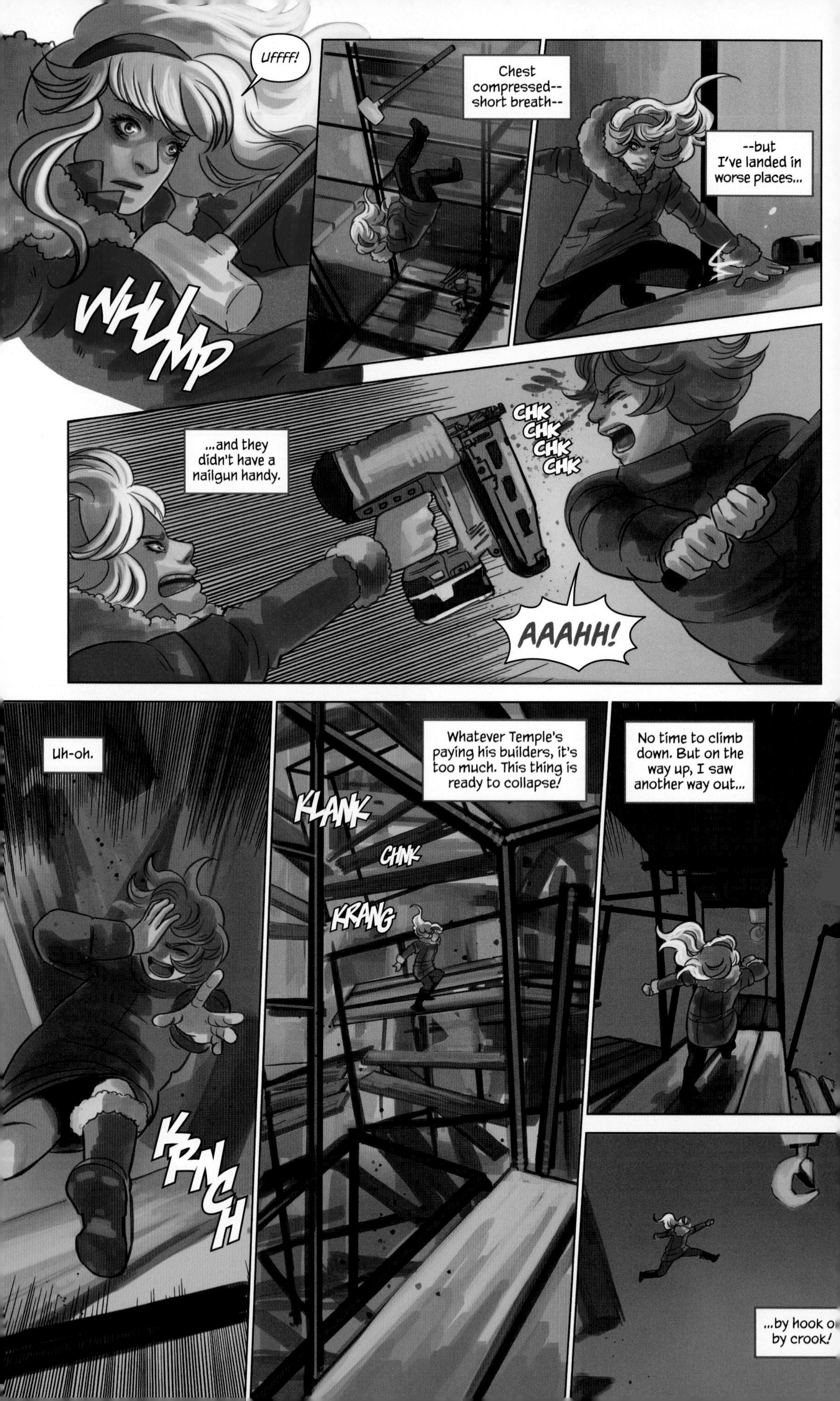
UFFFF!
Chest compressed-- short breath--
--but I've landed in worse places...
WHUMP
...and they didn't have a nailgun handy.
CHK CHK CHK CHK
AAAHH!
Uh-oh.
KRNCH
Whatever Temple's paying his builders, it's too much. This thing is ready to collapse!
KLANK
CHNK
KRANG
No time to climb down. But on the way up, I saw another way out...
...by hook o
by crook!

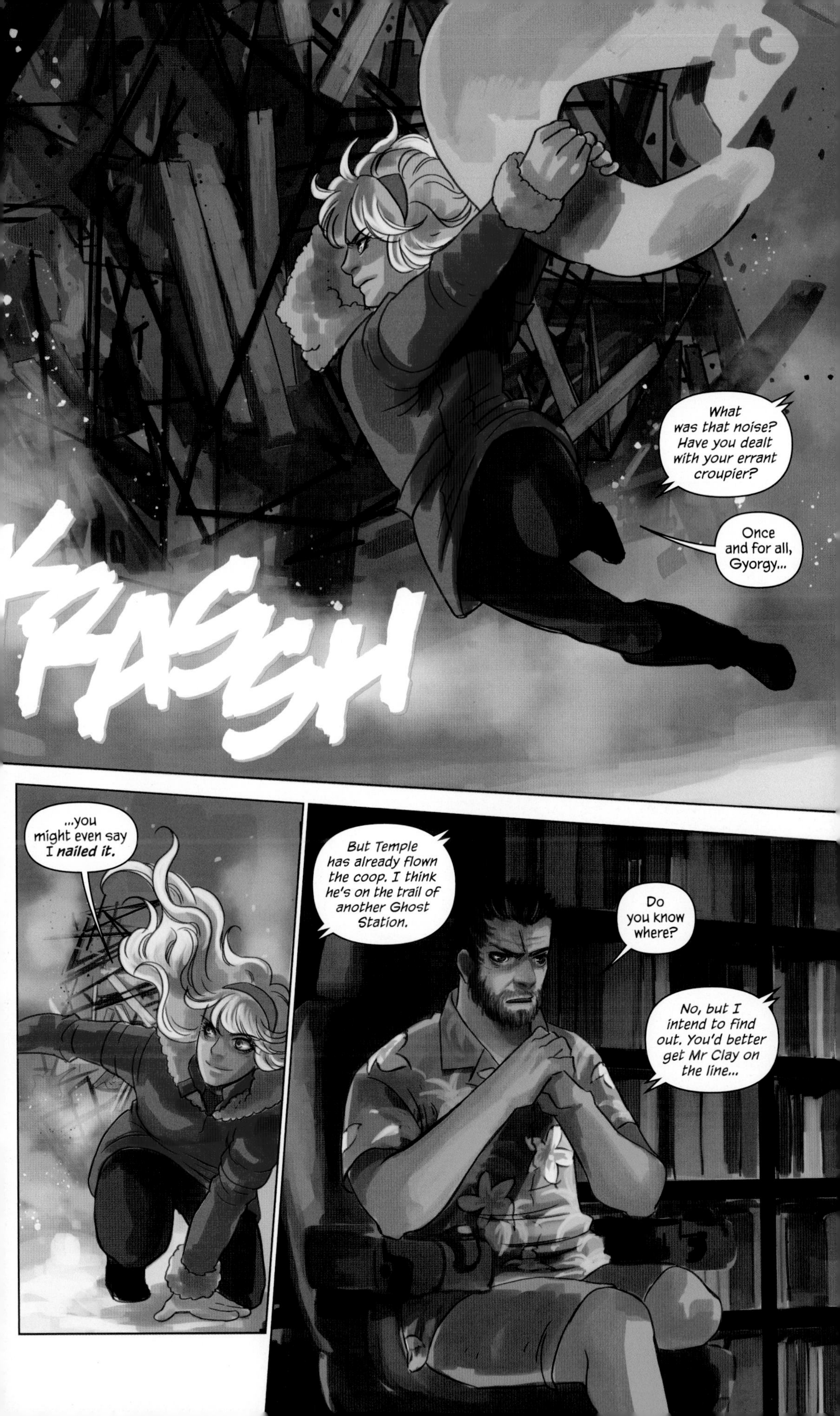
What was that noise? Have you dealt with your errant croupier?
Once and for all, Gyorgy...
KRASSH
...you might even say I ***nailed it.***
But Temple has already flown the coop. I think he's on the trail of another Ghost Station.
Do you know where?
No, but I intend to find out. You'd better get Mr Clay on the line...

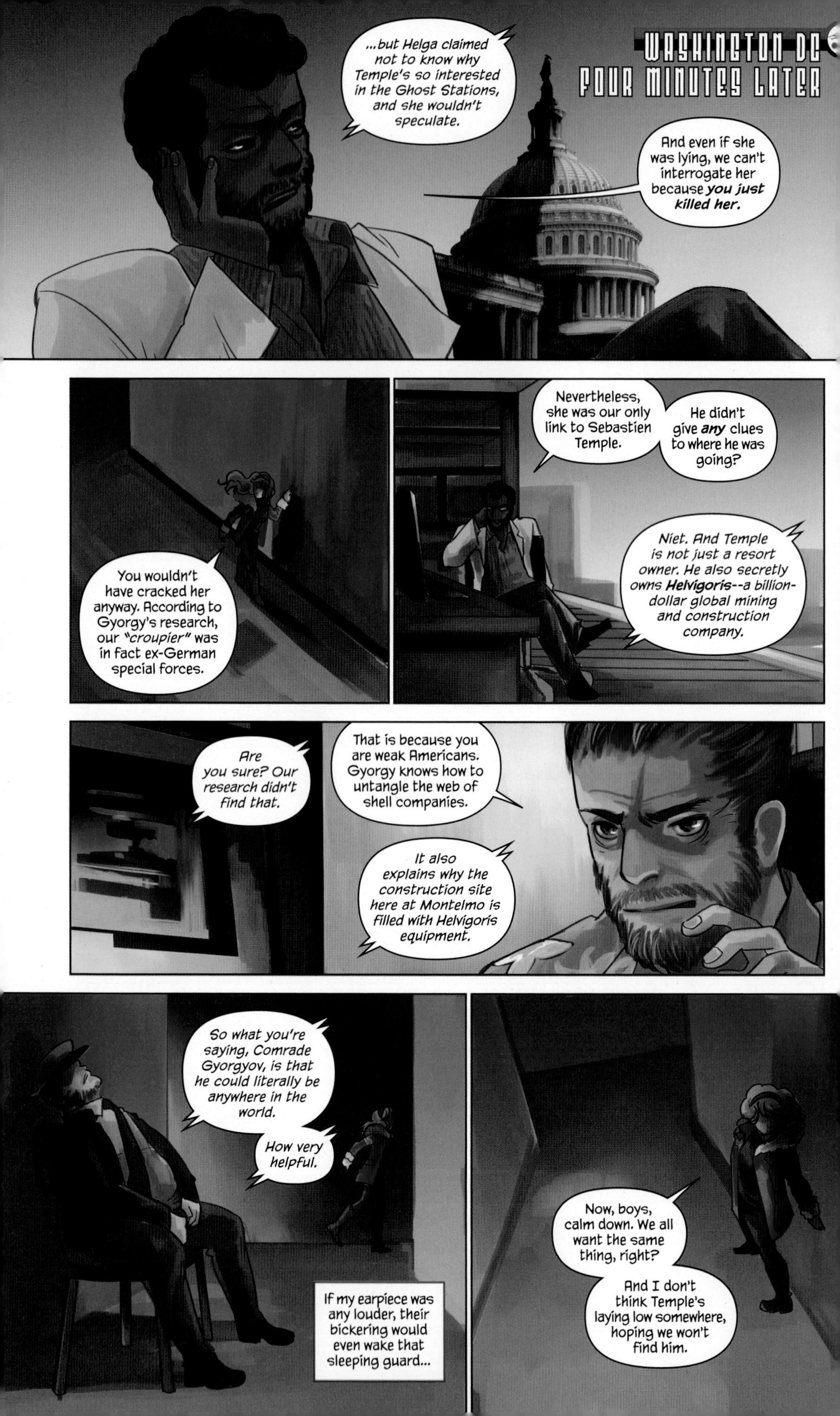
WASHINGTON DC
FOUR MINUTES LATER
...but Helga claimed not to know why Temple's so interested in the Ghost Stations, and she wouldn't speculate.
And even if she was lying, we can't interrogate her because you just killed her.
You wouldn't have cracked her anyway. According to Gyorgy's research, our "croupier" was in fact ex-German special forces.
Nevertheless, she was our only link to Sebastien Temple.
He didn't give any clues to where he was going?
Niet. And Temple is not just a resort owner. He also secretly owns Helvigoris--a billion-dollar global mining and construction company.
Are you sure? Our research didn't find that.
That is because you are weak Americans. Gyorgy knows how to untangle the web of shell companies.
It also explains why the construction site here at Montelmo is filled with Helvigoris equipment.
So what you're saying, Comrade Gyorgyov, is that he could literally be anywhere in the world.
How very helpful.
If my earpiece was any louder, their bickering would even wake that sleeping guard...
Now, boys, calm down. We all want the same thing, right?
And I don't think Temple's laying low somewhere, hoping we won't find him.

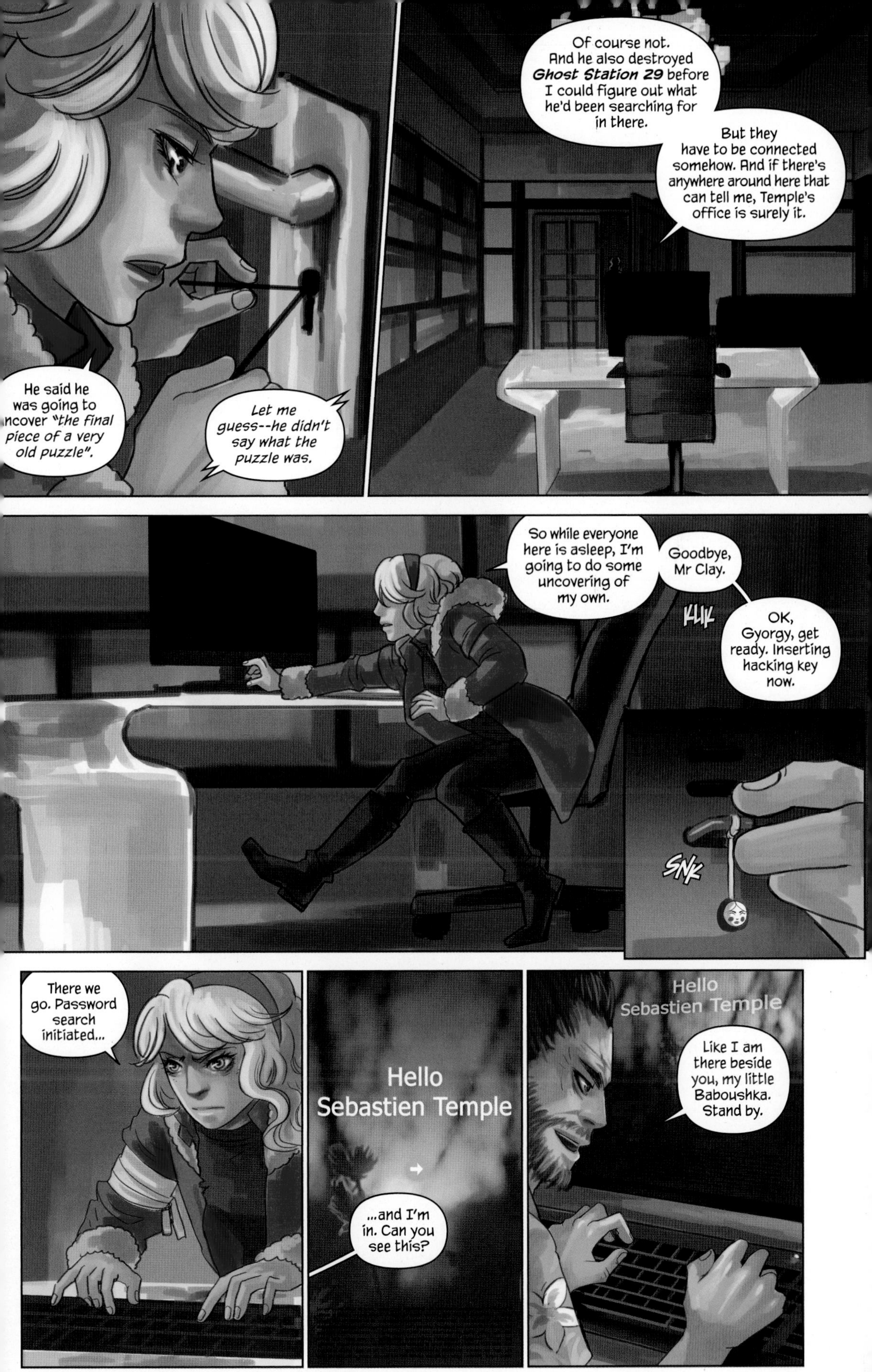
He said he was going to ncover "the final piece of a very old puzzle".
Let me guess--he didn't say what the puzzle was.
Of course not. And he also destroyed Ghost Station 29 before I could figure out what he'd been searching for in there.
But they have to be connected somehow. And if there's anywhere around here that can tell me, Temple's office is surely it.
So while everyone here is asleep, I'm going to do some uncovering of my own.
Goodbye, Mr Clay.
KLIK
OK, Gyorgy, get ready. Inserting hacking key now.
SNK
There we go. Password search initiated...
Hello Sebastien Temple
...and I'm in. Can you see this?
Hello Sebastien Temple
Like I am there beside you, my little Baboushka. Stand by.

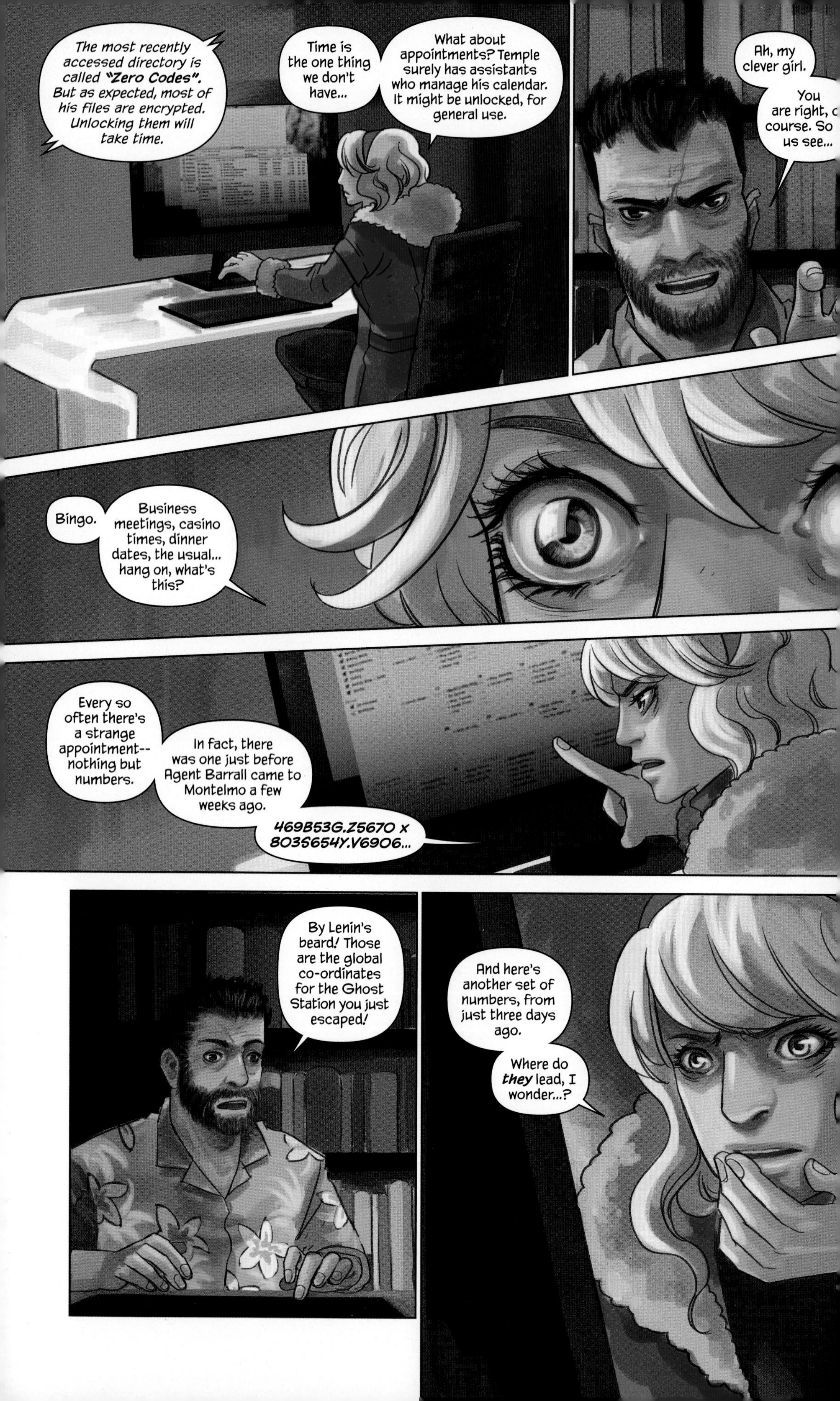

The most recently accessed directory is called "Zero Codes". But as expected, most of his files are encrypted. Unlocking them will take time.
Time is the one thing we don't have...
What about appointments? Temple surely has assistants who manage his calendar. It might be unlocked, for general use.
Ah, my clever girl.
You are right, o course. So us see...
Bingo.
Business meetings, casino times, dinner dates, the usual... hang on, what's this?
Every so often there's a strange appointment-- nothing but numbers.
In fact, there was one just before Agent Barrall came to Montelmo a few weeks ago.
469B53G.Z5670 x 803S654Y.V6906...
By Lenin's beard! Those are the global co-ordinates for the Ghost Station you just escaped!
And here's another set of numbers, from just three days ago.
Where do they lead, I wonder...?

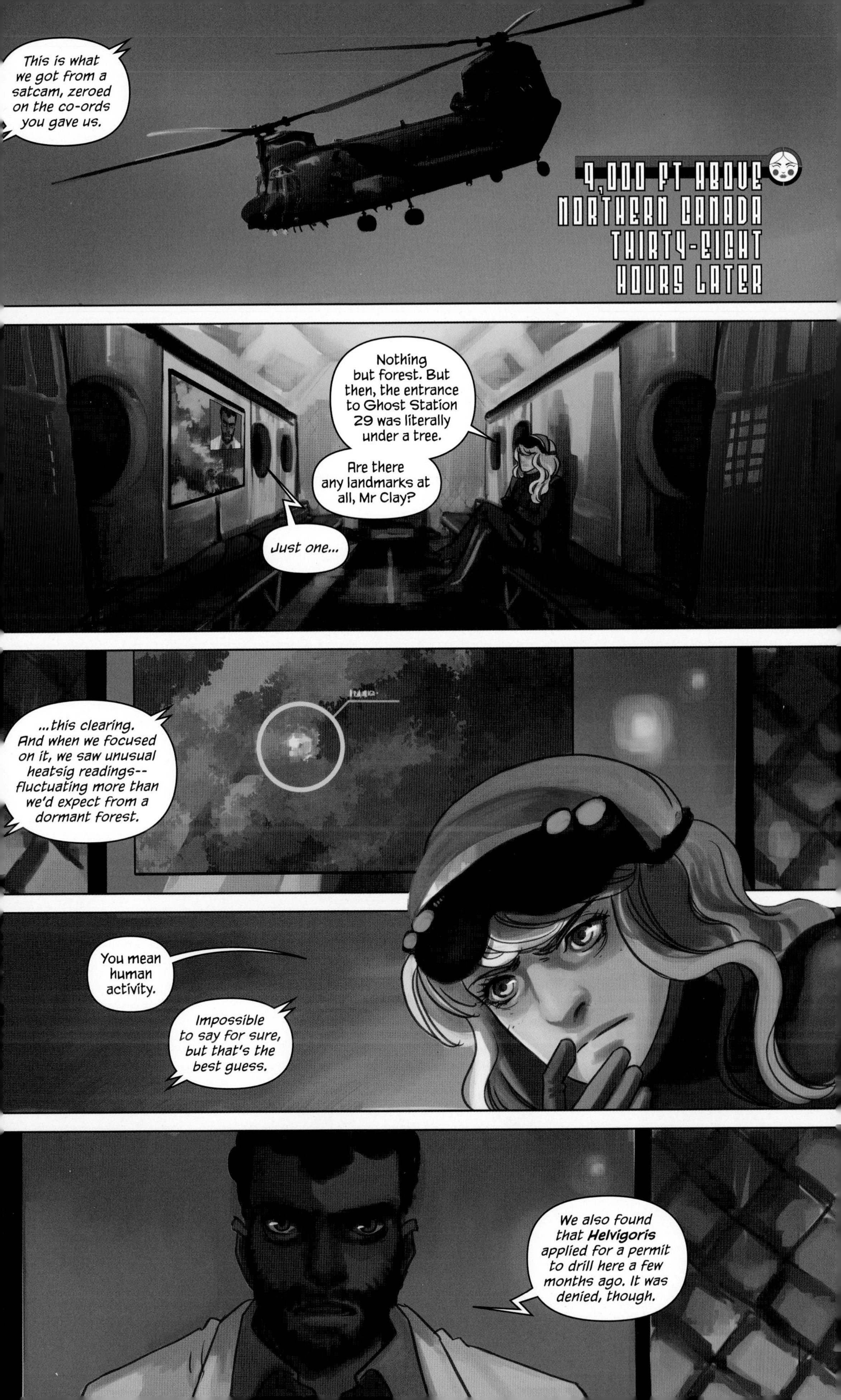
This is what we got from a satcam, zeroed on the co-ords you gave us.
4,000 FT ABOVE NORTHERN CANADA THIRTY-EIGHT HOURS LATER
Nothing but forest. But then, the entrance to Ghost Station 29 was literally under a tree.
Are there any landmarks at all, Mr Clay?
Just one...
...this clearing. And when we focused on it, we saw unusual heatsig readings-- fluctuating more than we'd expect from a dormant forest.
You mean human activity.
Impossible to say for sure, but that's the best guess.
We also found that **Helvigoris** applied for a permit to drill here a few months ago. It was denied, though.

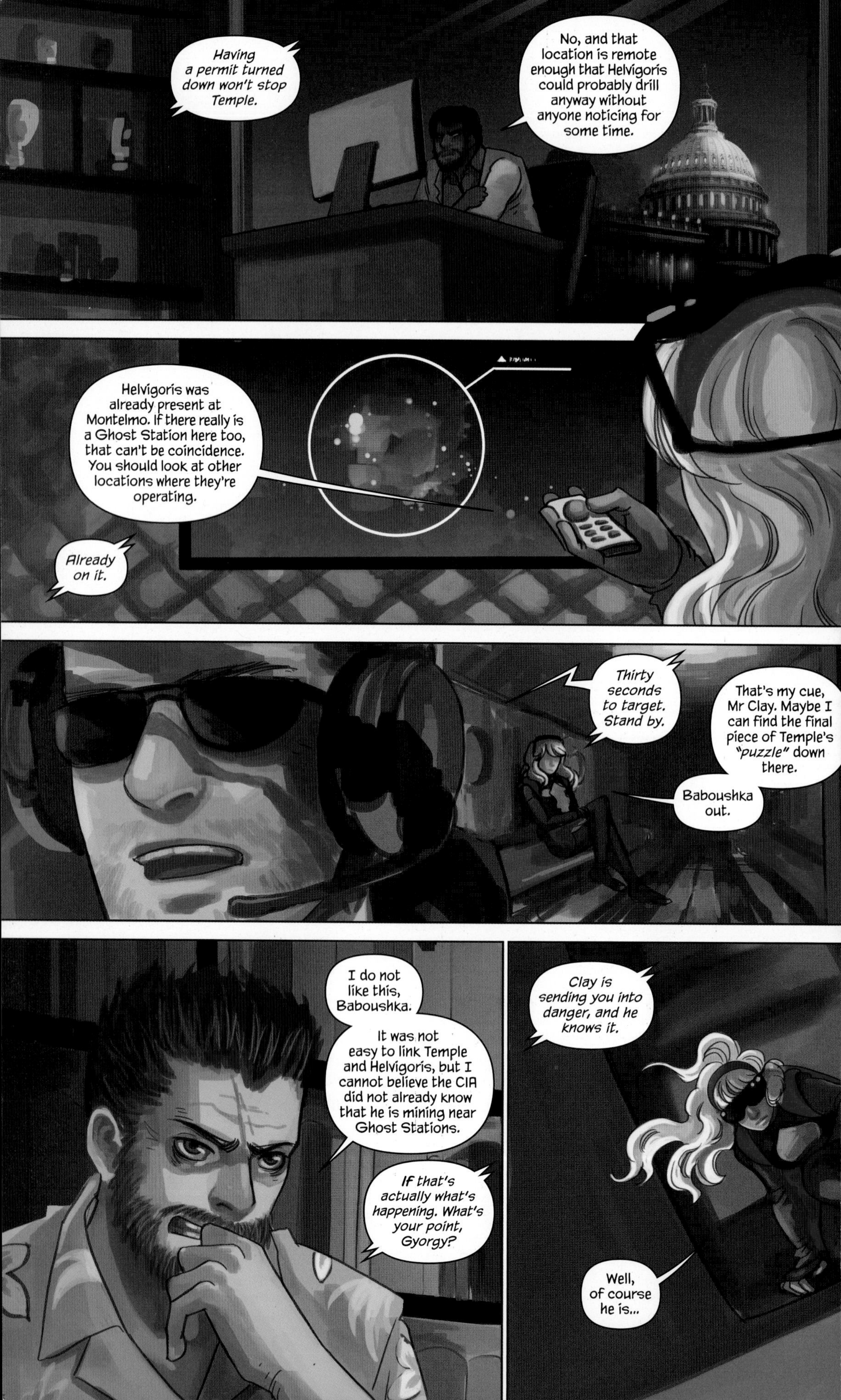
Having a permit turned down won't stop Temple.
No, and that location is remote enough that Helvigoris could probably drill anyway without anyone noticing for some time.
Helvigoris was already present at Montelmo. If there really is a Ghost Station here too, that can't be coincidence. You should look at other locations where they're operating.
Already on it.
Thirty seconds to target. Stand by.
That's my cue, Mr Clay. Maybe I can find the final piece of Temple's "puzzle" down there.
Baboushka out.
I do not like this, Baboushka.
It was not easy to link Temple and Helvigoris, but I cannot believe the CIA did not already know that he is mining near Ghost Stations.
If that's actually what's happening. What's your point, Gyorgy?
Clay is sending you into danger, and he knows it.
Well, of course he is...

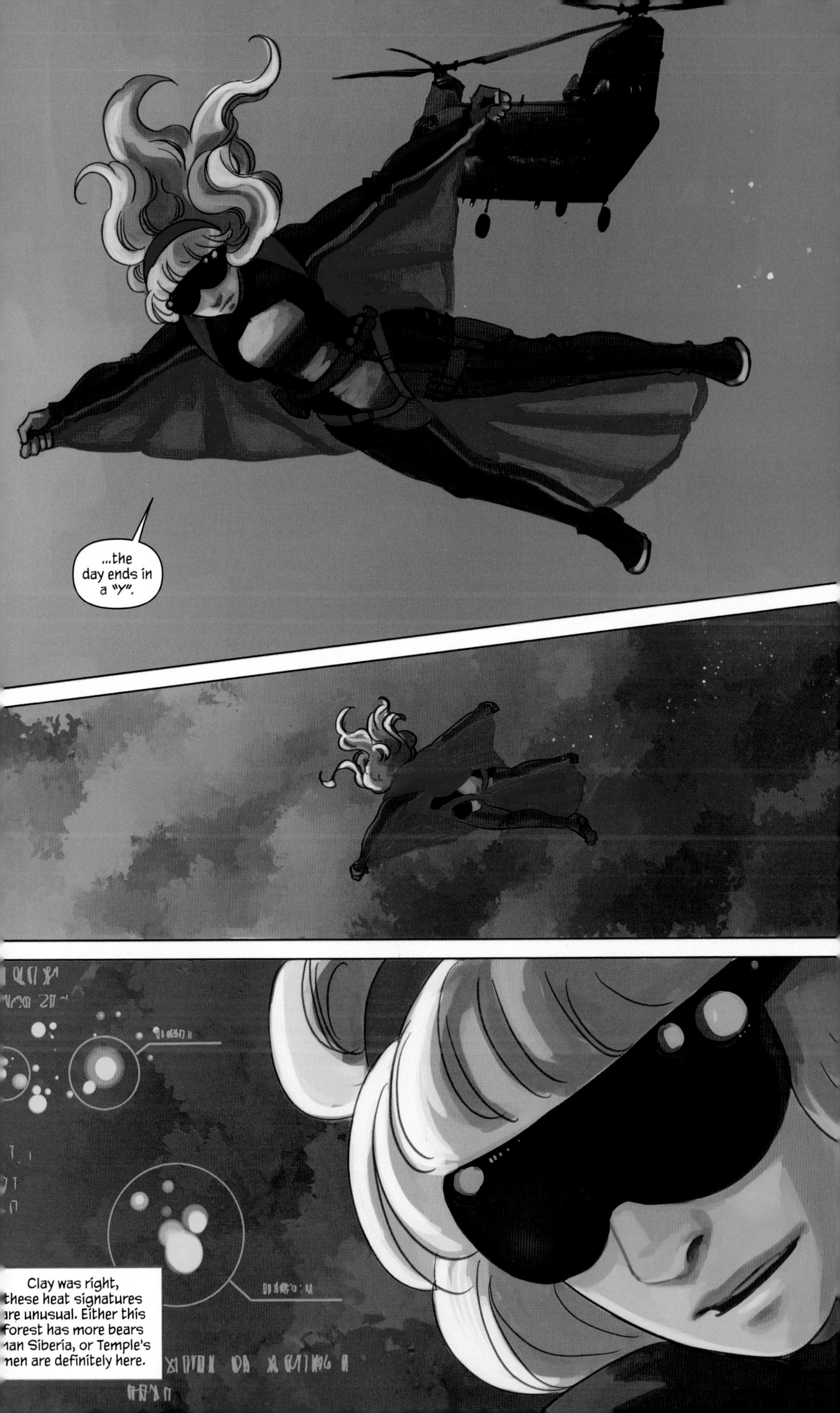
...the day ends in a "Y".
Clay was right,
these heat signatures
are unusual. Either this
forest has more bears
han Siberia, or Temple's
nen are definitely here.

Down we go!

CHNK

FLOOF

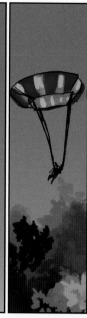

SNAG

Dammit! Parachuting into a forest: rarely a good idea.

KUK KUK KUK

And now the release is locked. This just gets better...!

Well, then...

SLTCH

...I'll just have to cut my losses.

Not like I was going to parachute back out again anyway.

So let's see what Temple's up to. If this really another Ghost Station, maybe can find a way in

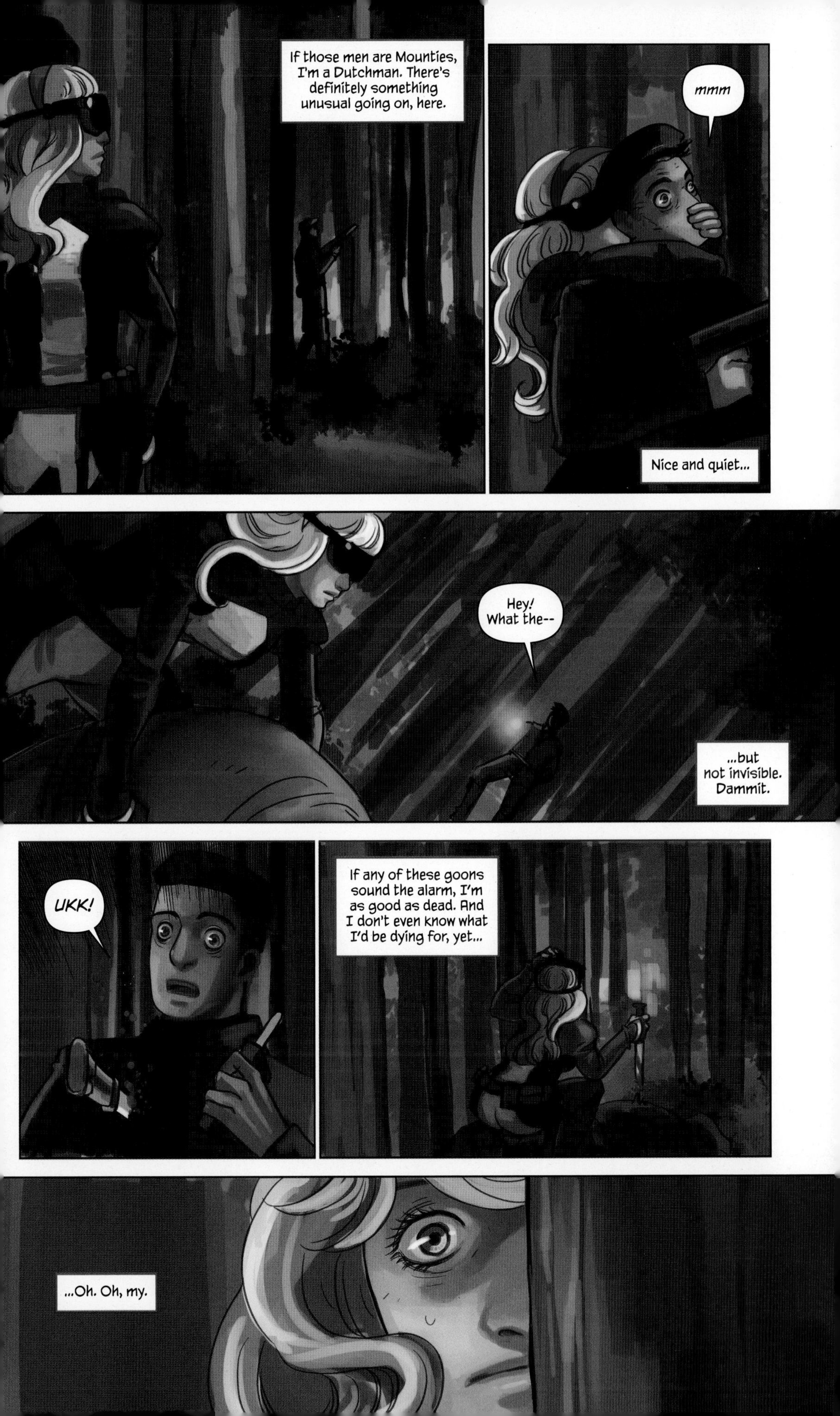
If those men are Mounties, I'm a Dutchman. There's definitely something unusual going on, here.
mmm
Nice and quiet...
Hey! What the--
...but not invisible. Dammit.
UKK!
If any of these goons sound the alarm, I'm as good as dead. And I don't even know what I'd be dying for, yet...
...Oh. Oh, my.

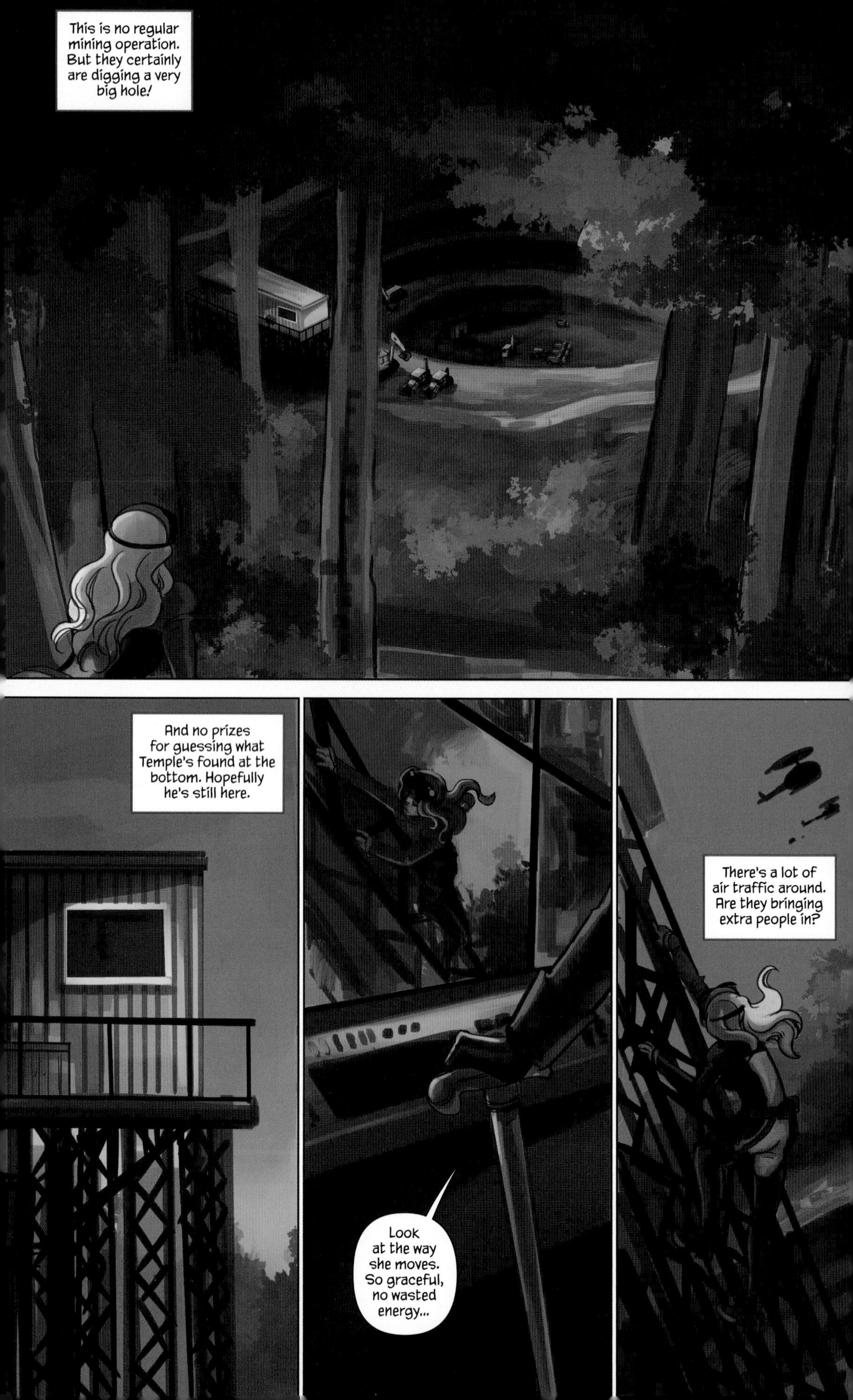
This is no regular mining operation. But they certainly are digging a very big hole!
And no prizes for guessing what Temple's found at the bottom. Hopefully he's still here.
Look at the way she moves. So graceful, no wasted energy...
There's a lot of air traffic around. Are they bringing extra people in?

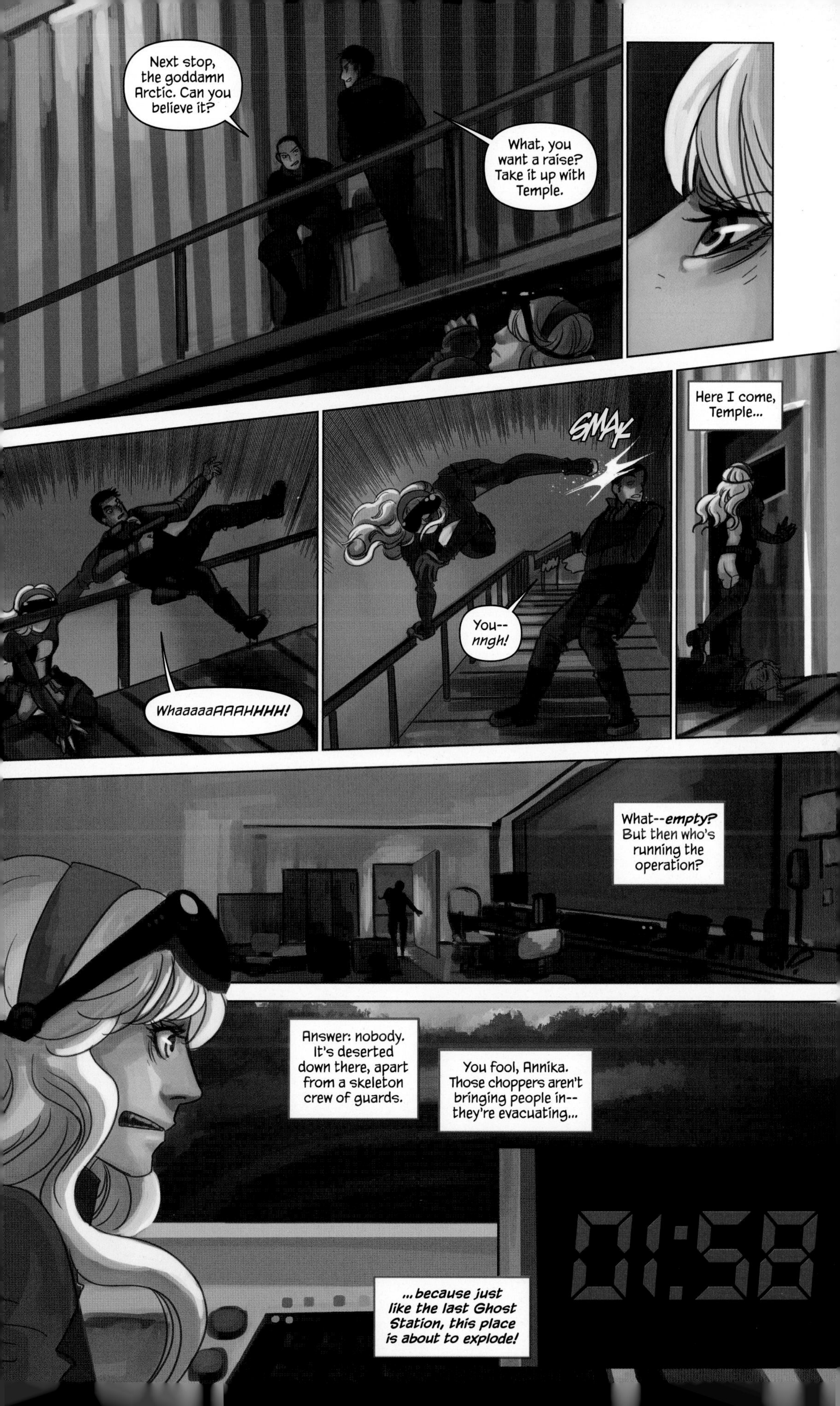

Next stop, the goddamn Arctic. Can you believe it?
What, you want a raise? Take it up with Temple.
WhaaaaaAAAHHHH!
SMAK
You-- nngh!
Here I come, Temple...
What--*empty?* But then who's running the operation?
Answer: nobody. It's deserted down there, apart from a skeleton crew of guards.
You fool, Annika. Those choppers aren't bringing people in-- they're evacuating...
01:58
...because just like the last Ghost Station, this place is about to explode!

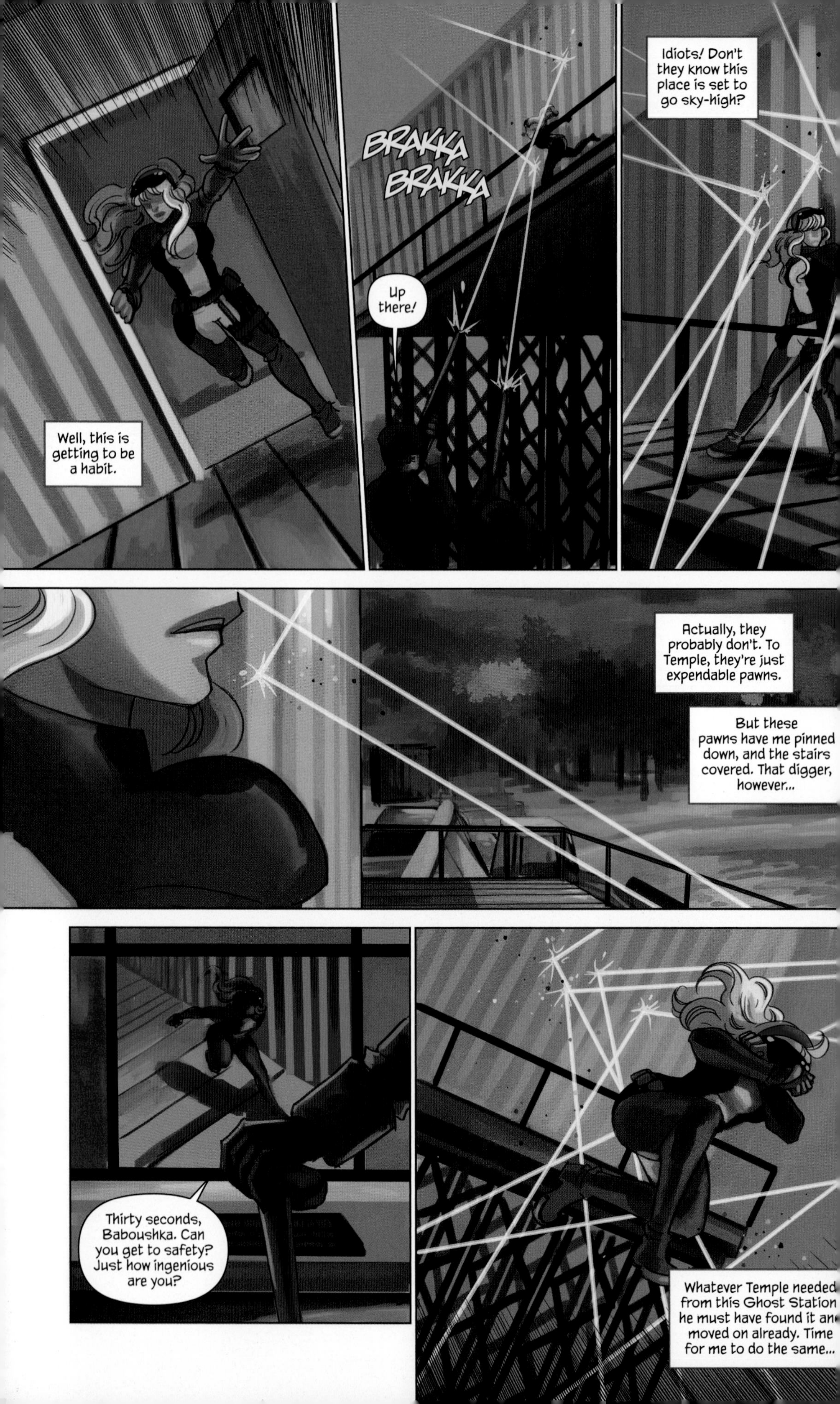
Well, this is getting to be a habit.
BRAKKA BRAKKA
Up there!
Idiots! Don't they know this place is set to go sky-high?
Actually, they probably don't. To Temple, they're just expendable pawns.
But these pawns have me pinned down, and the stairs covered. That digger, however...
Thirty seconds, Baboushka. Can you get to safety? Just how ingenious are you?
Whatever Temple needed from this Ghost Station he must have found it an moved on already. Time for me to do the same...

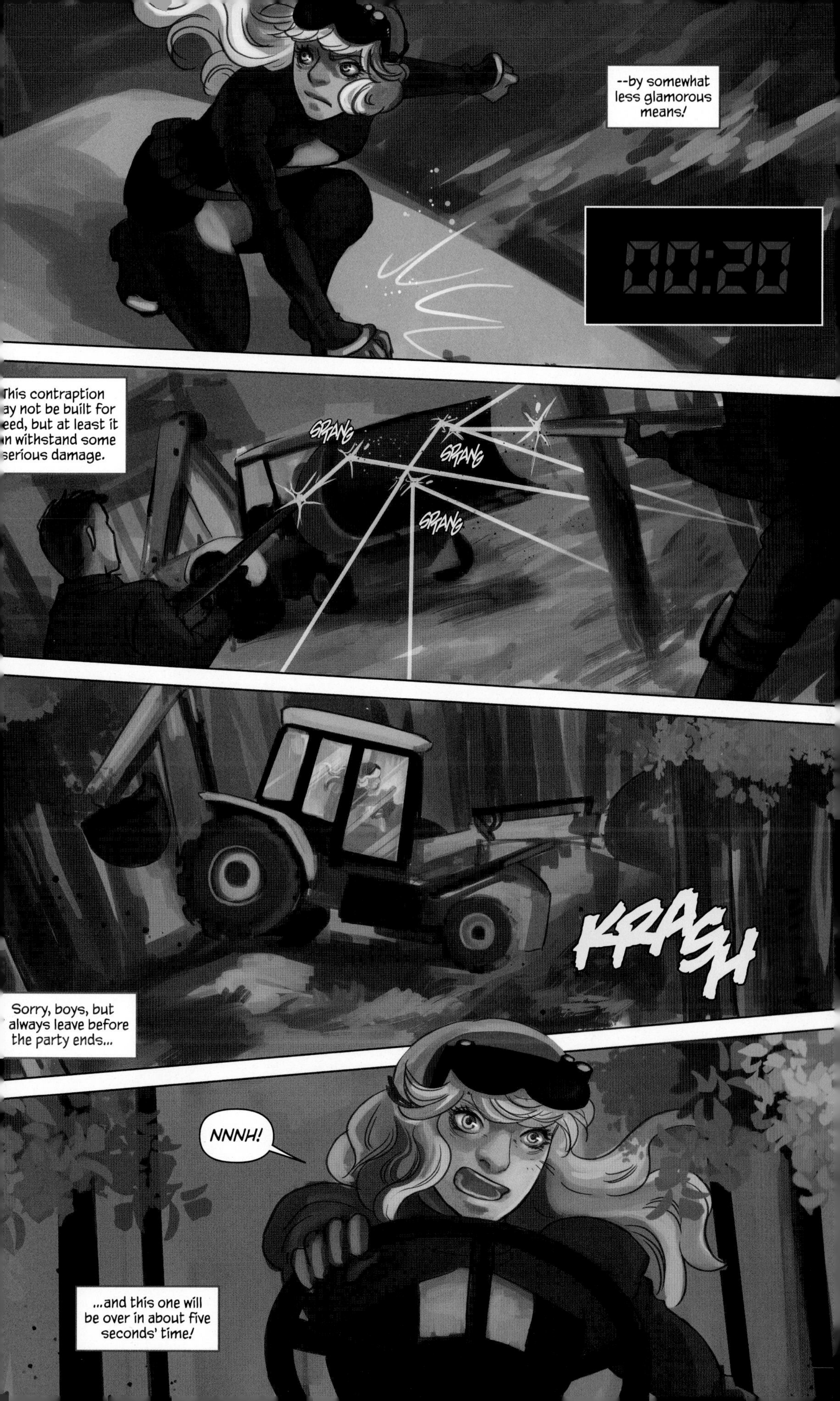
--by somewhat less glamorous means!
00:20
This contraption ay not be built for eed, but at least it n withstand some serious damage.
SPRANG
SPRANG
SPRANG
KRASH
Sorry, boys, but always leave before the party ends...
NNNH!
...and this one will be over in about five seconds' time!

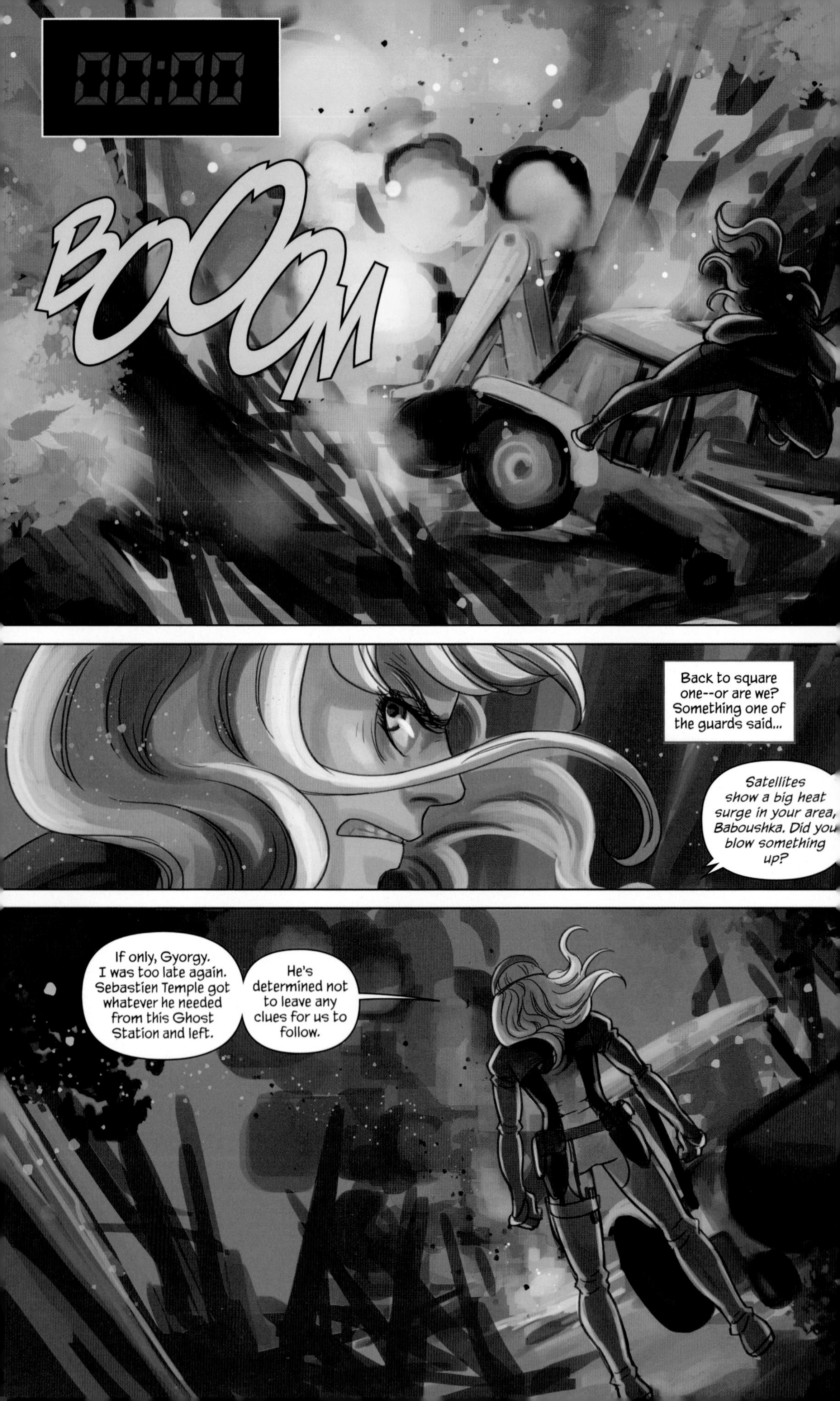
00:00
BOOOM
Back to square one--or are we? Something one of the guards said...
Satellites show a big heat surge in your area, Baboushka. Did you blow something up?
If only, Gyorgy. I was too late again. Sebastien Temple got whatever he needed from this Ghost Station and left.
He's determined not to leave any clues for us to follow.

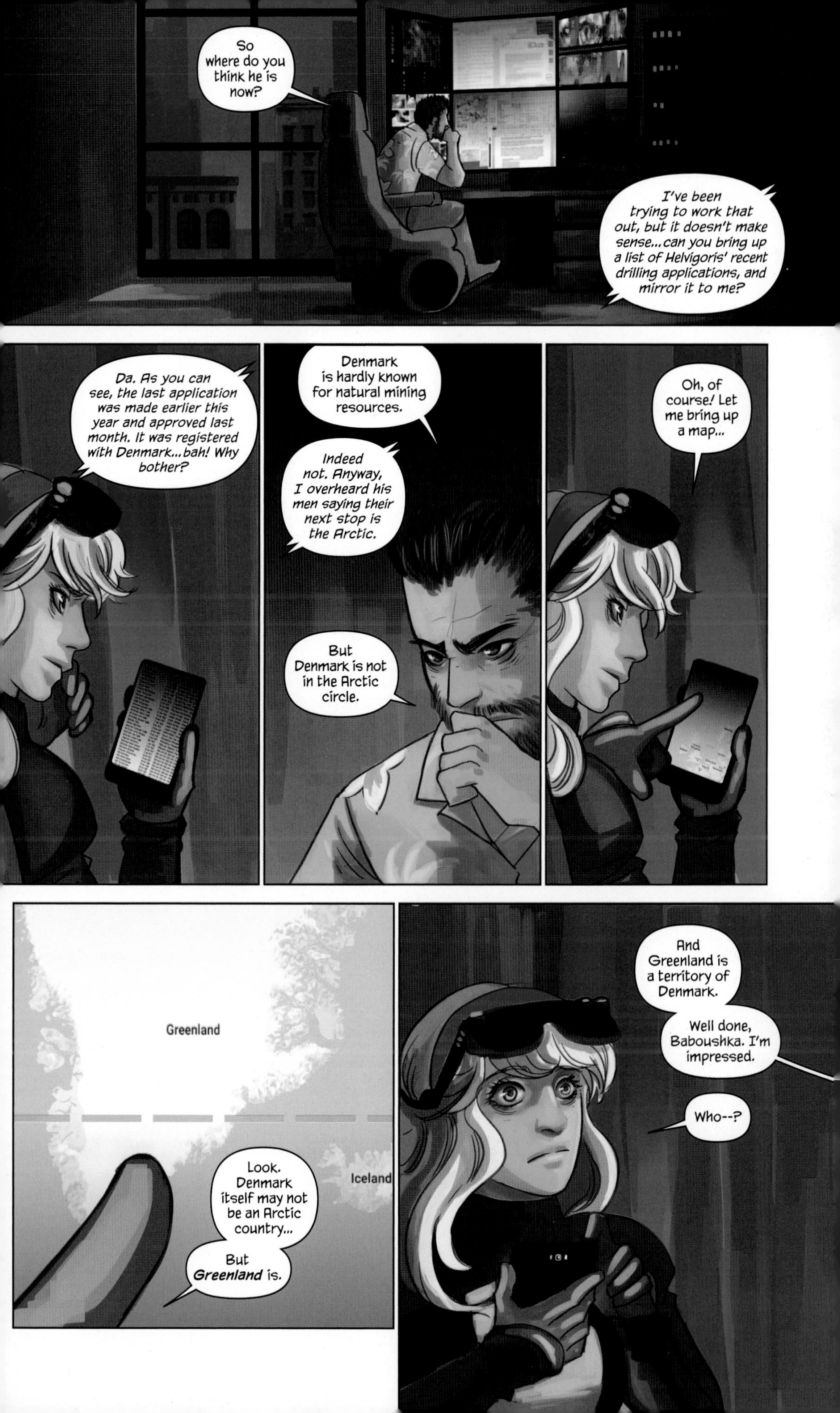
So where do you think he is now?
I've been trying to work that out, but it doesn't make sense...can you bring up a list of Helvigoris' recent drilling applications, and mirror it to me?
Da. As you can see, the last application was made earlier this year and approved last month. It was registered with Denmark...bah! Why bother?
Denmark is hardly known for natural mining resources.
Indeed not. Anyway, I overheard his men saying their next stop is the Arctic.
But Denmark is not in the Arctic circle.
Oh, of course! Let me bring up a map...
Greenland
Iceland
Look. Denmark itself may not be an Arctic country...
But Greenland is.
And Greenland is a territory of Denmark.
Well done, Baboushka. I'm impressed.
Who--?

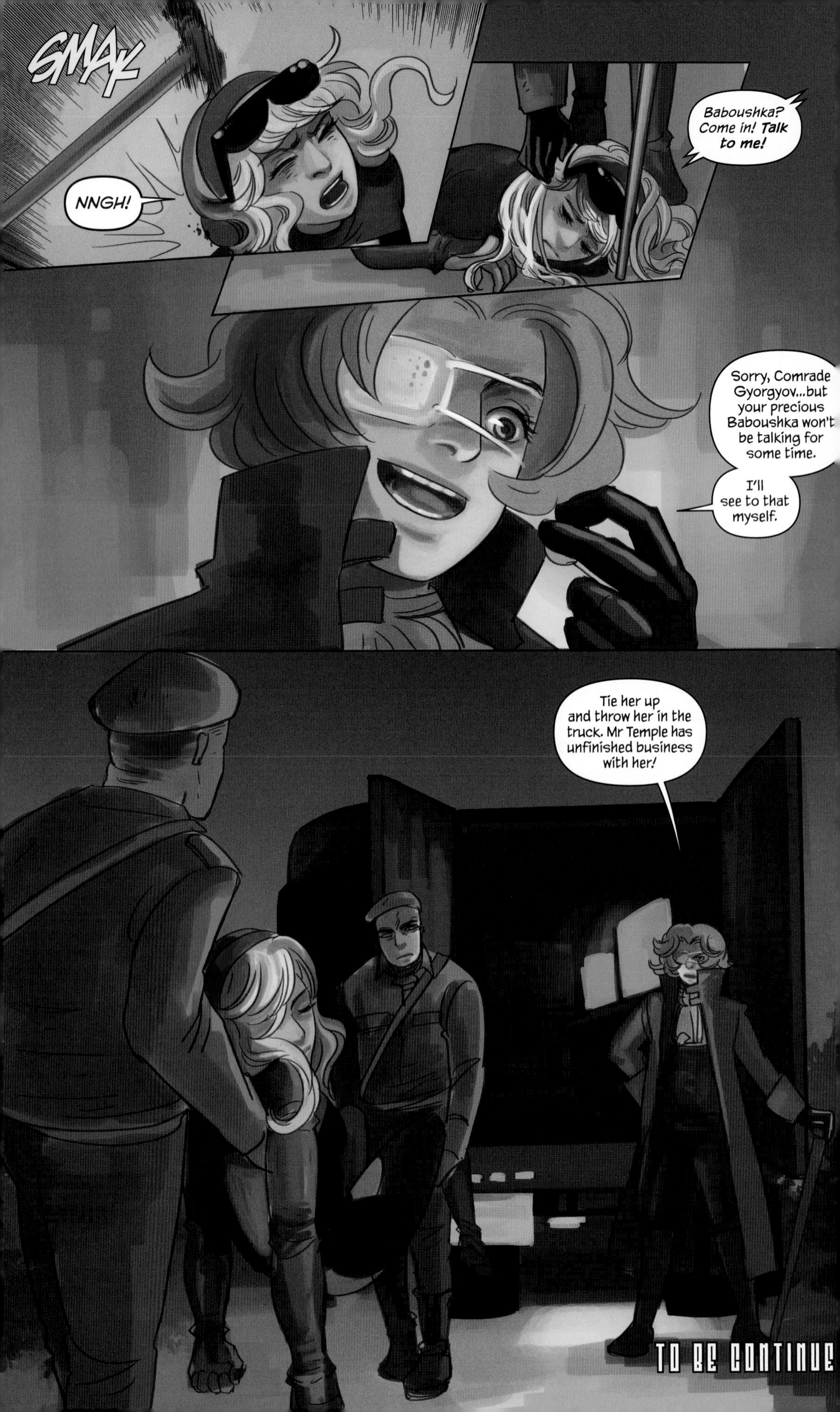
SMAK
NNGH!
Baboushka? Come in! Talk to me!
Sorry, Comrade Gyorgyov...but your precious Baboushka won't be talking for some time.
I'll see to that myself.
Tie her up and throw her in the truck. Mr Temple has unfinished business with her!
TO BE CONTINUE

PART ★ FOUR

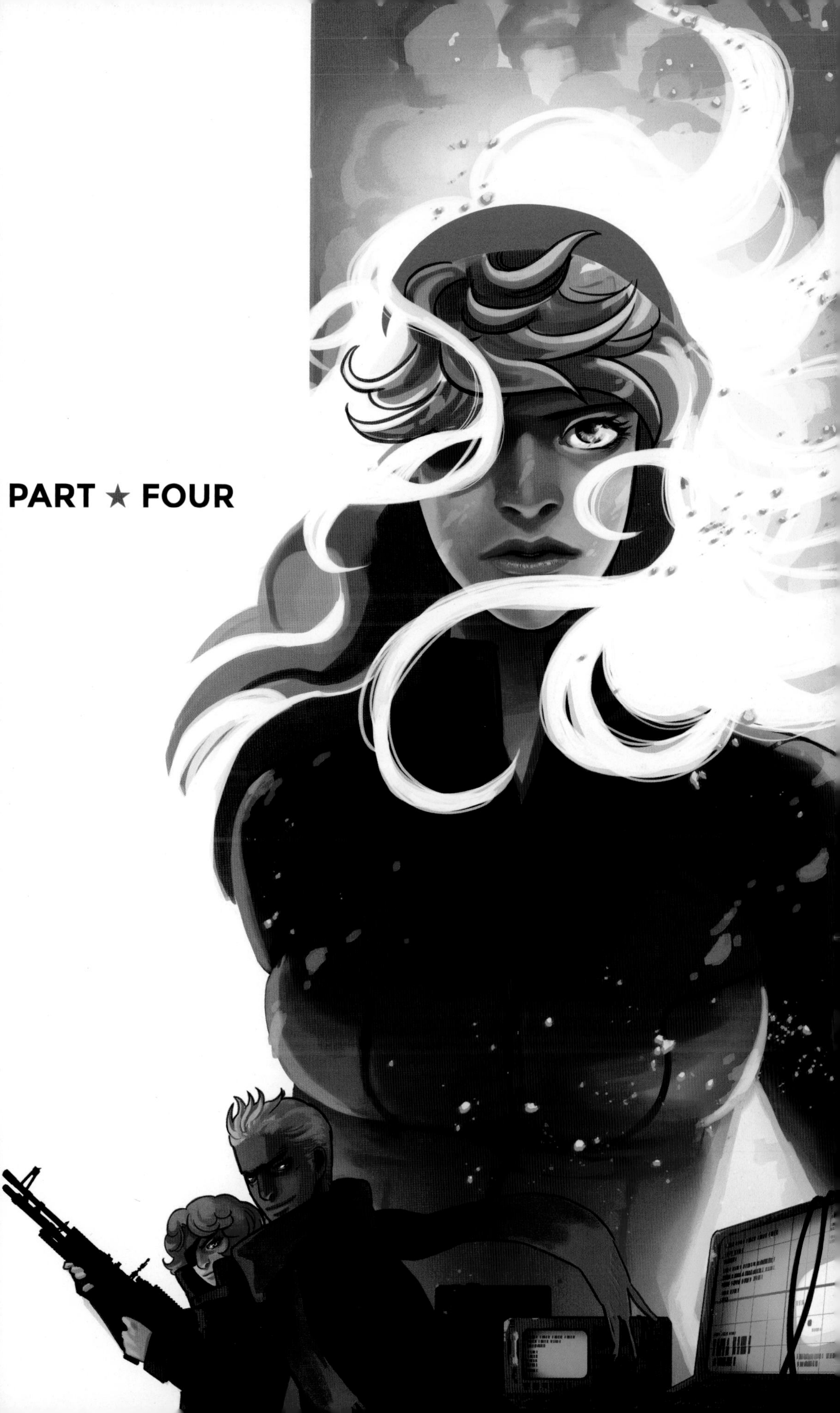

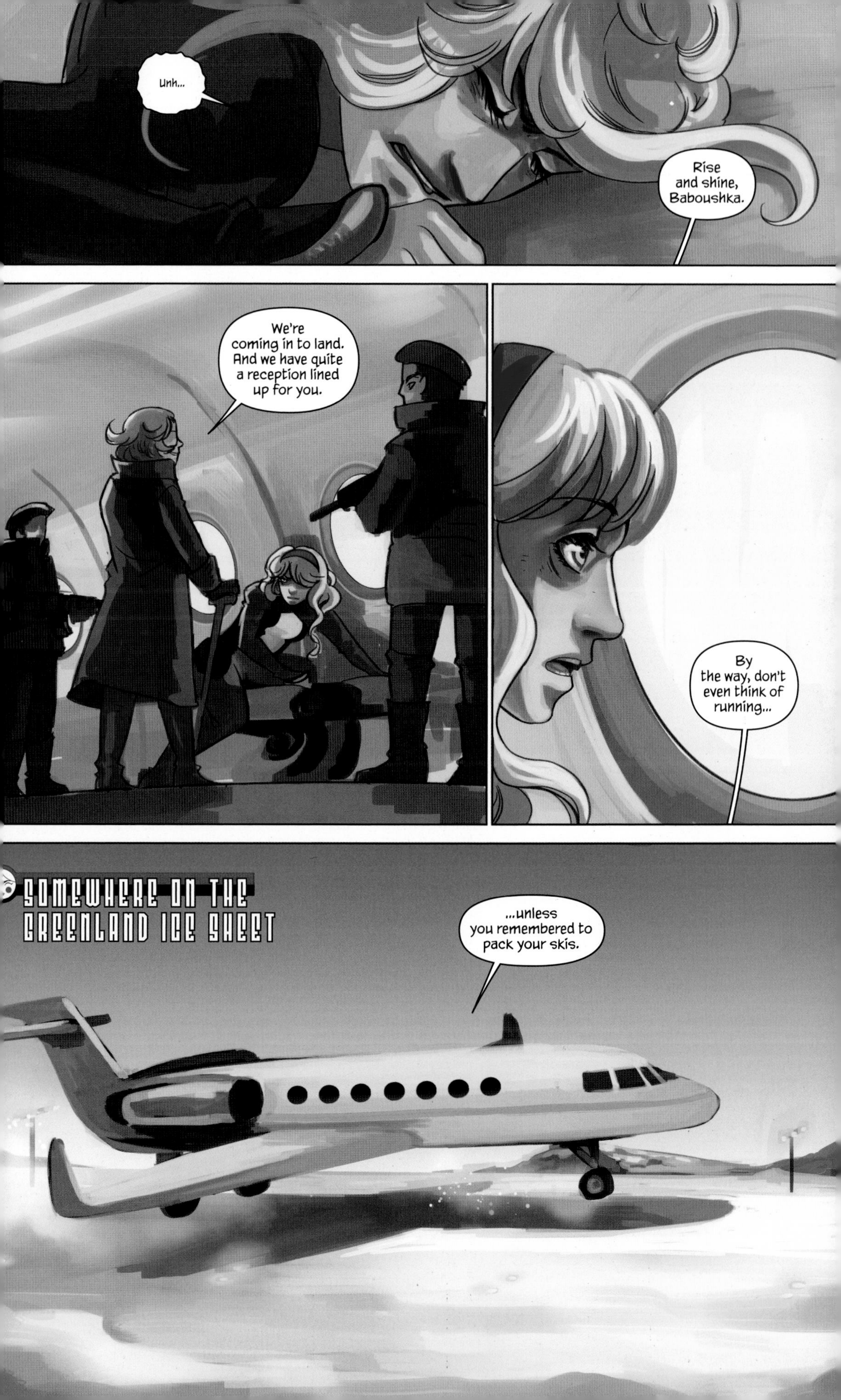
Unh...
Rise and shine, Baboushka.
We're coming in to land. And we have quite a reception lined up for you.
By the way, don't even think of running...
SOMEWHERE ON THE GREENLAND ICE SHEET
...unless you remembered to pack your skis.

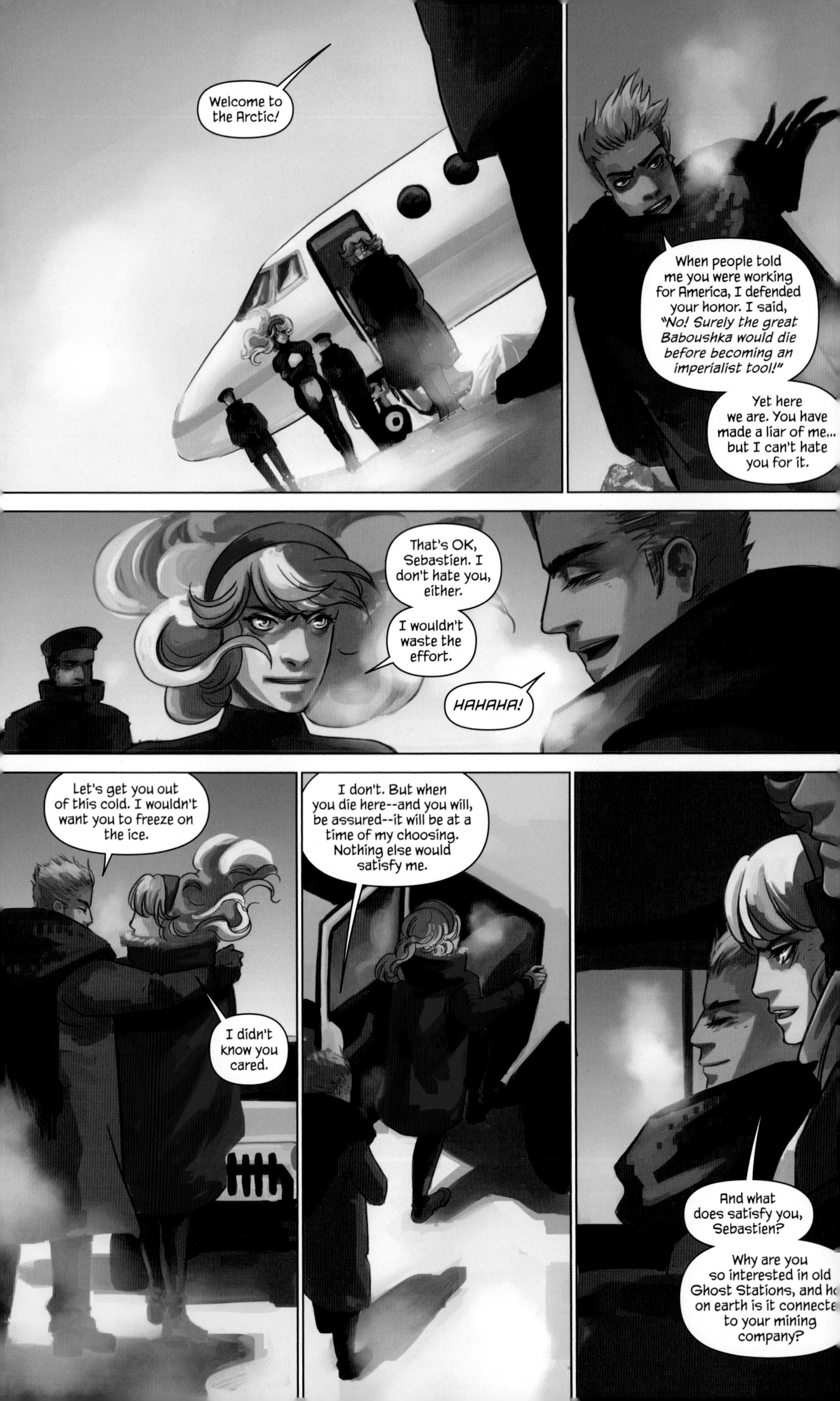
Welcome to the Arctic!
When people told me you were working for America, I defended your honor. I said, *"No! Surely the great Baboushka would die before becoming an imperialist tool!"*
Yet here we are. You have made a liar of me... but I can't hate you for it.
That's OK, Sebastien. I don't hate you, either.
I wouldn't waste the effort.
HAHAHA!
Let's get you out of this cold. I wouldn't want you to freeze on the ice.
I didn't know you cared.
I don't. But when you die here--and you will, be assured--it will be at a time of my choosing. Nothing else would satisfy me.
And what does satisfy you, Sebastien?
Why are you so interested in old Ghost Stations, and h on earth is it connecte to your mining company?

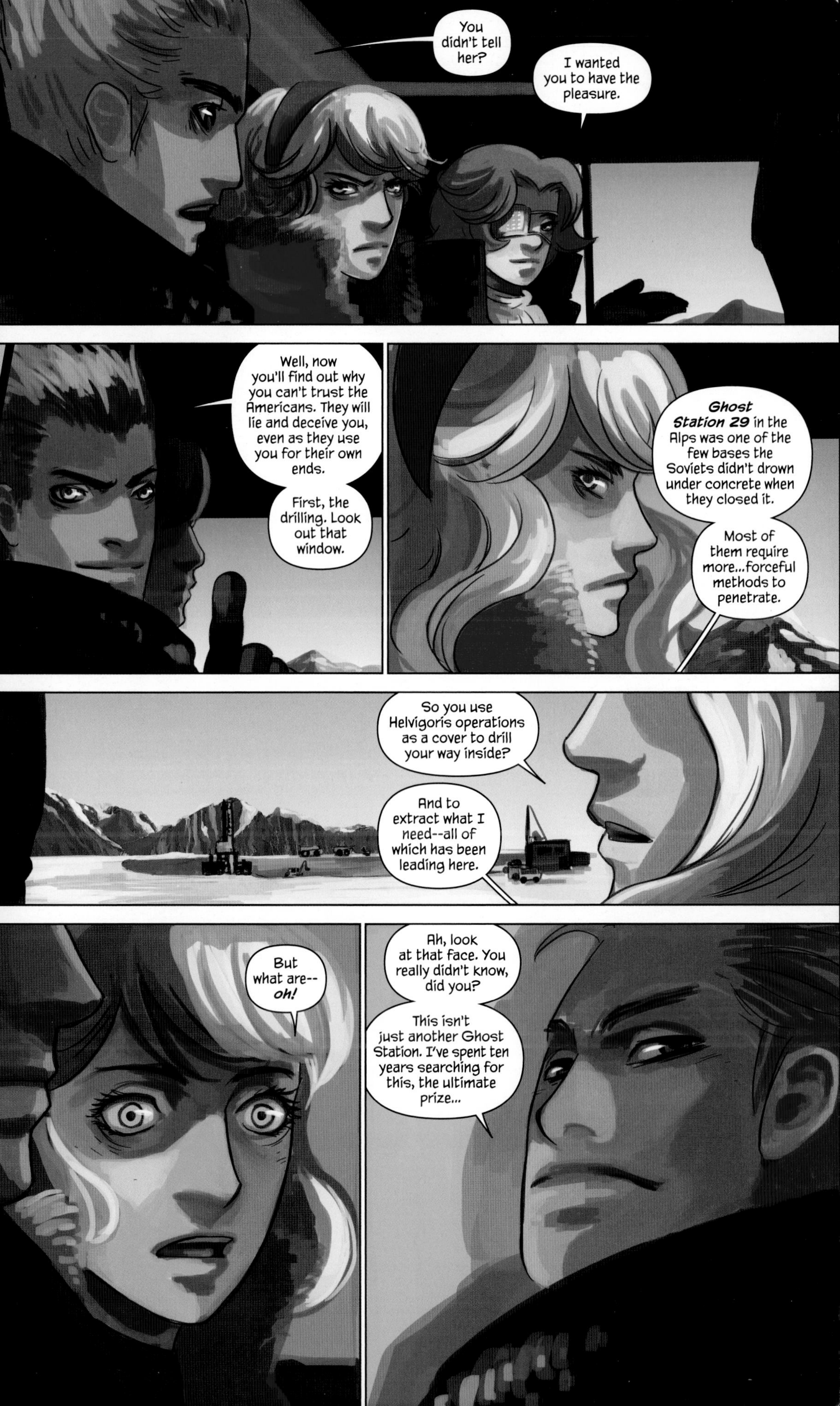

You didn't tell her?
I wanted you to have the pleasure.
Well, now you'll find out why you can't trust the Americans. They will lie and deceive you, even as they use you for their own ends.
First, the drilling. Look out that window.
Ghost Station 29 in the Alps was one of the few bases the Soviets didn't drown under concrete when they closed it.
Most of them require more...forceful methods to penetrate.
So you use Helvigoris operations as a cover to drill your way inside?
And to extract what I need--all of which has been leading here.
But what are-- oh!
Ah, look at that face. You really didn't know, did you?
This isn't just another Ghost Station. I've spent ten years searching for this, the ultimate prize...

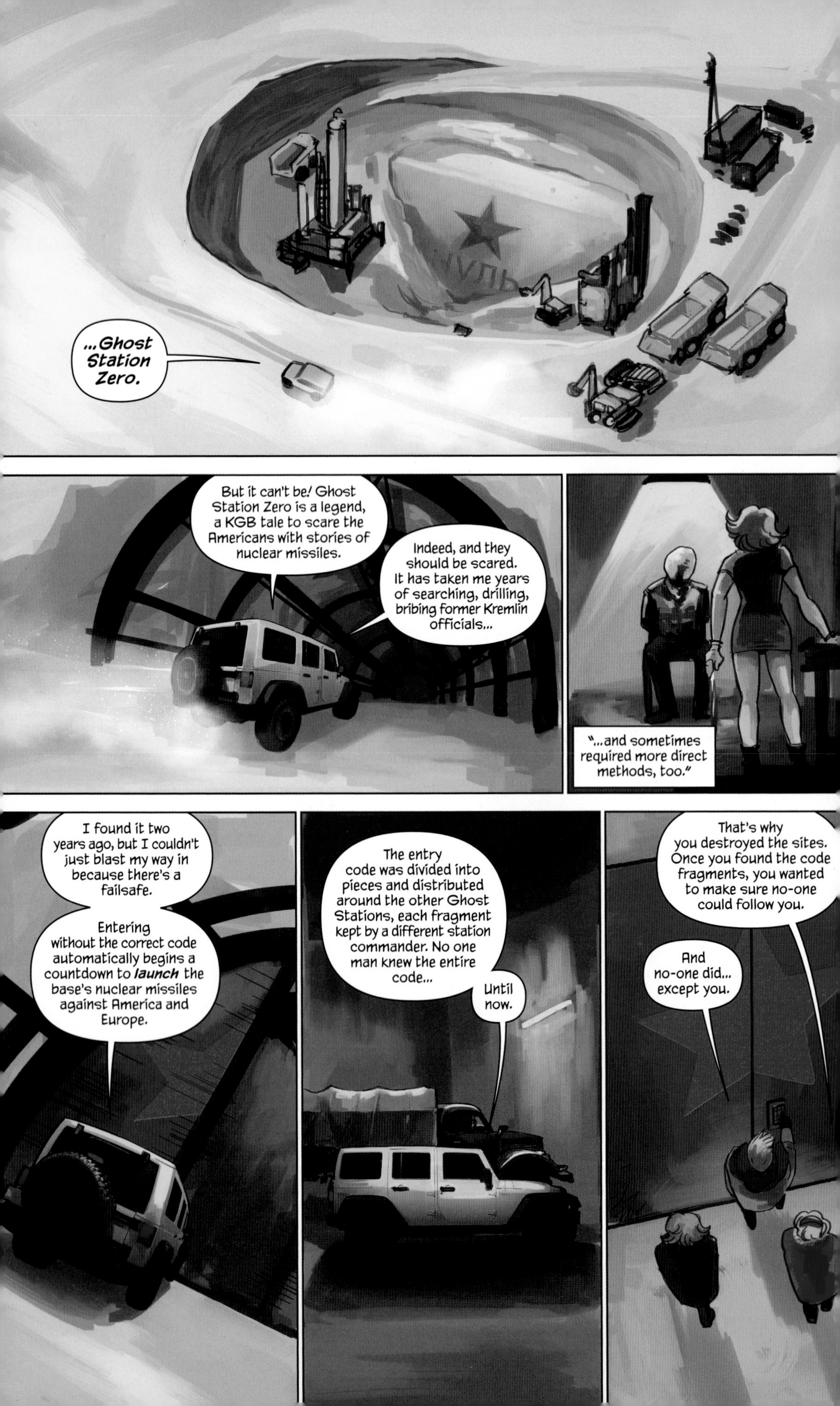

...Ghost Station Zero.
But it can't be! Ghost Station Zero is a legend, a KGB tale to scare the Americans with stories of nuclear missiles.
Indeed, and they should be scared. It has taken me years of searching, drilling, bribing former Kremlin officials...
"...and sometimes required more direct methods, too."
I found it two years ago, but I couldn't just blast my way in because there's a failsafe.
Entering without the correct code automatically begins a countdown to *launch* the base's nuclear missiles against America and Europe.
The entry code was divided into pieces and distributed around the other Ghost Stations, each fragment kept by a different station commander. No one man knew the entire code...
Until now.
That's why you destroyed the sites. Once you found the code fragments, you wanted to make sure no-one could follow you.
And no-one did... except you.

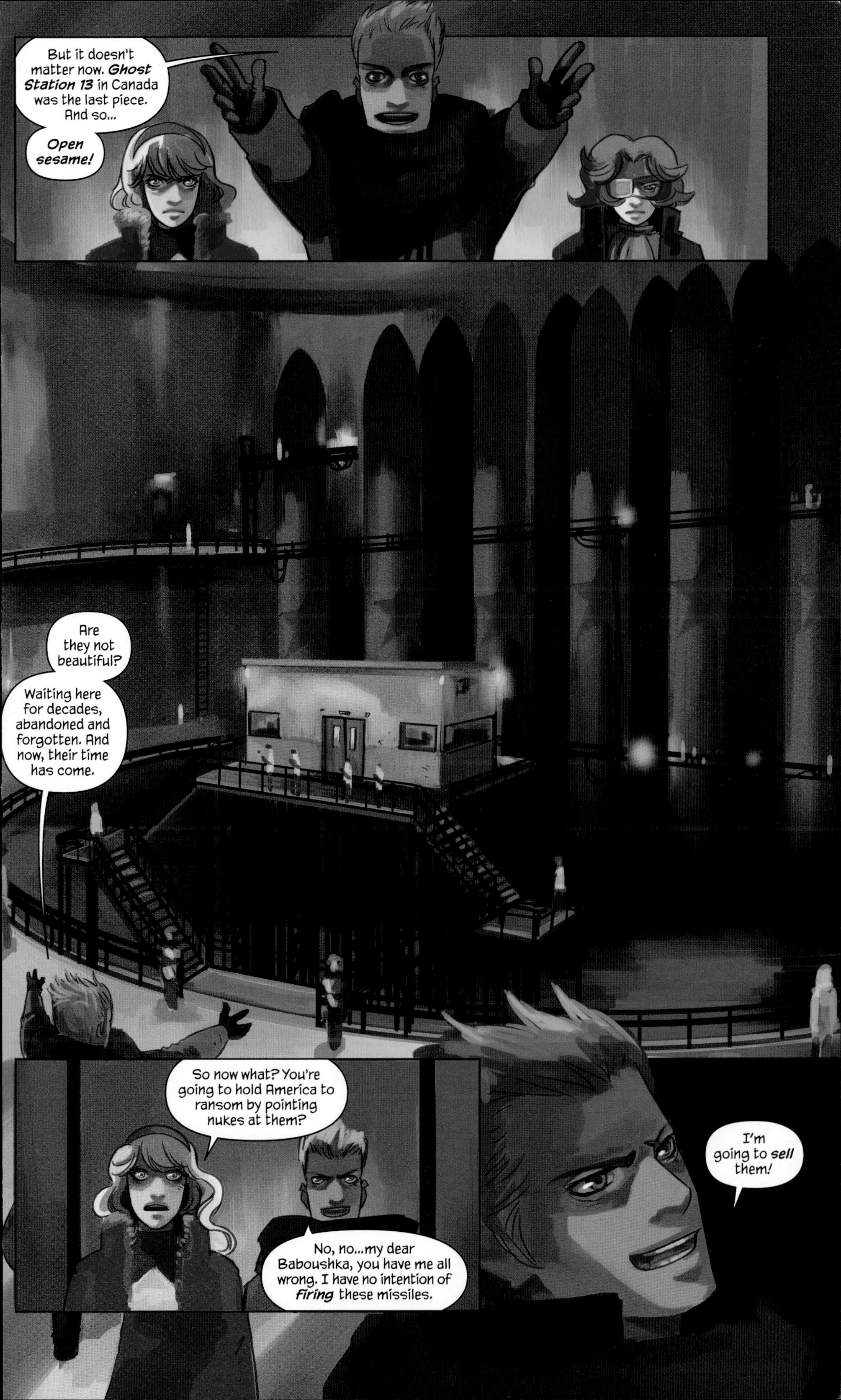

But it doesn't matter now. *Ghost Station 13* in Canada was the last piece. And so...
Open sesame!
Are they not beautiful?
Waiting here for decades, abandoned and forgotten. And now, their time has come.
So now what? You're going to hold America to ransom by pointing nukes at them?
No, no...my dear Baboushka, you have me all wrong. I have no intention of *firing* these missiles.
I'm going to *sell* them!

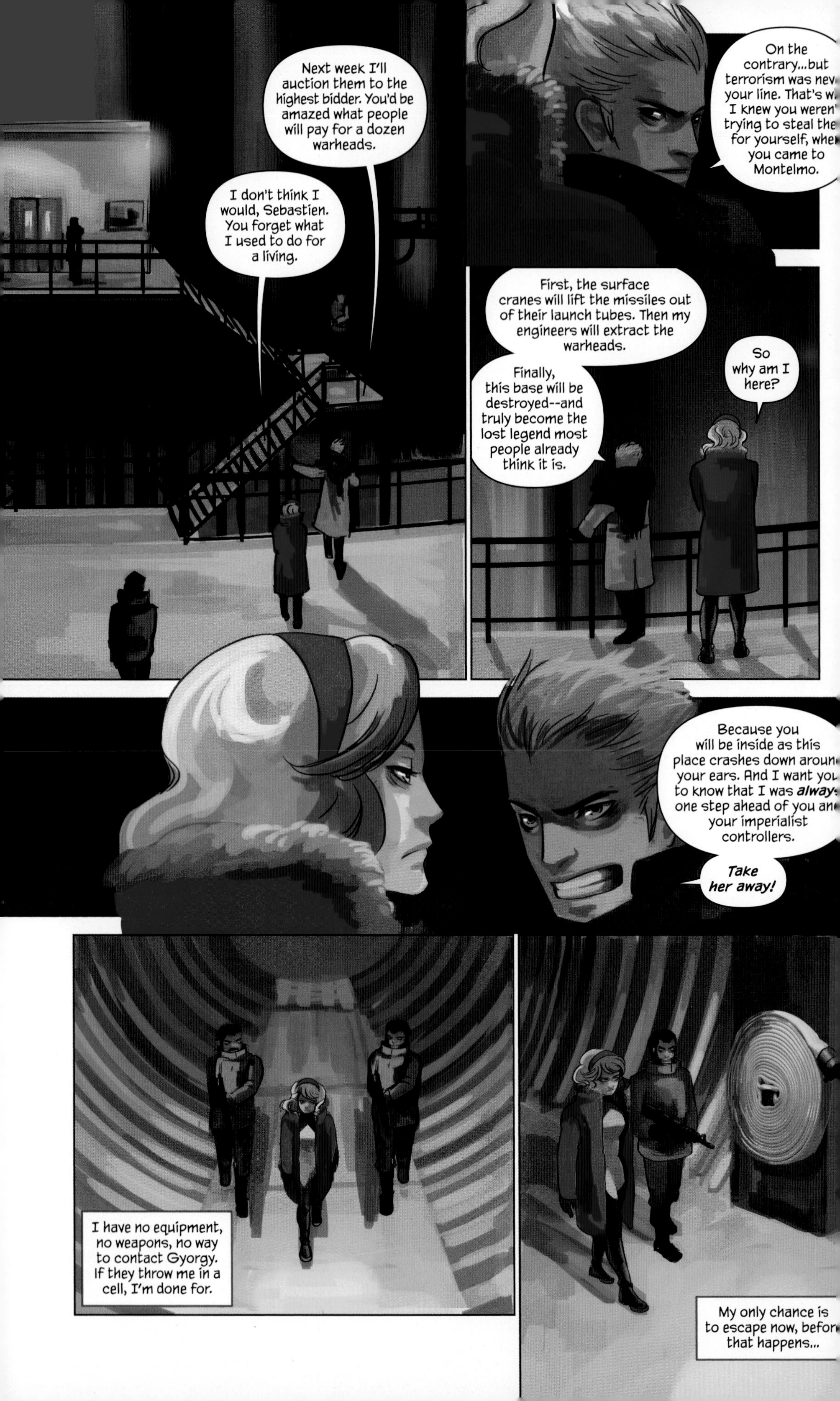

Next week I'll auction them to the highest bidder. You'd be amazed what people will pay for a dozen warheads.
I don't think I would, Sebastien. You forget what I used to do for a living.
On the contrary...but terrorism was nev your line. That's w I knew you weren' trying to steal the for yourself, whe you came to Montelmo.
First, the surface cranes will lift the missiles out of their launch tubes. Then my engineers will extract the warheads.
Finally, this base will be destroyed--and truly become the lost legend most people already think it is.
So why am I here?
Because you will be inside as this place crashes down aroun your ears. And I want yo to know that I was alway one step ahead of you an your imperialist controllers.
Take her away!
I have no equipment, no weapons, no way to contact Gyorgy. If they throw me in a cell, I'm done for.
My only chance is to escape now, befor that happens...

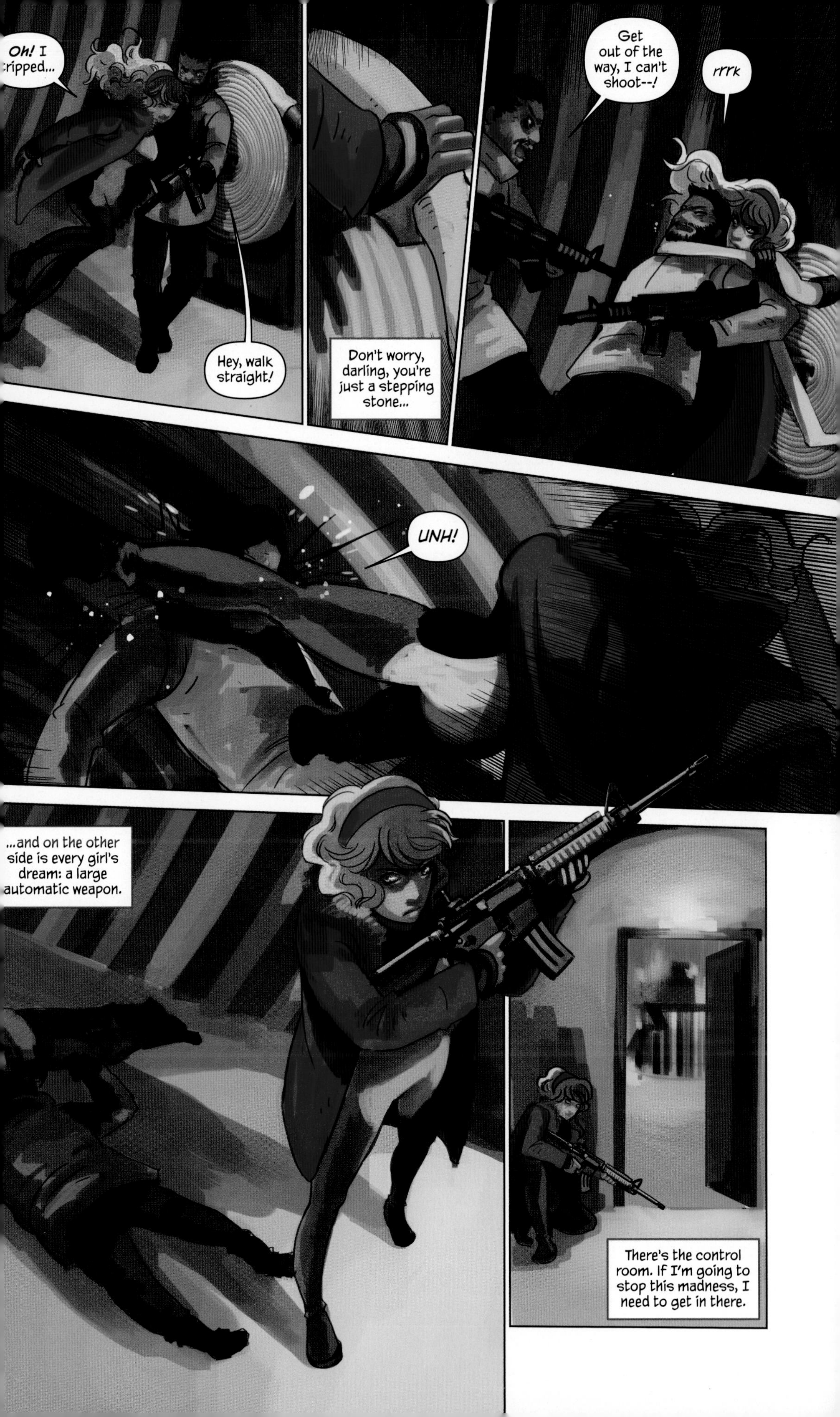
Oh! I tripped...
Hey, walk straight!
Don't worry, darling, you're just a stepping stone...
Get out of the way, I can't shoot--!
rrrk
UNH!
...and on the other side is every girl's dream: a large automatic weapon.
There's the control room. If I'm going to stop this madness, I need to get in there.

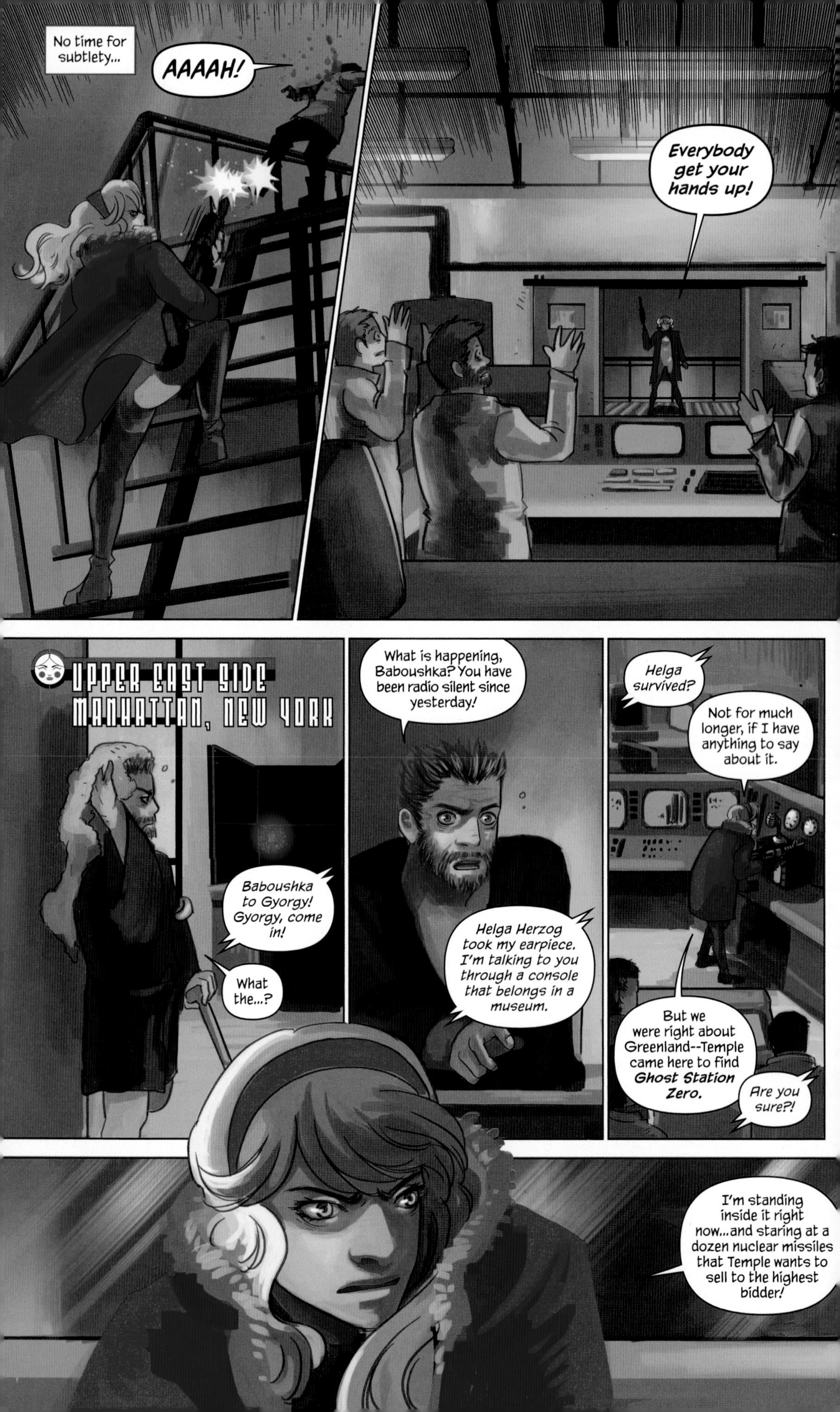
No time for subtlety...
AAAAH!
Everybody get your hands up!
UPPER EAST SIDE
MANHATTAN, NEW YORK
Baboushka to Gyorgy! Gyorgy, come in!
What the...?
What is happening, Baboushka? You have been radio silent since yesterday!
Helga Herzog took my earpiece. I'm talking to you through a console that belongs in a museum.
Helga survived?
Not for much longer, if I have anything to say about it.
But we were right about Greenland--Temple came here to find Ghost Station Zero.
Are you sure?!
I'm standing inside it right now...and staring at a dozen nuclear missiles that Temple wants to sell to the highest bidder!

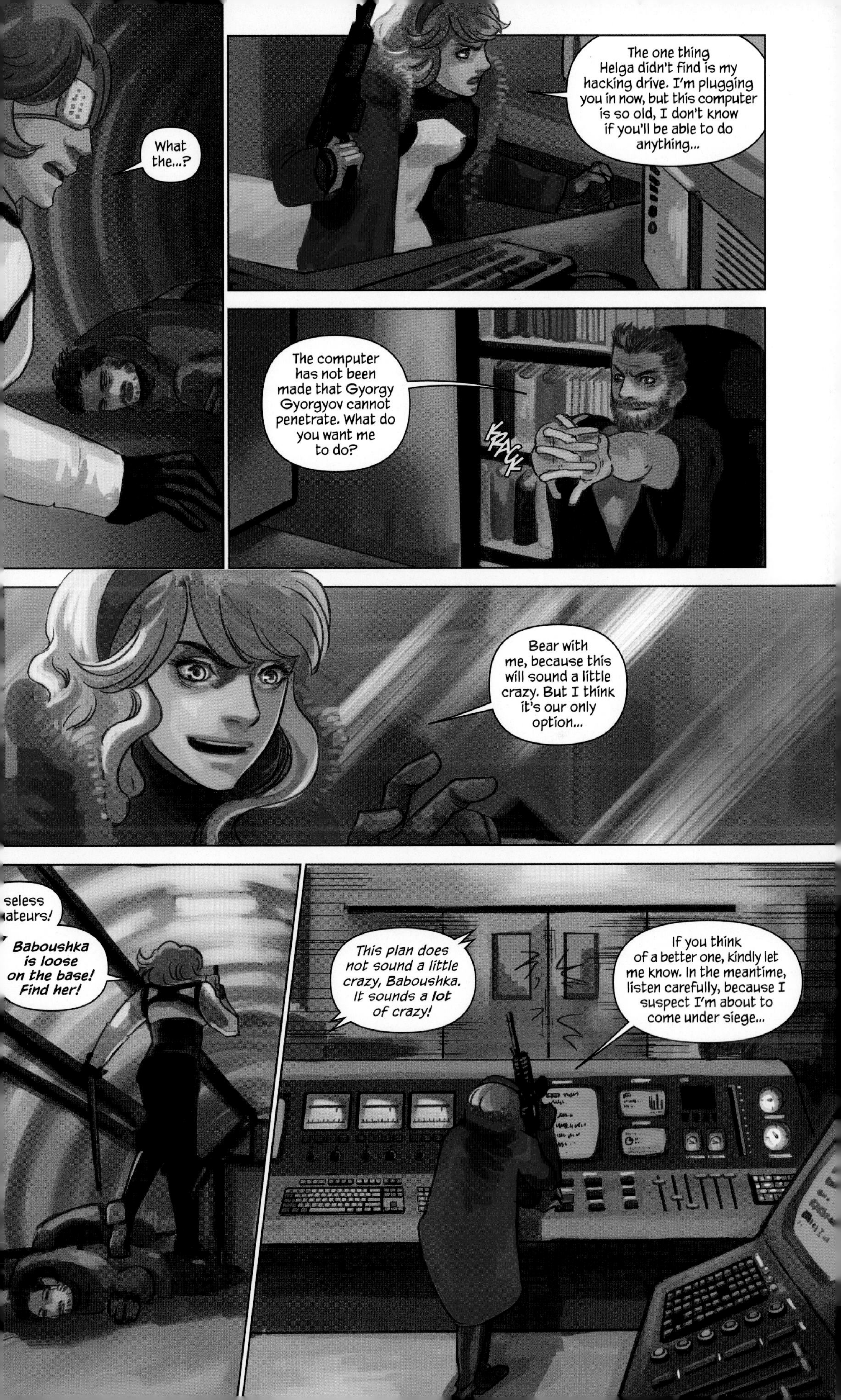
What the...?
The one thing Helga didn't find is my hacking drive. I'm plugging you in now, but this computer is so old, I don't know if you'll be able to do anything...
The computer has not been made that Gyorgy Gyorgyov cannot penetrate. What do you want me to do?
KRACK
Bear with me, because this will sound a little crazy. But I think it's our only option...
seless
ateurs!
Baboushka is loose on the base! Find her!
*This plan does not sound a little crazy, Baboushka. It sounds a **lot** of crazy!*
If you think of a better one, kindly let me know. In the meantime, listen carefully, because I suspect I'm about to come under siege...

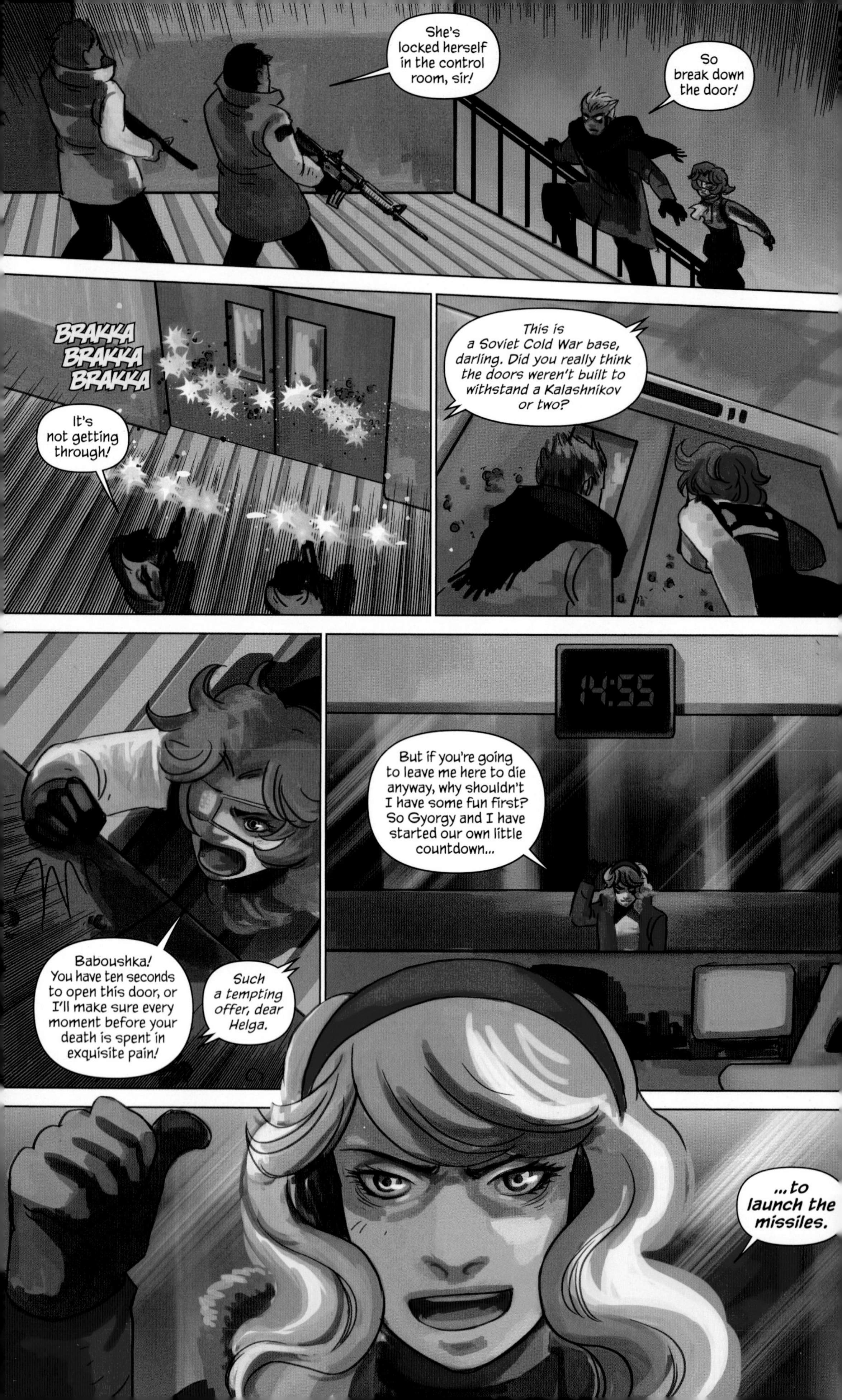
She's locked herself in the control room, sir!
So break down the door!
BRAKKA BRAKKA BRAKKA
It's not getting through!
This is a Soviet Cold War base, darling. Did you really think the doors weren't built to withstand a Kalashnikov or two?
Baboushka! You have ten seconds to open this door, or I'll make sure every moment before your death is spent in exquisite pain!
Such a tempting offer, dear Helga.
14:55
But if you're going to leave me here to die anyway, why shouldn't I have some fun first? So Gyorgy and I have started our own little countdown...
...to launch the missiles.

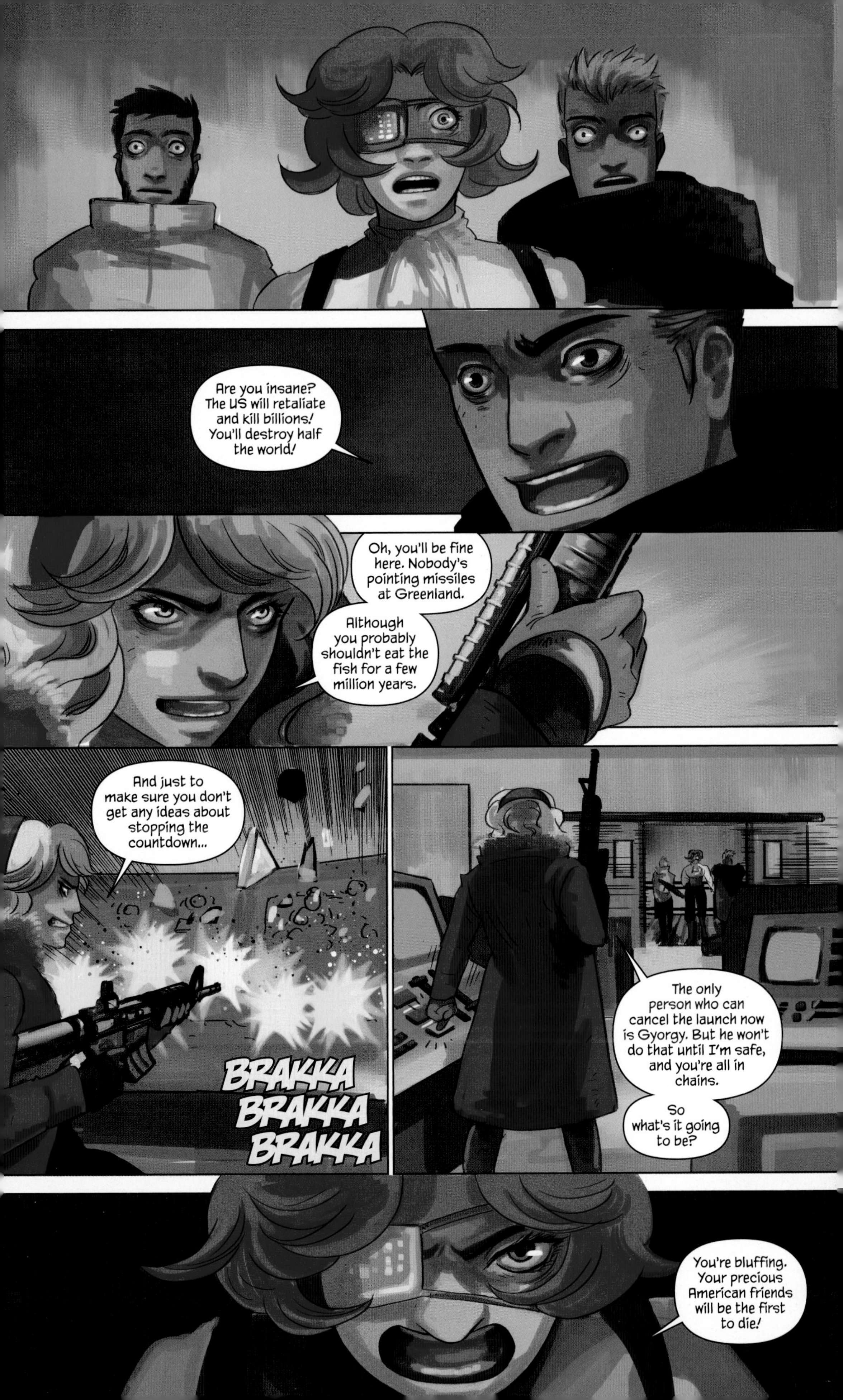

Are you insane? The US will retaliate and kill billions! You'll destroy half the world!
Oh, you'll be fine here. Nobody's pointing missiles at Greenland.
Although you probably shouldn't eat the fish for a few million years.
And just to make sure you don't get any ideas about stopping the countdown...
BRAKKA BRAKKA BRAKKA
The only person who can cancel the launch now is Gyorgy. But he won't do that until I'm safe, and you're all in chains.
So what's it going to be?
You're bluffing. Your precious American friends will be the first to die!

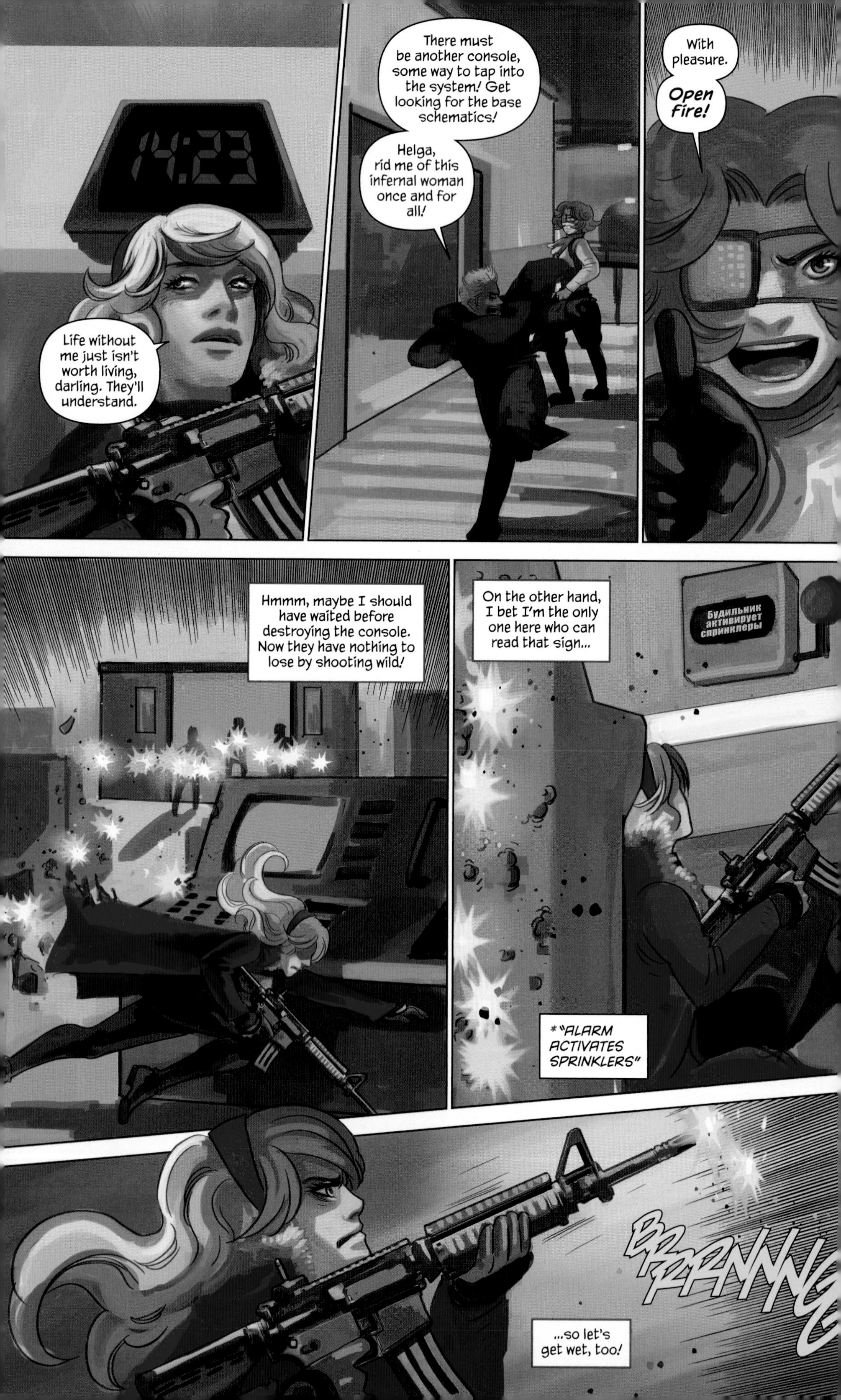
Life without me just isn't worth living, darling. They'll understand.
There must be another console, some way to tap into the system! Get looking for the base schematics!
Helga, rid me of this infernal woman once and for all!
With pleasure.
Open fire!
Hmmm, maybe I should have waited before destroying the console. Now they have nothing to lose by shooting wild!
On the other hand, I bet I'm the only one here who can read that sign...
Будильник активирует спринклеры
*"ALARM ACTIVATES SPRINKLERS"
BRRRNNNNG
...so let's get wet, too!

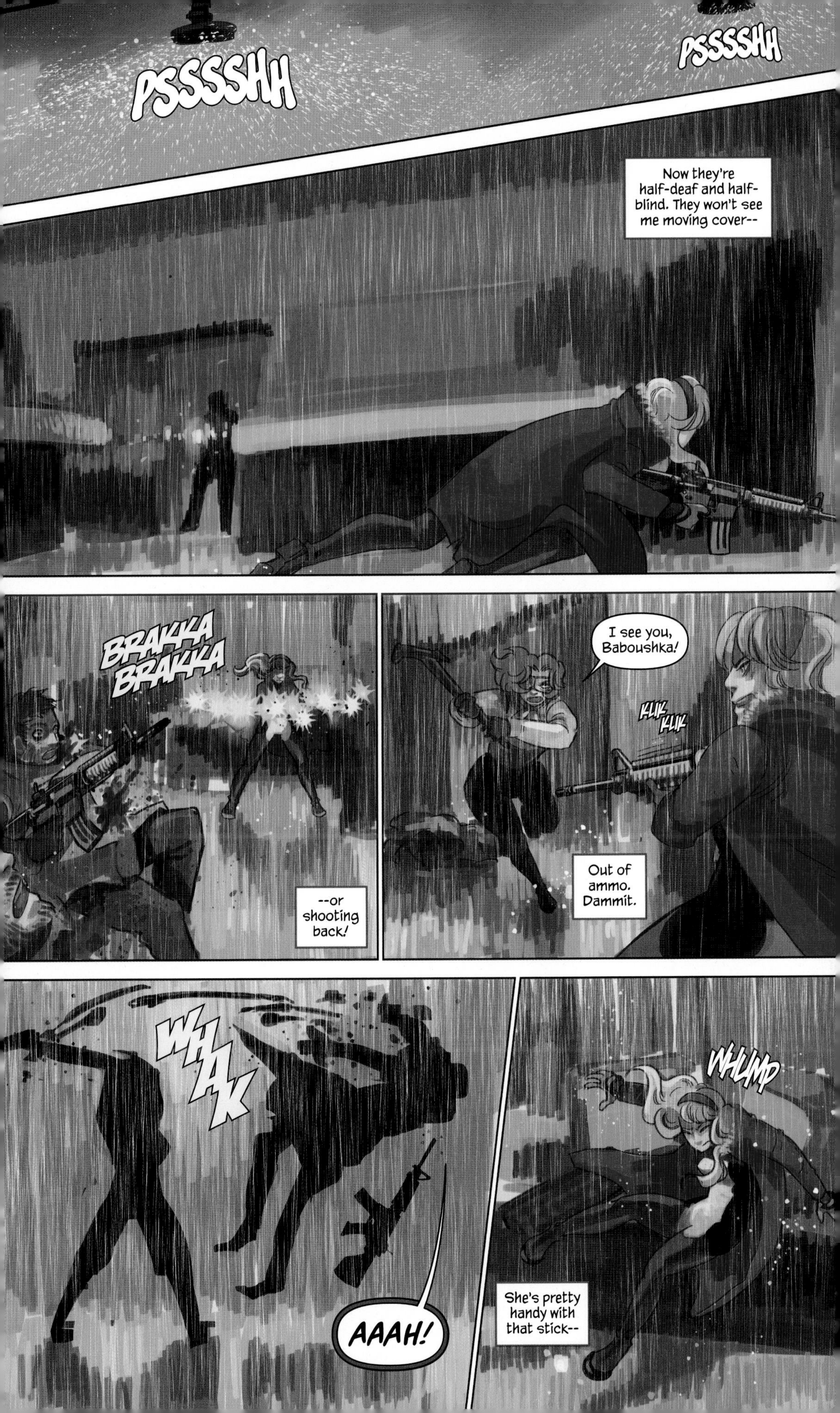
PSSSSHH
PSSSSHH
Now they're half-deaf and half-blind. They won't see me moving cover--
BRAKKA BRAKKA
--or shooting back!
I see you, Baboushka!
KLIK KLIK
Out of ammo. Dammit.
WHAK
AAAH!
WHUMP
She's pretty handy with that stick--

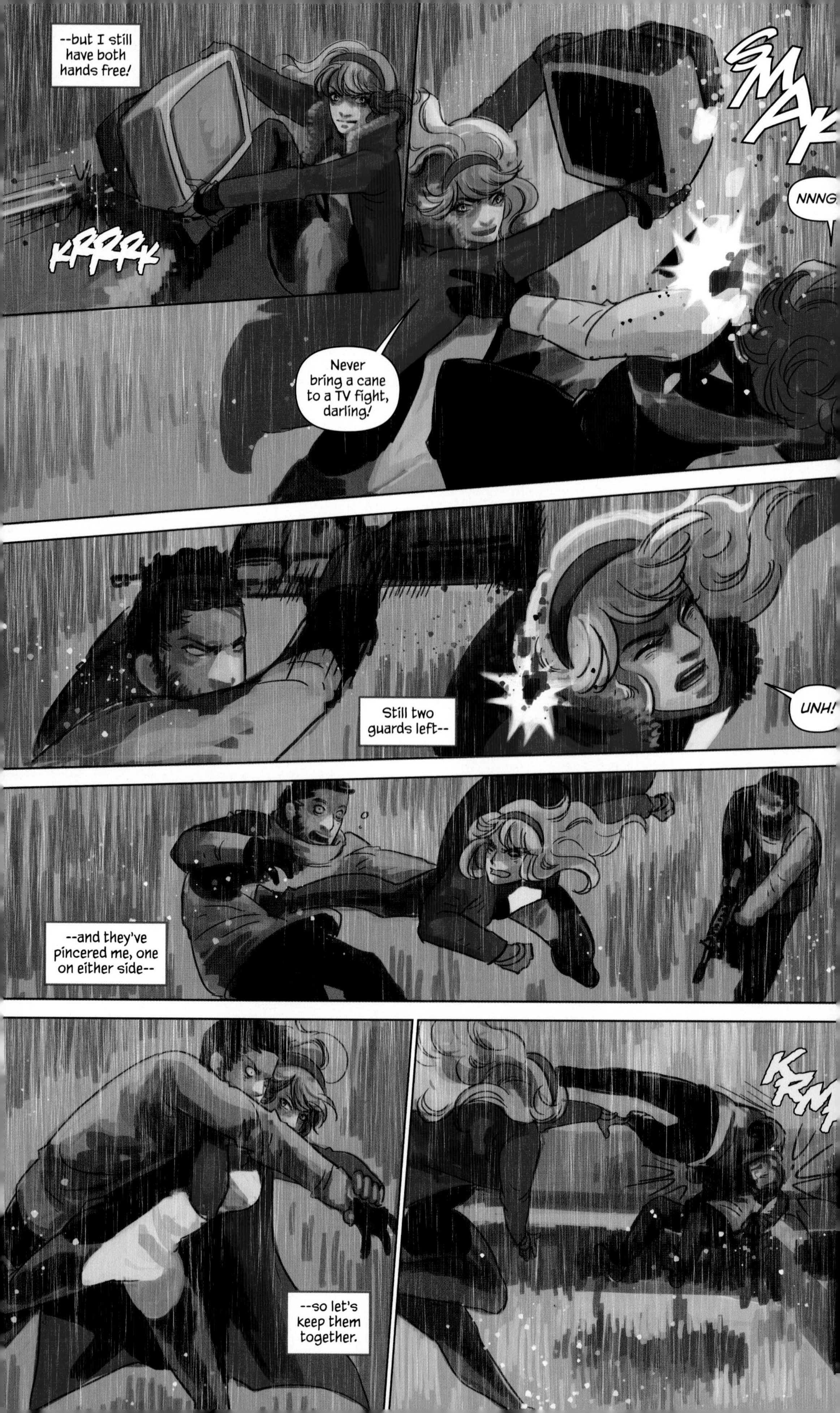
--but I still have both hands free!
KRRRK
SMAK
NNNG!
Never bring a cane to a TV fight, darling!
Still two guards left--
UNH!
--and they've pincered me, one on either side--
--so let's keep them together.
KRMP

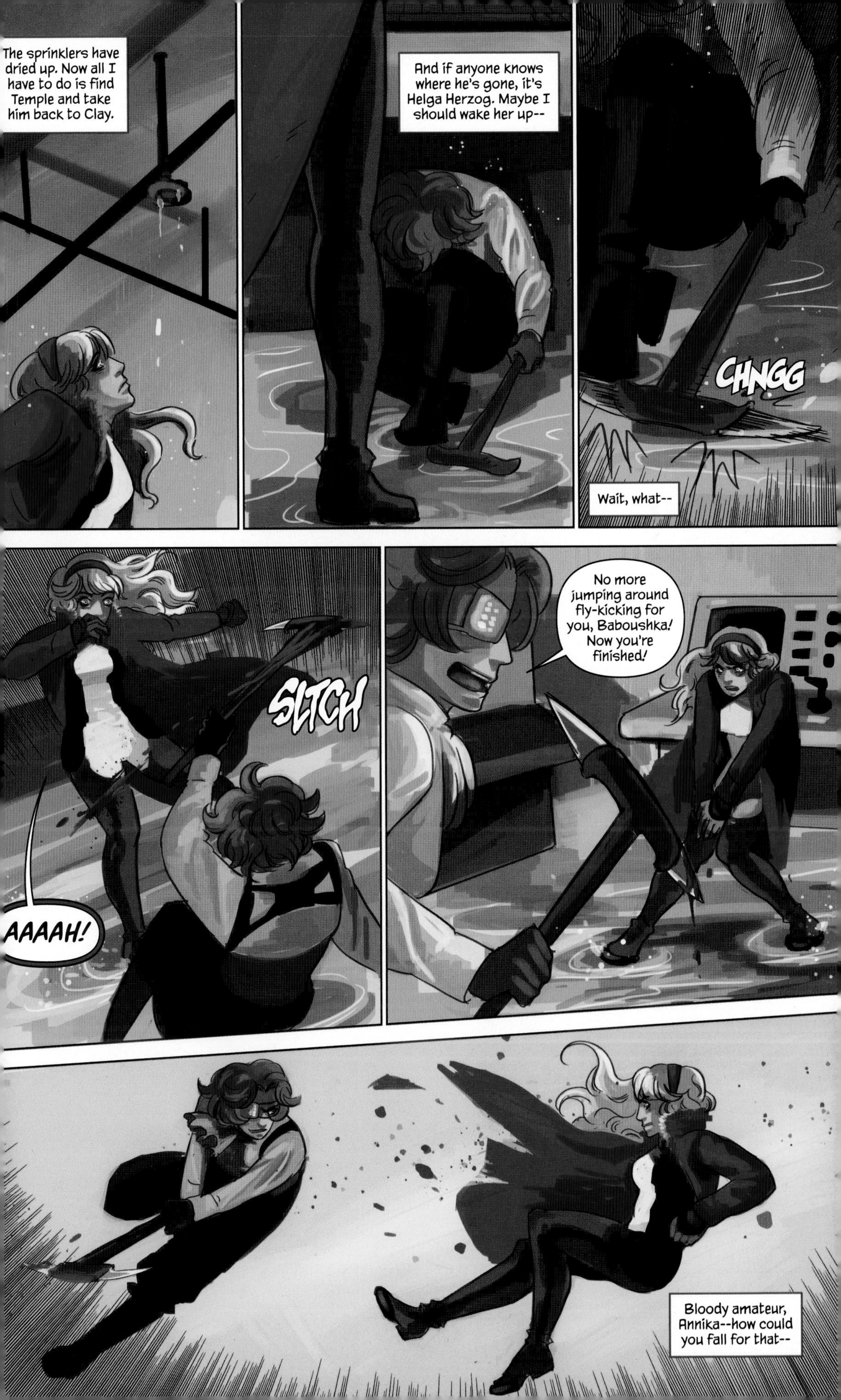

The sprinklers have dried up. Now all I have to do is find Temple and take him back to Clay.
And if anyone knows where he's gone, it's Helga Herzog. Maybe I should wake her up--
CHNGG
Wait, what--
SLTCH
AAAAH!
No more jumping around fly-kicking for you, Baboushka! Now you're finished!
Bloody amateur, Annika--how could you fall for that--

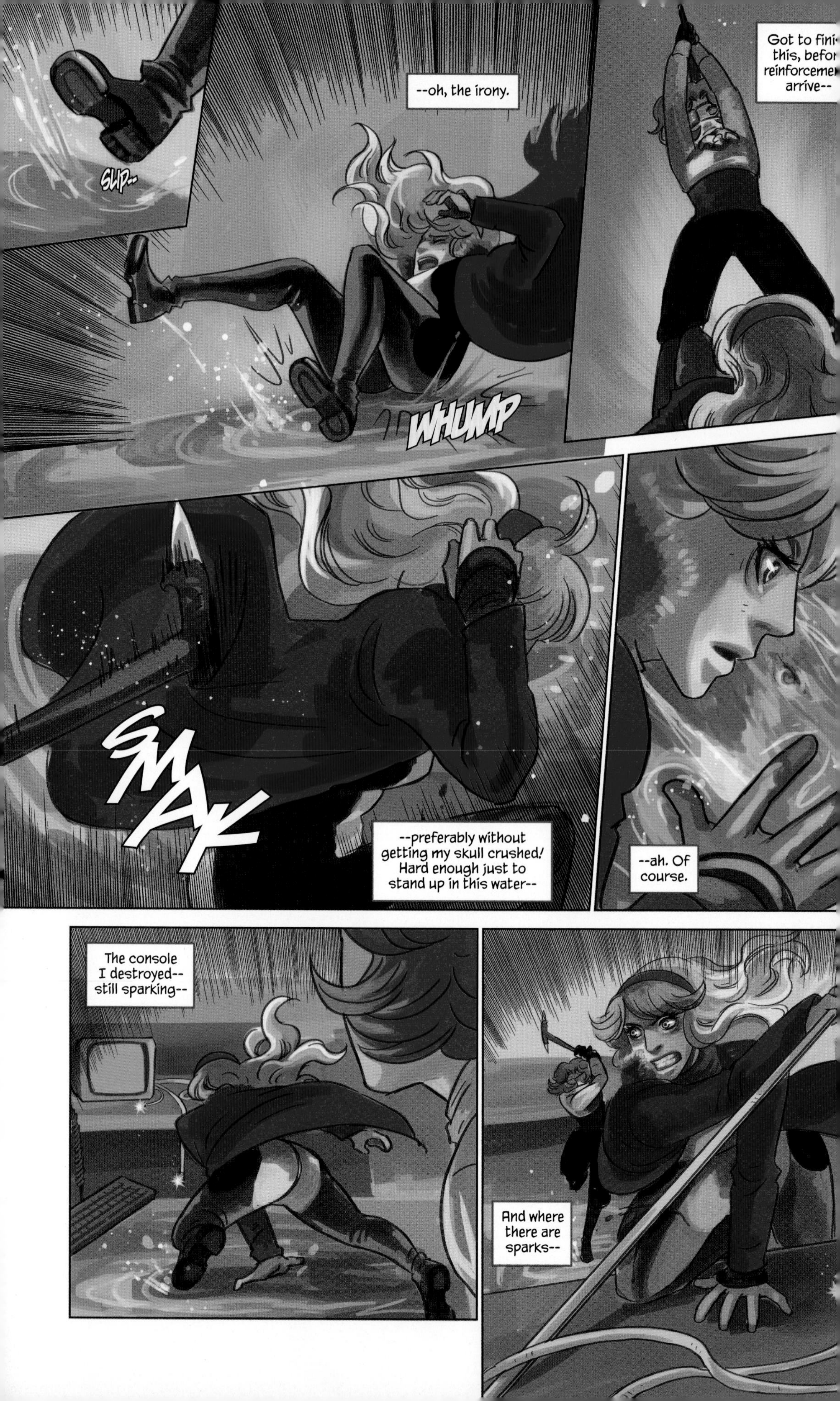
SLIP--
--oh, the irony.
WHUMP
Got to fini-
this, befor
reinforceme
arrive--
SMAK
--preferably without getting my skull crushed! Hard enough just to stand up in this water--
--ah. Of course.
The console I destroyed-- still sparking--
And where there are sparks--

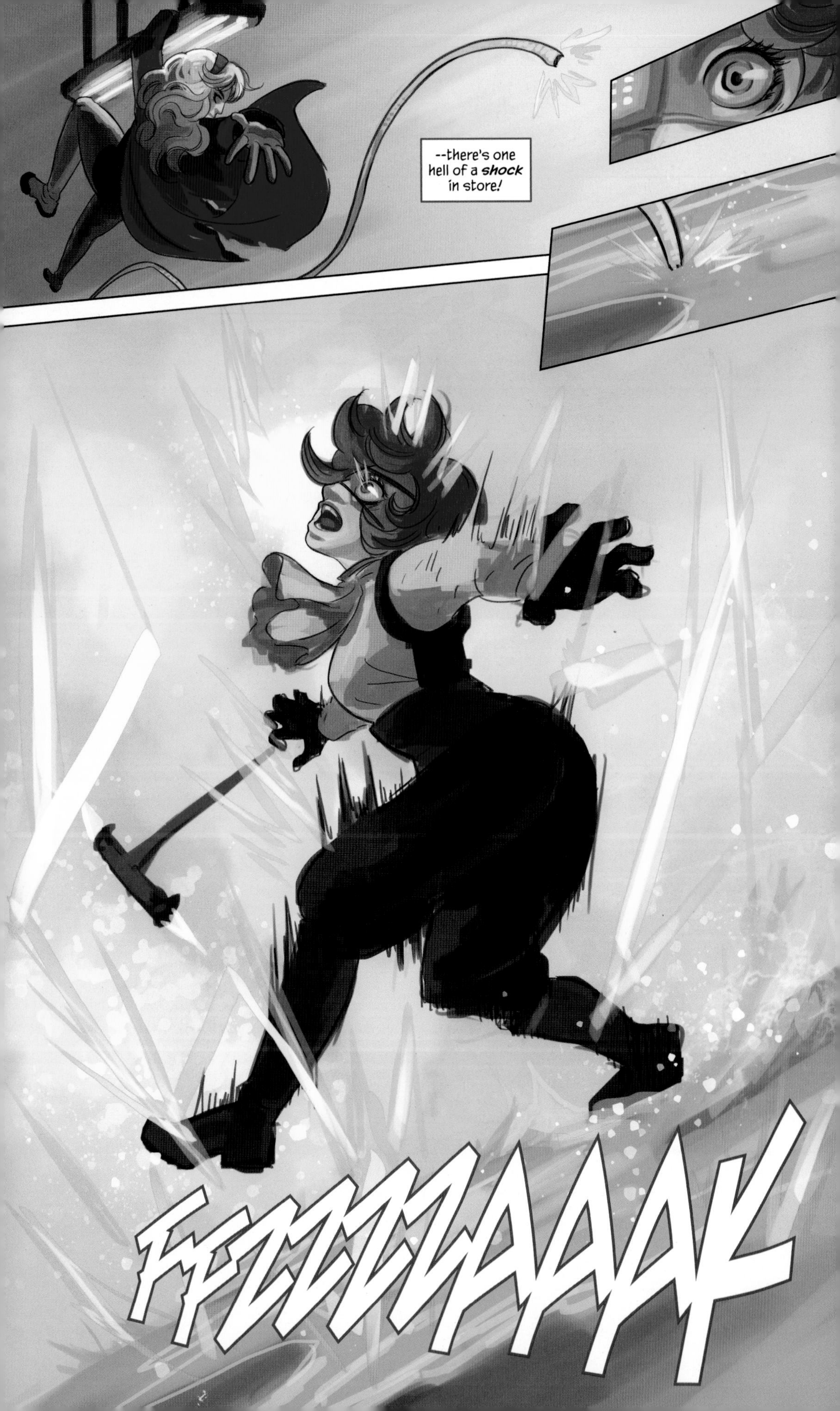
--there's one hell of a *shock* in store!
FFZZZZAAAAK

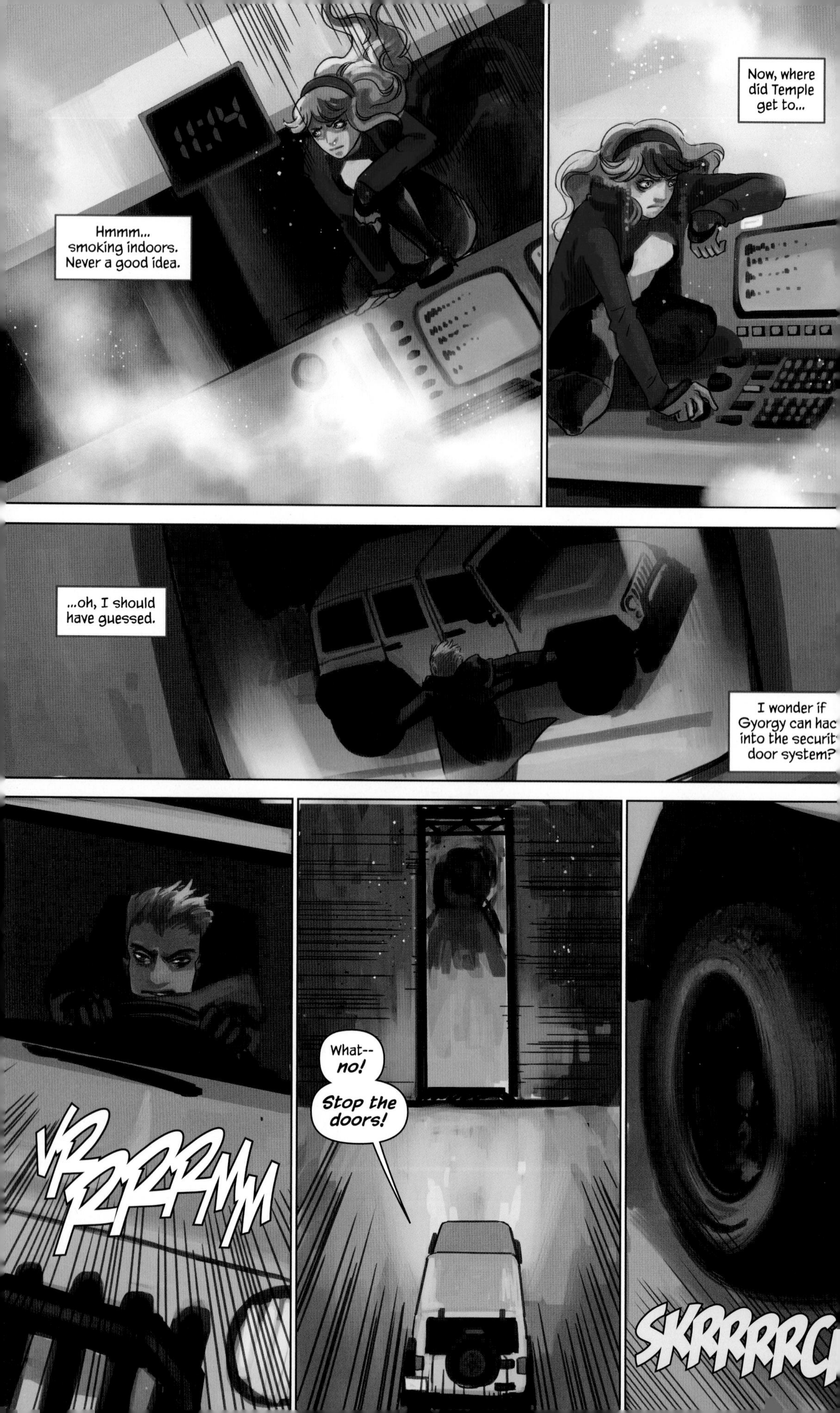
Hmmm... smoking indoors. Never a good idea.
Now, where did Temple get to...
...oh, I should have guessed.
I wonder if Gyorgy can hac into the securit door system?
VRRRRRMMM
What-- no!
Stop the doors!
SKRRRRC

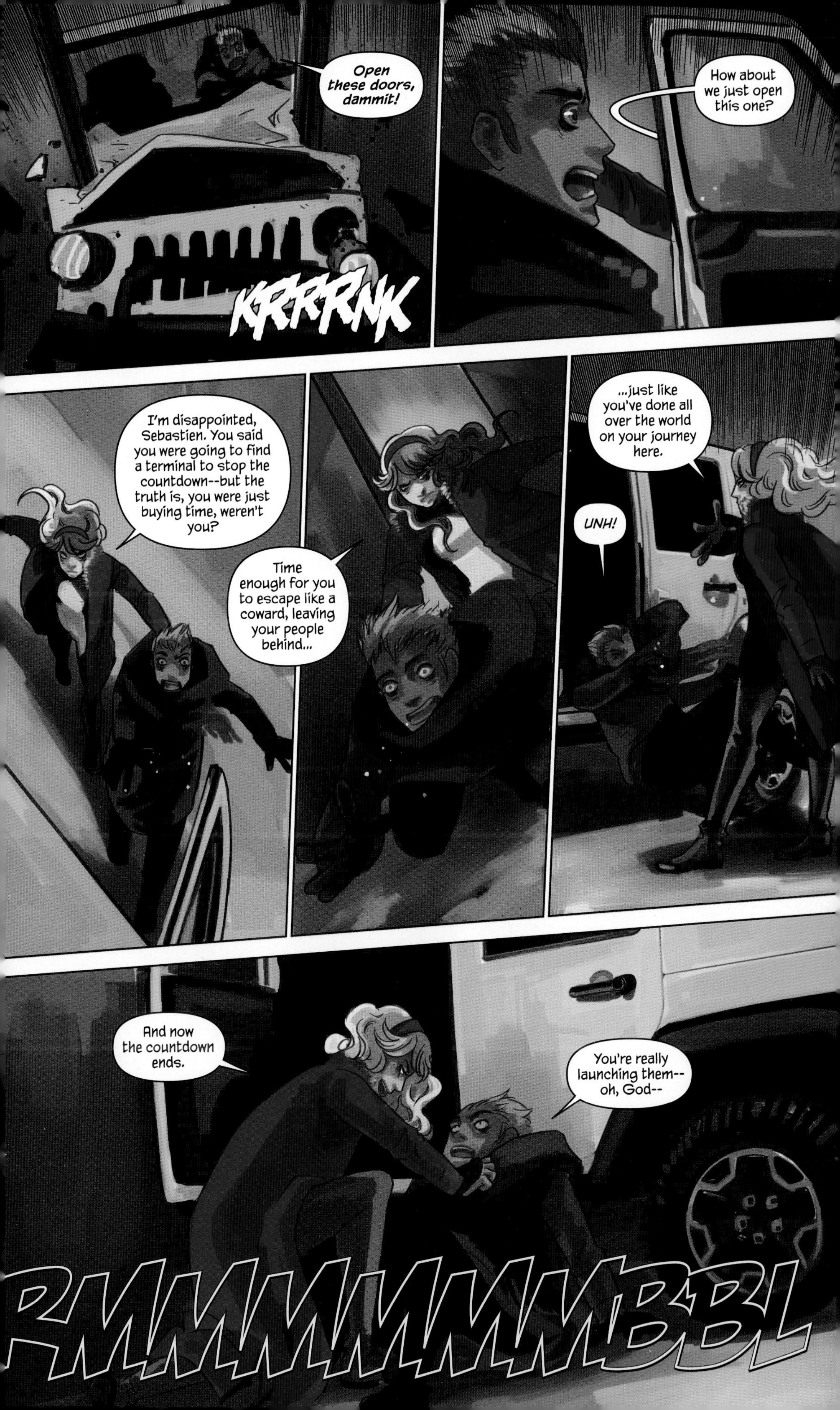

Open these doors, dammit!
KRRRNK
How about we just open this one?
I'm disappointed, Sebastien. You said you were going to find a terminal to stop the countdown--but the truth is, you were just buying time, weren't you?
Time enough for you to escape like a coward, leaving your people behind...
...just like you've done all over the world on your journey here.
UNH!
And now the countdown ends.
You're really launching them--oh, God--
RMMMMMMBBL

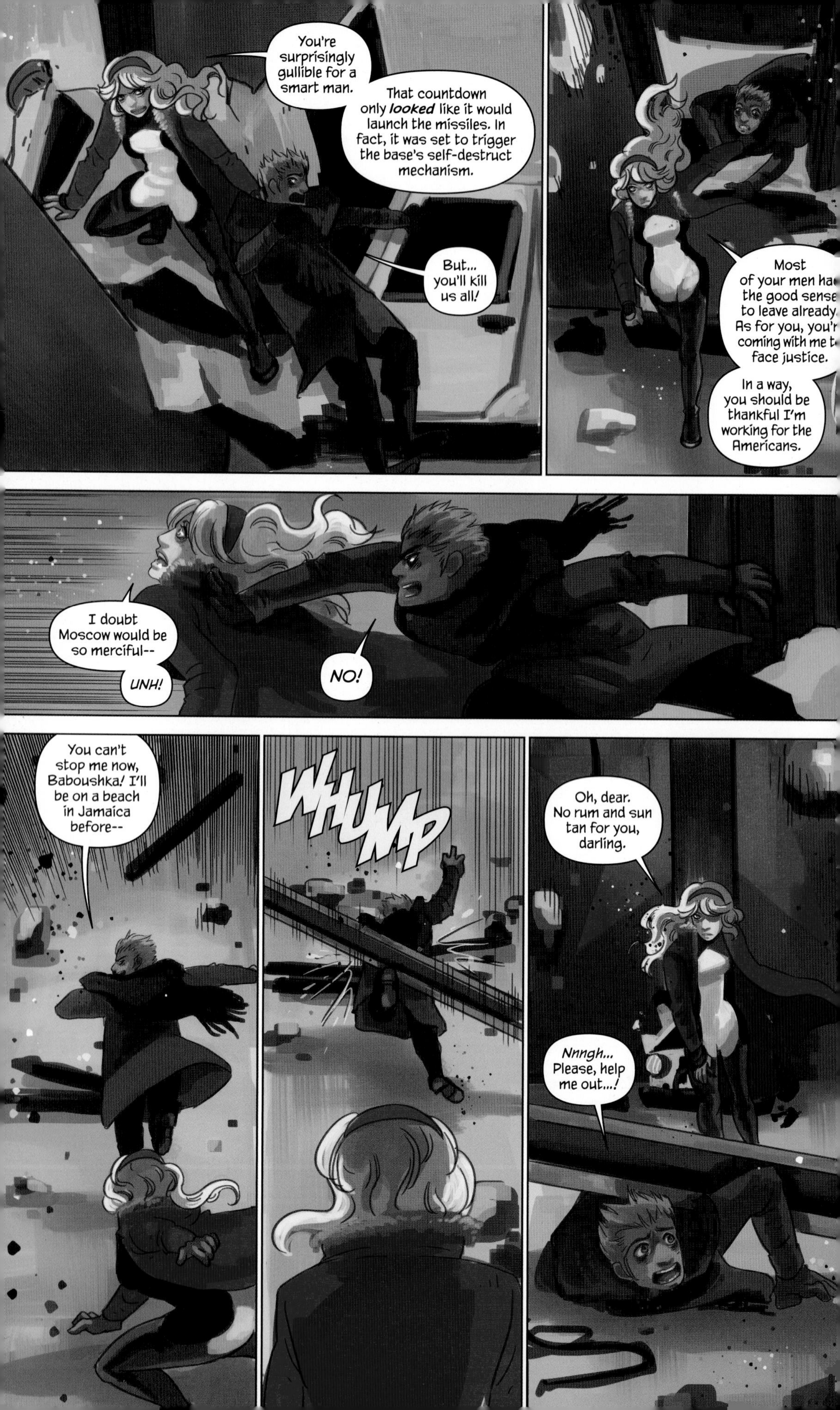

You're surprisingly gullible for a smart man.
That countdown only *looked* like it would launch the missiles. In fact, it was set to trigger the base's self-destruct mechanism.
But... you'll kill us all!
Most of your men ha the good sense to leave already As for you, you'r coming with me t face justice.
In a way, you should be thankful I'm working for the Americans.
I doubt Moscow would be so merciful--
UNH!
NO!
You can't stop me now, Baboushka! I'll be on a beach in Jamaica before--
WHUMP
Oh, dear. No rum and sun tan for you, darling.
Nnngh... Please, help me out...!

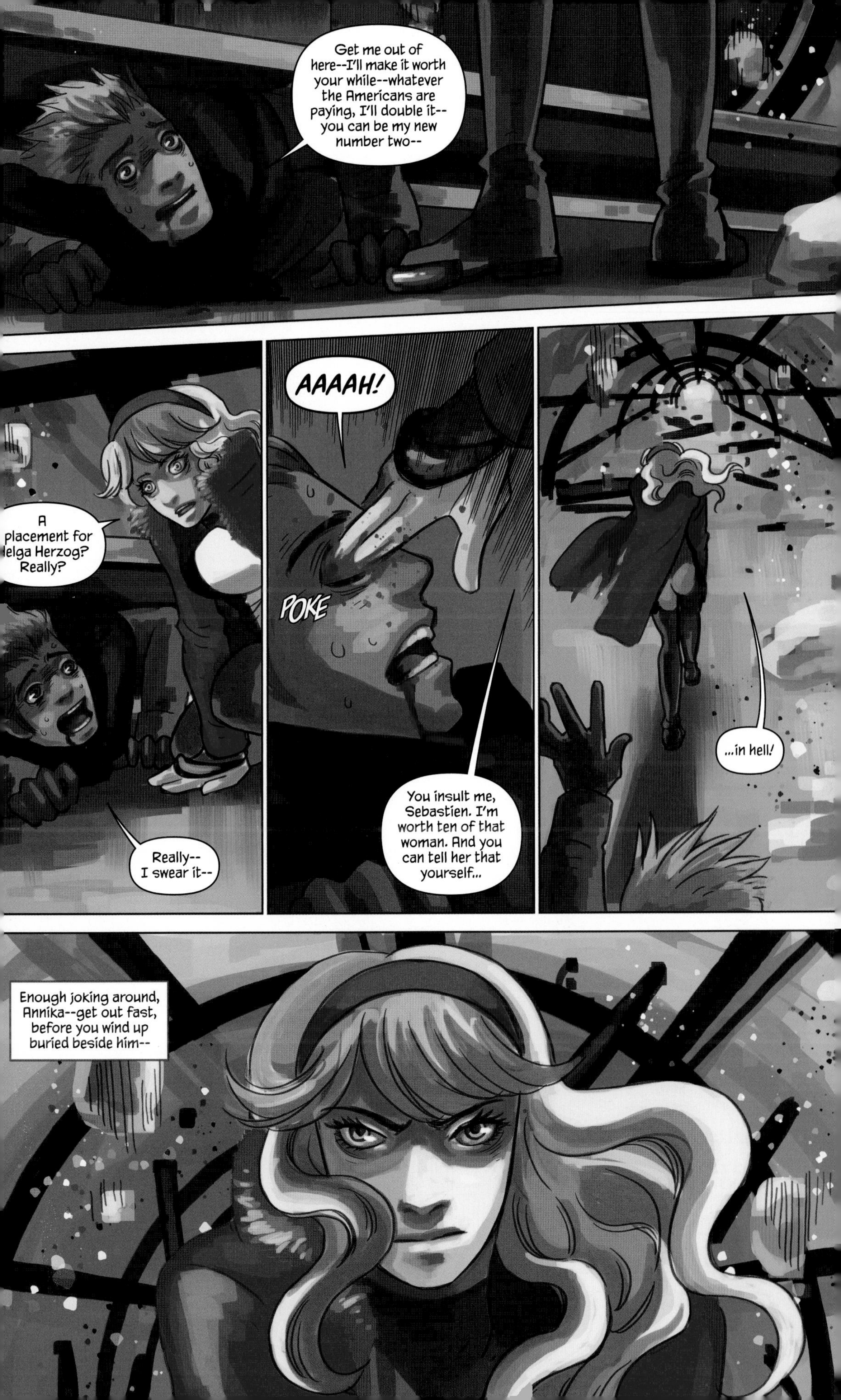
Get me out of here--I'll make it worth your while--whatever the Americans are paying, I'll double it--you can be my new number two--
A placement for elga Herzog? Really?
Really-- I swear it--
AAAAH!
POKE
You insult me, Sebastien. I'm worth ten of that woman. And you can tell her that yourself...
...in hell!
Enough joking around, Annika--get out fast, before you wind up buried beside him--

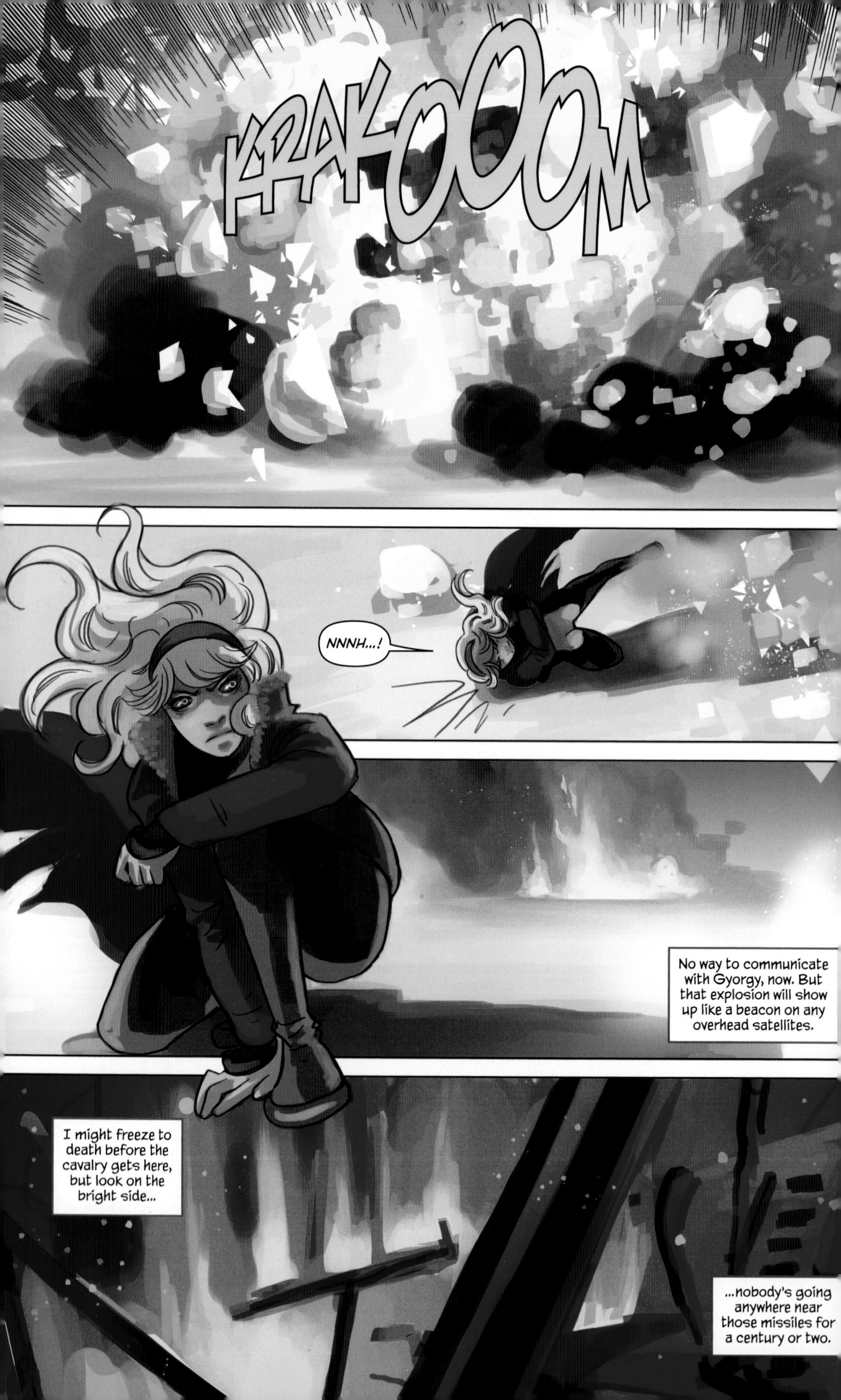
KRAKOOOM
NNNH...!
No way to communicate with Gyorgy, now. But that explosion will show up like a beacon on any overhead satellites.
I might freeze to death before the cavalry gets here, but look on the bright side...
...nobody's going anywhere near those missiles for a century or two.

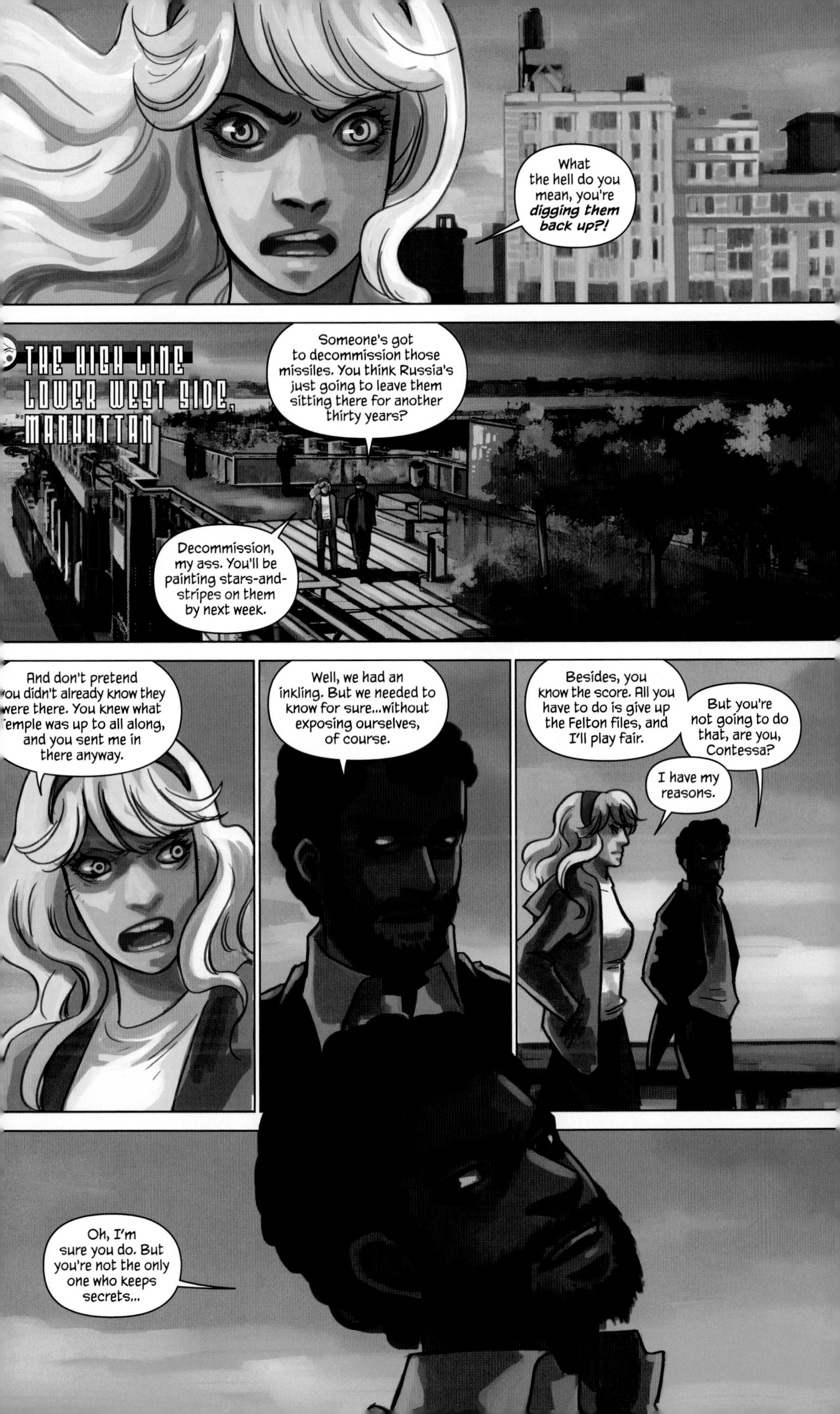
What the hell do you mean, you're ***digging them back up?!***
THE HIGH LINE LOWER WEST SIDE, MANHATTAN
Someone's got to decommission those missiles. You think Russia's just going to leave them sitting there for another thirty years?
Decommission, my ass. You'll be painting stars-and-stripes on them by next week.
And don't pretend you didn't already know they were there. You knew what Temple was up to all along, and you sent me in there anyway.
Well, we had an inkling. But we needed to know for sure...without exposing ourselves, of course.
Besides, you know the score. All you have to do is give up the Felton files, and I'll play fair.
But you're not going to do that, are you, Contessa?
I have my reasons.
Oh, I'm sure you do. But you're not the only one who keeps secrets...

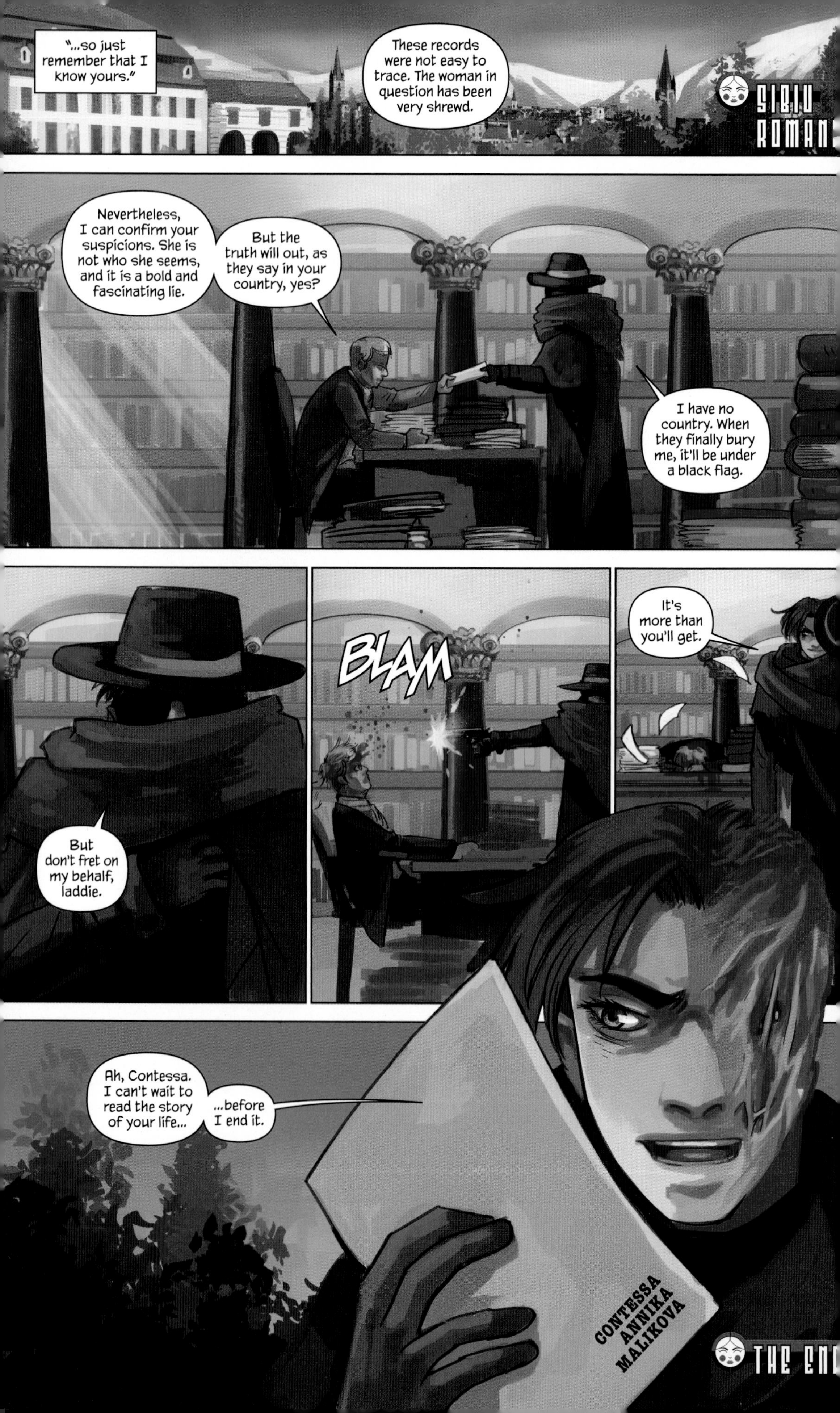
"...so just remember that I know yours."
These records were not easy to trace. The woman in question has been very shrewd.
SIBIU ROMAN
Nevertheless, I can confirm your suspicions. She is not who she seems, and it is a bold and fascinating lie.
But the truth will out, as they say in your country, yes?
I have no country. When they finally bury me, it'll be under a black flag.
But don't fret on my behalf, laddie.
BLAM
It's more than you'll get.
Ah, Contessa. I can't wait to read the story of your life...
...before I end it.
CONTESSA ANNIKA MALIKOVA
THE END

CODENAME BABOUSHKA

WILL RETURN

IN

"THE MALIKOV GAMBIT"

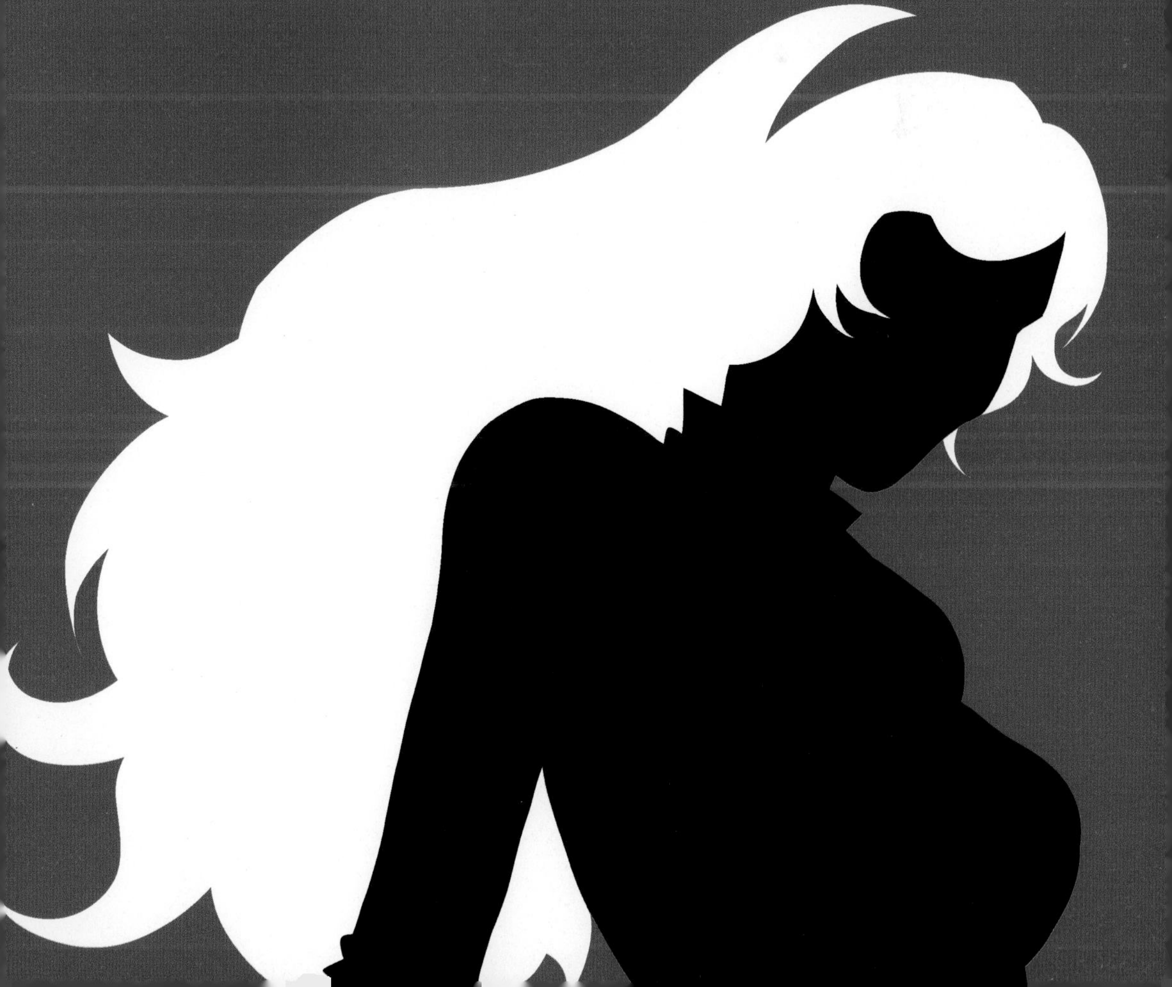

PORTRAIT GALLERY

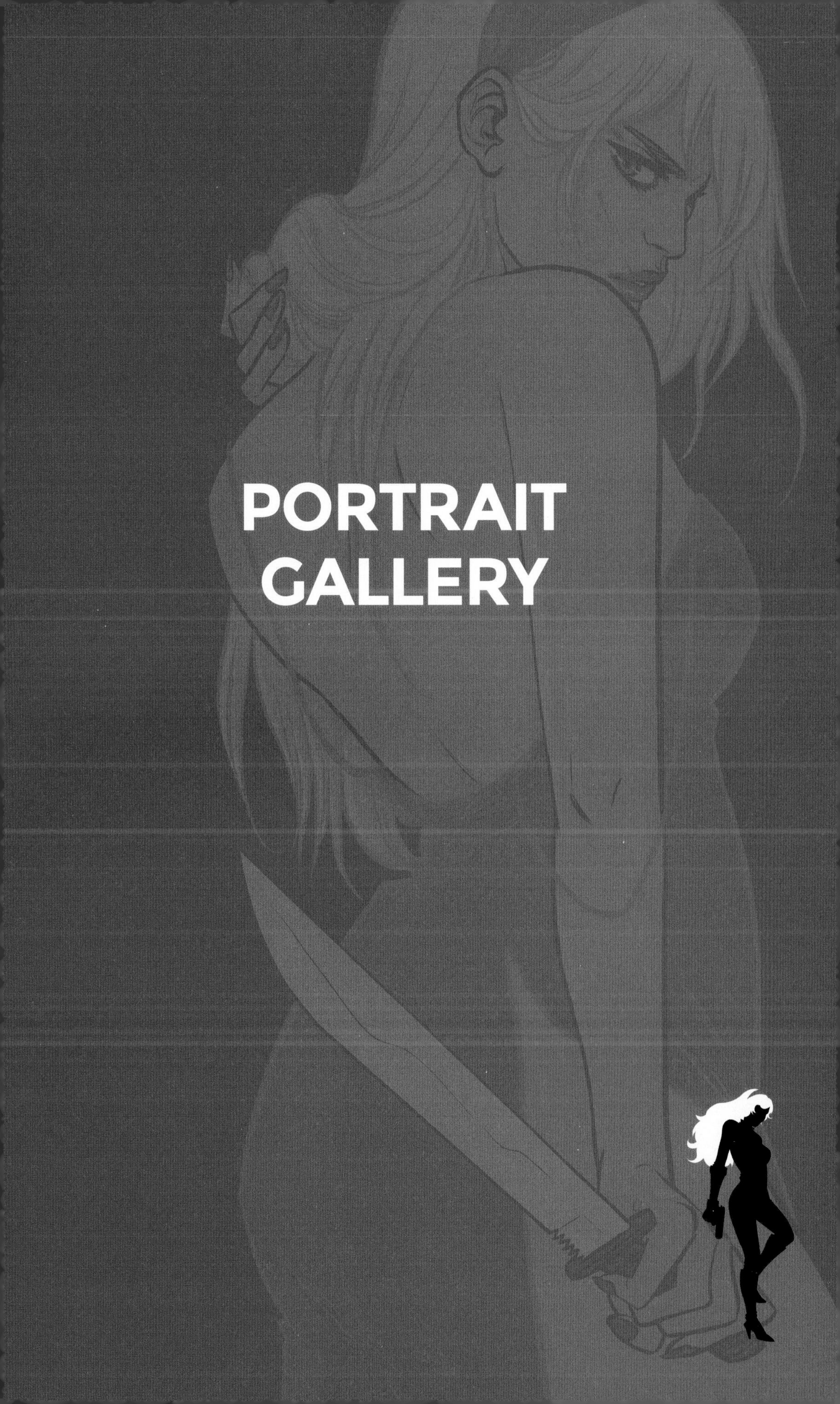

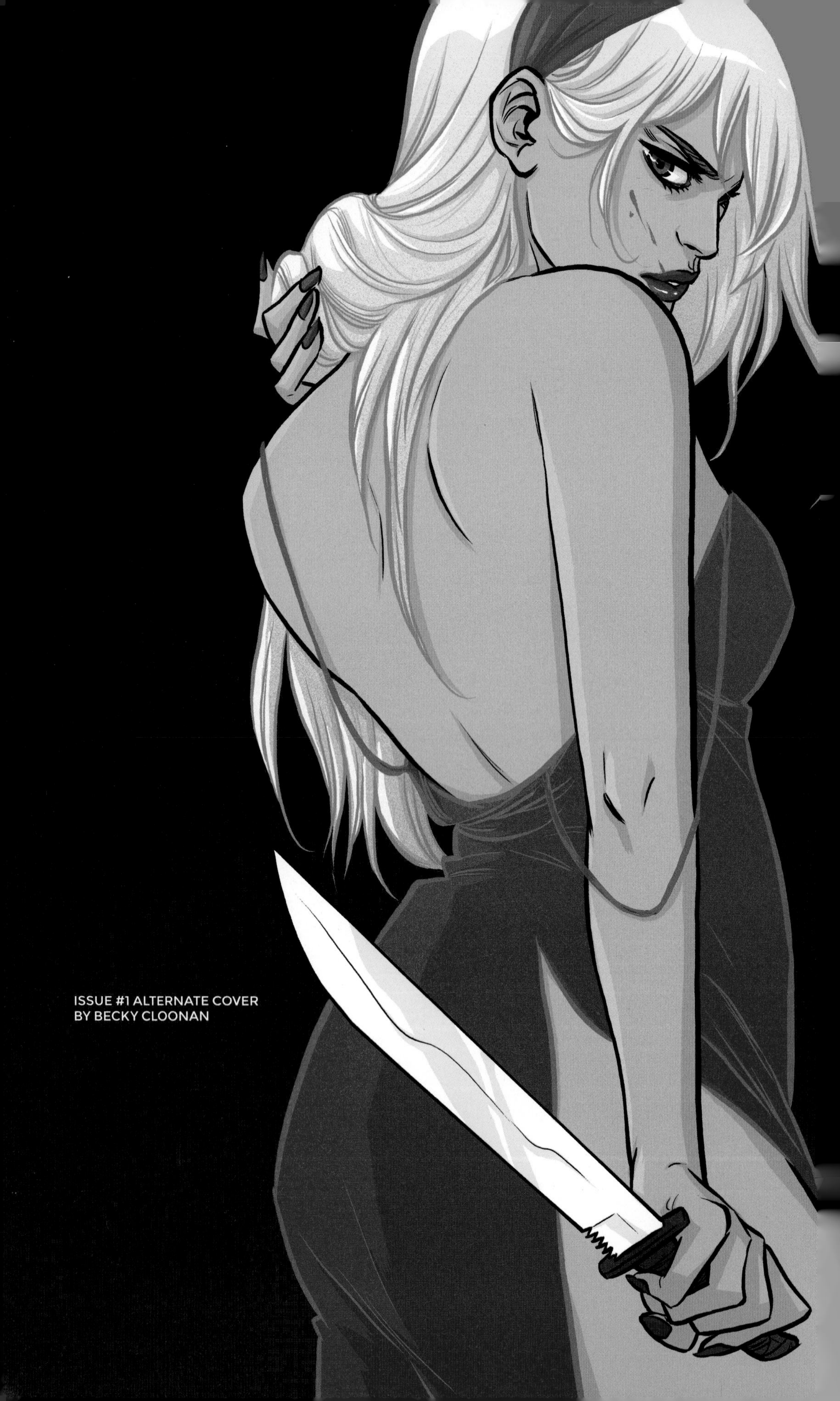

ISSUE #1 ALTERNATE COVER
BY BECKY CLOONAN

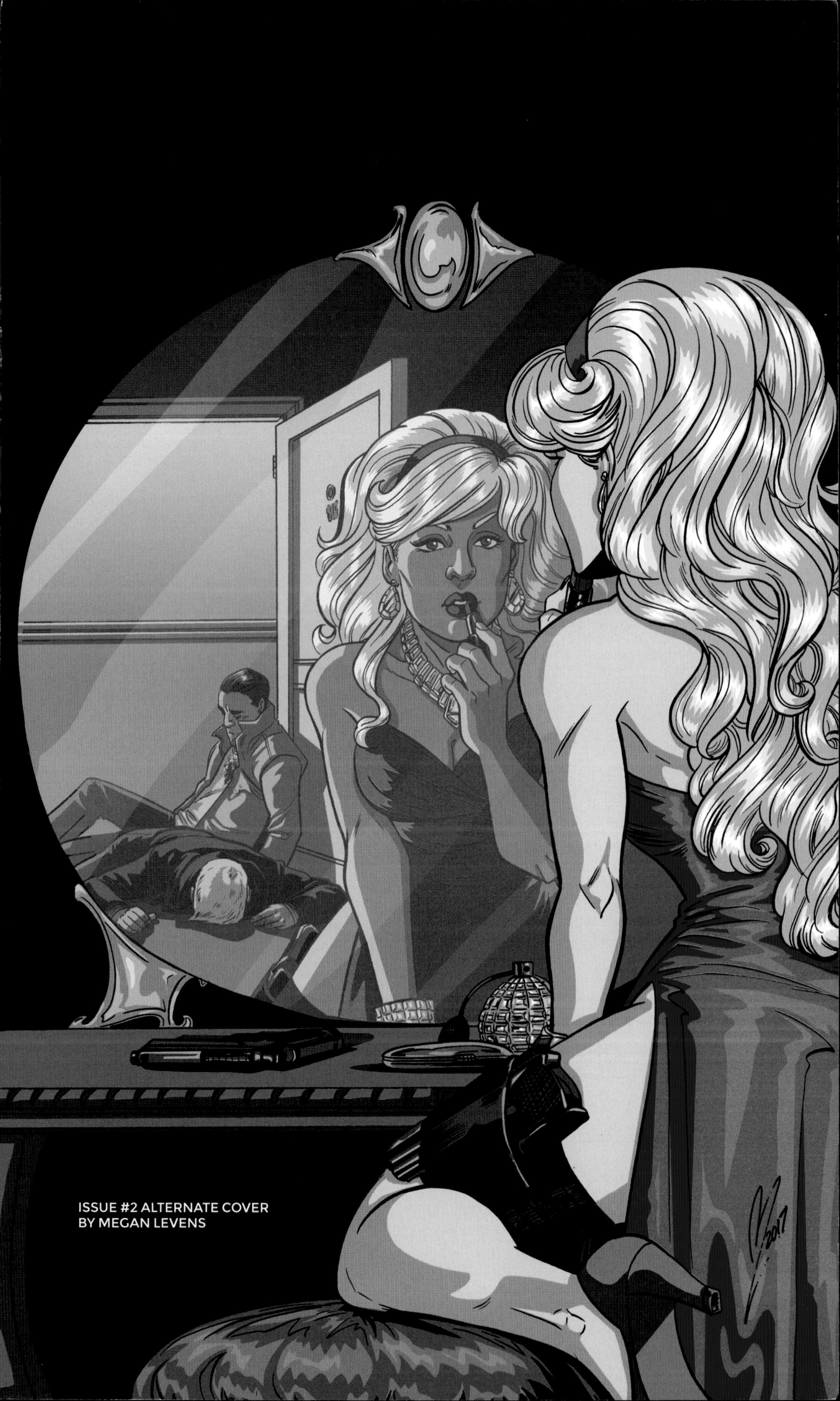

ISSUE #2 ALTERNATE COVER
BY MEGAN LEVENS

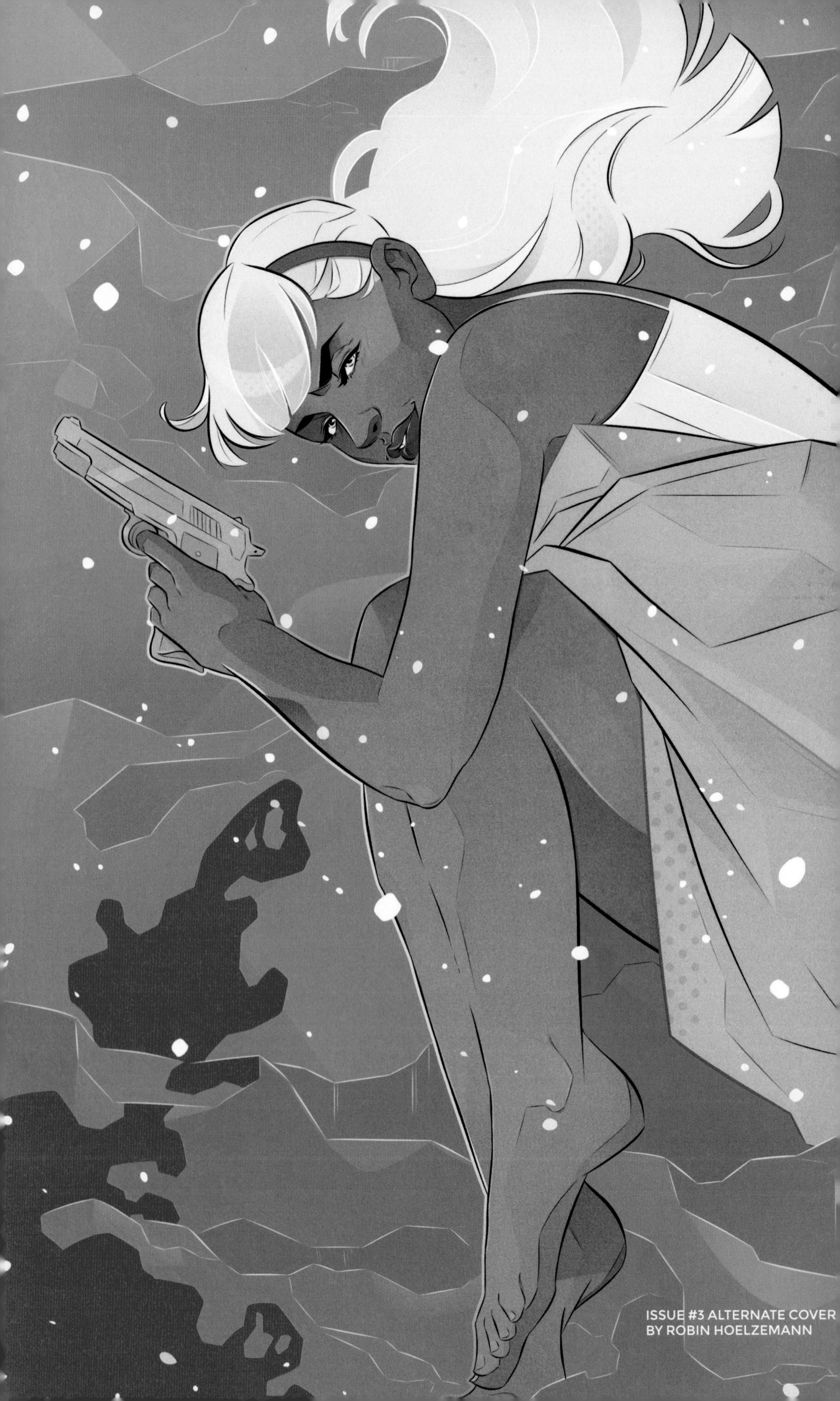

ISSUE #3 ALTERNATE COVER
BY ROBIN HOELZEMANN

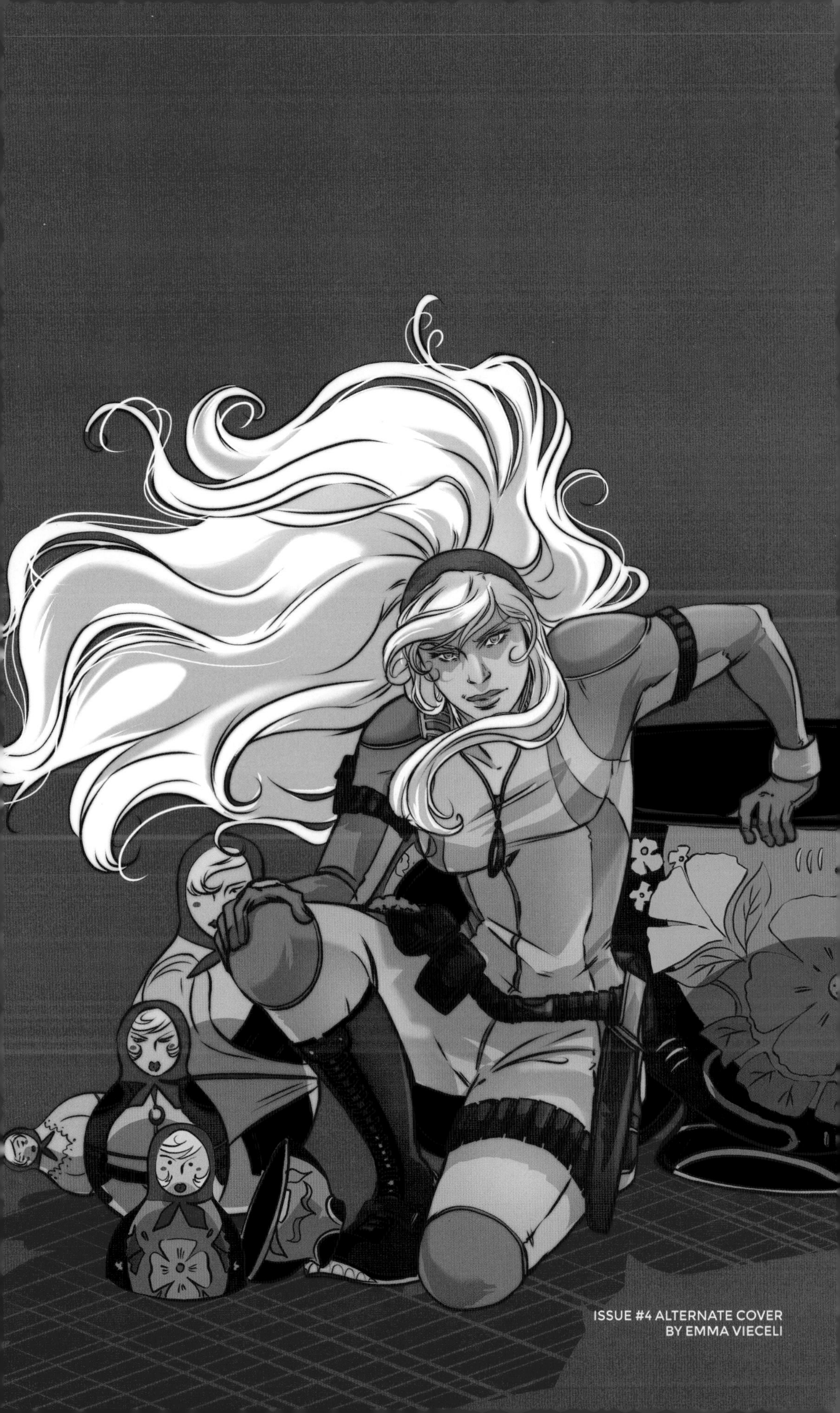
ISSUE #4 ALTERNATE COVER
BY EMMA VIECELI

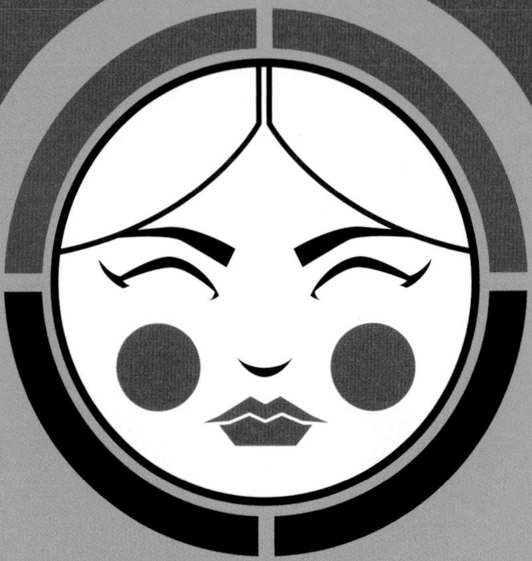

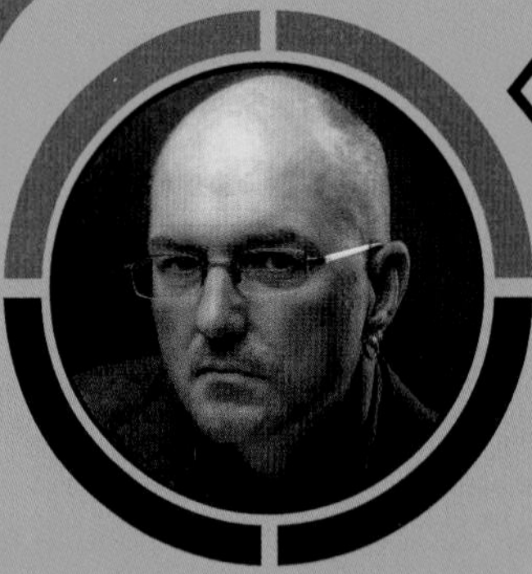

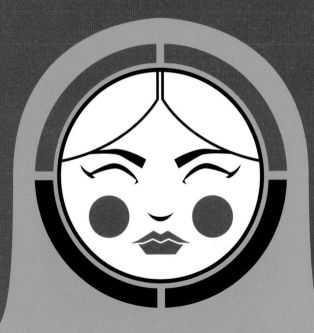

ANTONY JOHNSTON

is a *New York Times* bestselling graphic novelist, author, and games writer. His work includes *The Coldest City* (which became the hit movie *Atomic Blonde*), *The Fuse* (colored by Shari), *The Exphoria Code*, *Wasteland*, *Julius*, *Dead Space*, and more. He lives and works in England.

ANTONYJOHNSTON.COM / @ANTONYJOHNSTON

SHARI CHANKHAMMA

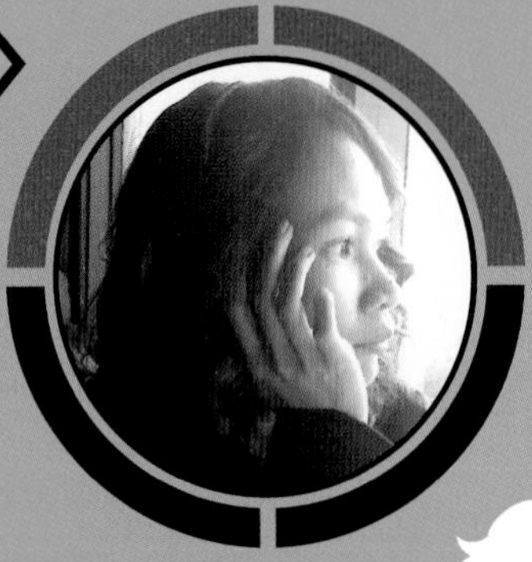

lives in Thailand and, as well as drawing *Codename Baboushka*, colors books like *The Fuse* (which Antony writes), *Sheltered*, and *Kill Shakespeare*. She also wrote and illustrated *The Sisters' Luck*, *The Clarence Principle*, *Pavlov's Dream*, and short stories in various anthologies.

SHARII.COM / @SHARIHES

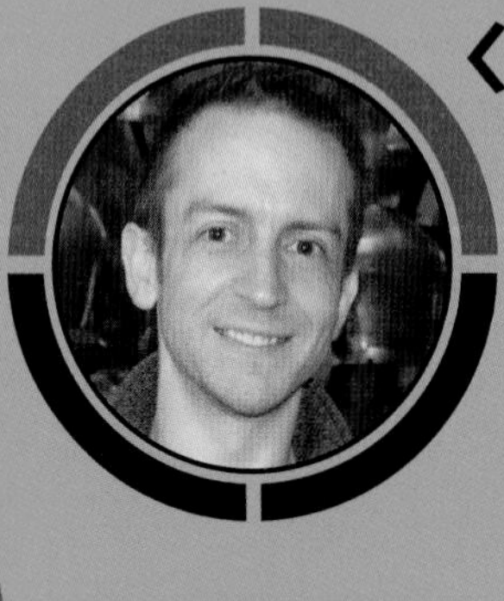

SIMON BOWLAND

is a comic book letterer, currently working for DC, Image, *2000AD*, Dark Horse, and Valiant, amongst others. He hails from the north-west of England, where he still lives today with his partner and their cat.

@SIMONBOWLAND

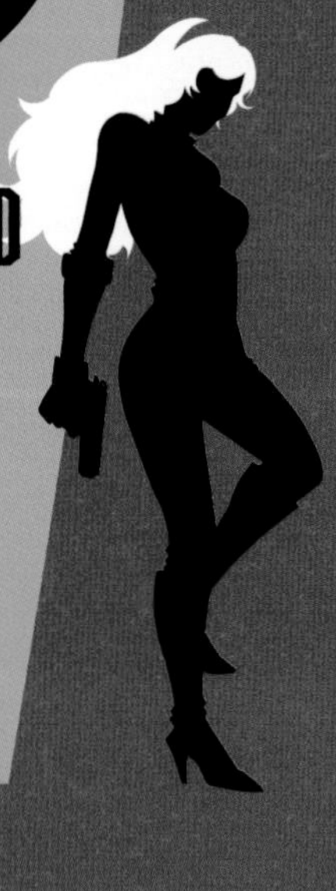

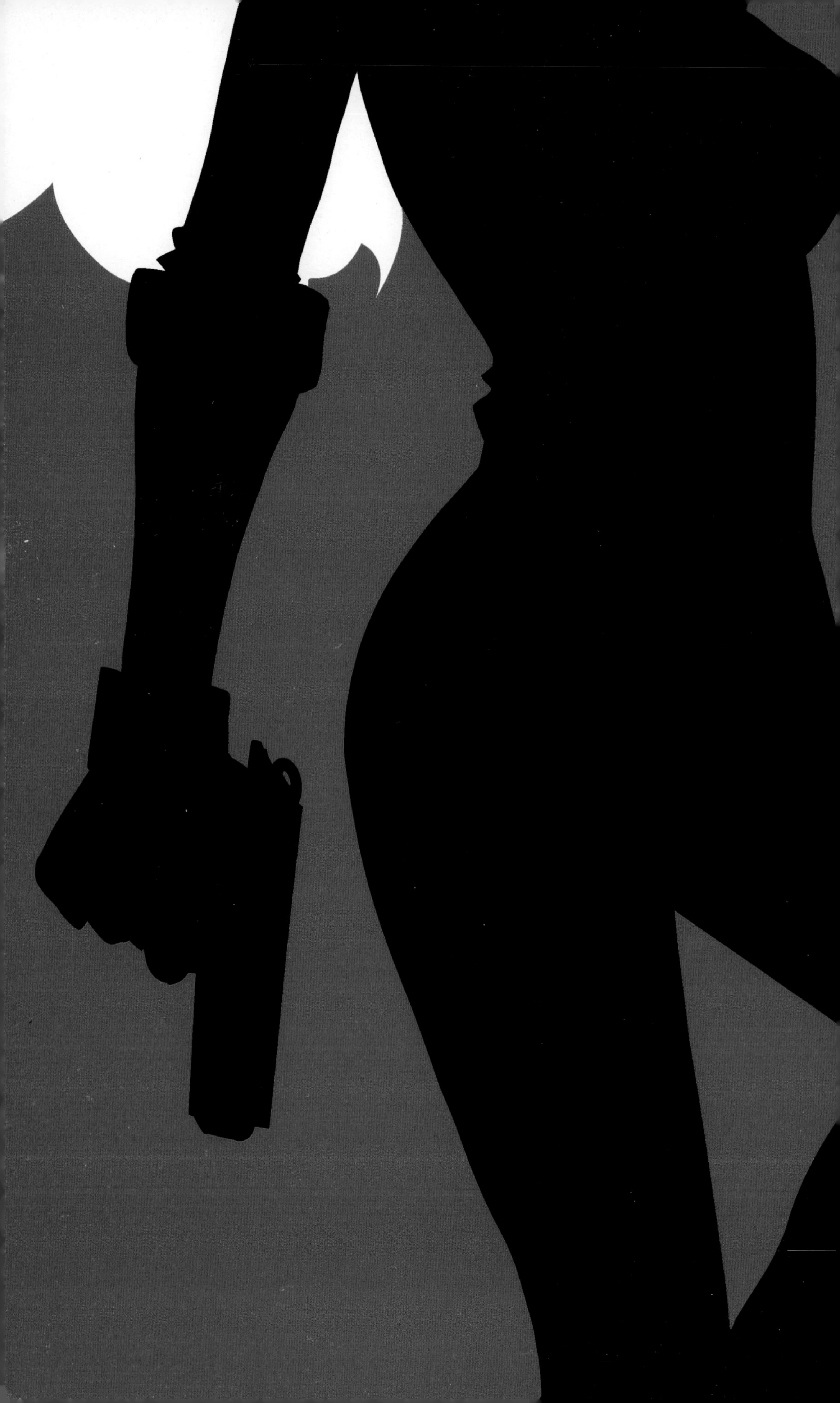